SMALL TOWN LAWYER

Defending Innocence

Influencing Justice

Interpreting Guilt

Burning Evidence

RELAY PUBLISHING EDITION, FEBRUARY 2023
Copyright © 2023 Relay Publishing Ltd.

Peter Kirkland is a pen name created by Relay Publishing for co-authored Legal Thriller projects. Relay Publishing works with incredible teams of writers and editors to collaboratively create the very best stories for our readers.

www.relaypub.com

SMALL TOWN LAWYER - BOOK THREE

INTERPRETING GUILT

PETER KIRKLAND

BLURB

A murder from the past hides an even darker secret.

A boating accident has left one Basking Rock teenager dead and three others traumatized. Defense attorney Leland Munroe is determined to prove his client wasn't responsible, but circuit solicitor Pat Ludlow will stop at nothing to keep his own son out of trouble. Even if it means ruining an innocent young man's life.

While Leland prepares his case, a second desperate client approaches him about an injustice from the past. Two decades ago, Maria Guerrero was convicted of murdering Peggy Ludlow, the solicitor's first wife. The evidence was stacked against her, but her son is positive his mother is innocent. If Maria didn't kill Peggy, though… who did?

As Leland navigates the two cases' twists and turns, he and his loved ones are caught in the crossfire. Leland has committed his life to fighting for justice… but this time both his career and his freedom may be on the line.

CONTENTS

1

MARCH 29, 2021

It was a pretty night—or it would've been, if we hadn't been talking about the death of a teenage boy. Terri and I were standing in the moonlight looking out over St. Helena Sound, trying to get a sense of how well folks on the shore could've seen the accident. The moon was right around full, like it had been on his last night a year or so earlier, so the black water was flickering with a million shards of white. A bridge loomed to our left. The boat he'd been riding on, or driving—that detail was in dispute—had crashed into a piling about forty feet out.

Terri took a few more photos and tucked her phone into her pocket.

She said, "You want to go get something back at that crab shack?"

"Yeah. I think we got what we need."

We walked under the cement arch of the bridge and up the empty beach. The air was chilly, but nothing a fried shrimp basket wouldn't fix.

I said, "It'd be easier if we could find some way of proving that couple lied."

The couple I was referring to had been down under the bridge, cheating on their spouses, when the crash occurred. They'd both identified my client as the driver.

"Unless they were wearing night-vision goggles," Terri said, "I don't see how they could be sure from that far away."

"When they heard the kids' names," I said, "I'm sure their memories got real clear all of a sudden."

Three boys and a girl had gone boating that night. Only two of the boys had come back, and only one of them—the one who was not my client—was the son of the circuit solicitor. The prosecutor, in other words. The man in charge of meting out justice over all six counties and 3,400 square miles of our judicial circuit.

The Ludlow name went a long way in these parts.

We walked on, silent. I could hear the water lapping on the shore.

Terri must've sensed my mood, because her voice was gentle when she asked, "You getting used to it yet? Being on the wrong side of the law all the time?"

We rounded a stand of palmettos, and I saw, a ways off yet, the yellow-lit windows of the crab shack. Ten or twelve people were inside enjoying themselves.

"I'm not on the wrong side of the *law*," I said.

To me, the law was a higher order, better than all of us.

But I knew what she meant. I'd spent most of my adult life as a prosecutor up in Charleston, until my own failings had cost me that career, and the only way to keep my son and myself afloat was to move back to my dirt-cheap hometown and turn to criminal defense.

"I guess what I'm on the wrong side of now is the law*man*."

"Mm. Well, you know, down here, that's the same thing."

———

A little over an hour later, after we'd eaten and caravanned back to town in our separate cars, I pulled up in front of my house. Noah was sitting on the porch with our Yorkie, Squatter, waiting for the crab legs he knew I was bringing. I saw the orange dot of his cigarette before he stubbed it out on a porch step.

I wished he wouldn't smoke, but we'd had that fight before. He claimed to be trying to stop. I knew there were far more dangerous vices he could have, so I decided not to mention it tonight.

Noah scooped Squatter into his carrier, came over to set him on the back seat, and then climbed in on the passenger side. We were heading for the causeway so he could eat at one of the picnic tables on the thin strip of beach there. He'd been stuck inside most of the day, working on a project for his criminal justice class, and had said he wanted a change of scene as much as he wanted the food.

Before I even put my foot back on the gas, he'd torn through the plastic bag and cracked a crab leg in half.

"I know you're hungry," I said, "but could you hold off on the crab legs until we're out of the car? They're a mess."

"Can I at least have some fries?"

"Yeah, if you're careful."

He ate one and said, "Isn't it about time you got your own car?"

I laughed. I was still driving the Chevy Malibu my boss, Roy, had leased for me back when I was at my lowest point financially. I'd had a beater whose broken rear windshield I'd replaced with plastic sheeting and duct tape, and the sight of that abomination sitting in the

3

parking lot of his law office, next to his sleek BMW, had driven **Roy** over the edge.

The abomination was Noah's now. Eating crab legs in that thing could only improve it.

"There's still a few months left on the lease," I said. "And besides, when do I have time to shop for a car? I've got three hearings next week alone."

"More drunk and disorderly rich boys?"

"Couple of those. But the other one's interesting. Preliminary hearing for a woman who shot her husband in self-defense."

"That the one where you'll be gone overnight?"

"Yep." That client was a two-and-a-half-hour drive northeast in Elkin Springs, a town about forty-five minutes outside Columbia.

"I guess you're famous now," he said, reaching between our seats to hand a fry to Squatter. "Jet-setting all over the state."

"I guess," I said. "Although I'm not sure driving a Malibu into the middle of nowhere counts as jet-setting."

At an intersection, passing headlights lit up Noah's hair. It was bright blue these days. I thought it looked ridiculous, but I hadn't said anything and wasn't going to. I knew how lucky I was. Of all the bad decisions a kid could make, that was nothing at all.

At the beach, or the strip of sand that passed for one, he set his meal on the nearest picnic table, then pulled a glow-in-the-dark ball out of the pocket of his hoodie and tossed it for Squatter to chase. The dog had some mobility issues, being well past his prime, but his enthusiasm was undimmed; his ears perked up, and he wobbled off into the darkness.

After Noah polished off a crab leg, he said, "I can't believe I've only got one semester left."

"I know." He was set to graduate in December with an associate's degree in criminal justice.

He sighed, looking out at the water, and said, "It sucks that Mom can't see it."

"Yeah."

I'd known a lot of people who would've added something comforting to that—something along the lines of how they were sure the person you'd lost was looking down from Heaven.

I wished I were one of those people.

I added what I could. "She'd be so damn proud of you."

He gave a little laugh and said, "Yeah, no. It's just community college. I mean, maybe if I was graduating from Vanderbilt."

"Naw, you don't need to go to the Harvard of the South to make her proud. She knew what you were going through. She was there."

In high school, he'd gotten addicted to prescription painkillers. We almost lost him, twice: to our own little family opioid crisis and then to Elise's DUI car crash, which had taken her life.

"Addiction's hard as hell," I said. "A lot of folks never make it out."

"Yeah," he said, picking up the ball that Squatter had dropped on the sand and tossing it again. "She sure didn't."

———

After Noah finished his take-out dinner, he reached into his other pocket, pulled out a baseball, and held it up to suggest a game of catch. The ball looked brand new, so bright white it was almost as glow-in-the-dark as the one Squatter was gnawing under the picnic table.

We got into position a few yards from the table, and Noah tossed the ball my way. It had been a good two years since he'd so much as watched a baseball game—the car accident had cost him a baseball scholarship to college, and for a long time, it had seemed to me he couldn't stand thinking about the sport at all—but his arm was as loose and natural as ever. I got farther back so he could enjoy the game more.

A perfectly aimed pitch smacked my hand. "Watch out for Squatter," I called out, throwing it back.

"Yeah, I can hear him."

Squatter's tags jangled as he toddled back and forth between us. The only other sound was the surf, and once in a while a car passing by on the causeway. We played without talking, until my own lack of talent sent the ball too far off to one side and Noah fell over trying to catch it. I winced. His legs still didn't have the strength and agility they'd had before the accident, and I doubted they ever would.

He picked himself up and tossed the ball to me. I caught it and threw it back. I'd taught him as a kid to get back in the saddle, not to give up because you failed or fell. It was good to see he'd taken it to heart. I just worried that he might take it too far.

Knowing your limits could be a good thing. Especially if you were planning on going into a dangerous field. He was enthused about becoming a private investigator, but he was twenty years old and correspondingly ignorant.

And I could tell from his throws that he was getting cocky. He threw a curveball, which I failed to catch. The next one, a changeup, had Squatter and me chasing after it and nearly going into the water. Noah raised both arms, cheering for himself.

I said, "You know there aren't any girls here. You don't need to show off."

He laughed and said, "You should talk. Saw your face on the front page the other day. What's next? You going to start doing infomercials?"

"God, no." I threw the ball back. "And you know it wasn't my choice to be in the paper."

"Yeah, I figured that out once I read it."

My throw had sent the ball into some spartina grass. Noah swept his hands through the long blades, looking for it.

I looked around to confirm we were still alone on the beach—the bad press coverage of my boat-crash case had made me extra cautious—and then said, "Seems like old Fourth wants to take me down a notch."

I was referring to our local media magnate, Dabney Barnes IV. His family had run all the newspapers in the nearest half-dozen counties for generations, and in recent decades they'd also started the first local internet provider and the biggest regional websites.

Noah said, "Just one notch? You sure?"

"I don't know," I said, walking over to help him look for the ball. "I didn't read past the first paragraph of that article."

"Huh," he said. "Well, you might want to."

2

APRIL 5, 2021

I headed west, the morning sun at my back. Driving gave me a chance to think, which I didn't often have time to do these days, now that I'd built up a caseload that kept me busy. The client I was going to meet had been in jail for nearly three weeks for killing her husband. She didn't deny doing it. I'd taken her case because, as she'd described it to me, she'd shot him in self-defense. She'd moved her three kids into an apartment and filed for divorce, and he hadn't taken it well.

Terri had pulled his record for me. In the past two years, the police had been by their marital home a few times on domestic violence calls. And he was apparently the type of man who didn't realize that you don't get a free pass on breaking and entering just because the apartment you're breaking into is your wife's.

I steered around a minor wreck, trying not to rubberneck, and put the Malibu back on cruise control. I felt a stab of guilt for not stopping, which didn't make sense; I'd seen the driver standing on the shoulder talking on his cell phone. He seemed to have things under control.

It occurred to me that my profession had turned me into something like the law's version of a paramedic. When someone wrecked his life against a legal guardrail or flipped it into a ravine, I pulled over. I applied the Jaws of Life to extricate him from the wreckage, if possible. I helicoptered him out.

And apparently, that habit was starting to bleed—as it were—over into other situations.

I was going to have to nip that in the bud. Trying to save everyone, or even just those who deserved it, was a losing proposition.

I headed into Elkin Springs on a two-lane rural highway running along some train tracks, flanked by fields and the occasional roadside business or farm. I let my phone guide me toward the Airbnb I'd reserved, and it took me down a few side streets until I reached a long avenue lined with gnarled oaks so huge and ancient that their branches met over the middle of the street, hiding the sky. That tunnel of trees with Spanish moss draping from the branches gave me a sense of rightness that no other landscape, apart from the shoreline in the Lowcountry, could.

It wasn't that I loved the South. I was no flag-waver of any kind. But it was a part of me, built in.

I turned down a one-block street and parked outside the green bungalow that I had booked. The preliminary hearing for my murder defendant, Britney LaSalle, was tomorrow morning. I checked myself in, scanned for roaches and bedbugs, and tossed my overnight bag onto the kitchen table. The fridge had nothing in it but a selection of off-brand bottled coffees, which was what I needed after a long drive.

I had thirty or forty minutes to kill before my appointed visit down at the jailhouse, so I grabbed a coffee and pulled out my laptop to check my email. All I'd gotten, apart from spam advertising various CLE classes and expert-witness services, was the county's legal newsletter.

Skimming through it, I saw a headline about a Mr. Lawrence Tucker receiving a pro bono services award.

That was the name of the man who'd been under the bridge by St. Helena Sound, getting busy with his mistress, on the night of the boat crash. I clicked the link; the photo was indeed him, smiling as he was presented with a plaque commemorating his award. He looked like the kind of man who got tapped to run for political office purely by virtue of his connections and his perfect hair. The article praised his skills in business litigation and the free legal services he occasionally provided to local entrepreneurs.

I wasn't sociable enough to be tapped into local legal gossip, and I found myself wondering if Mr. Tucker's indiscretion had been talked about. I knew far too much about it, thanks to my case file, but I hadn't given much attention to Tucker or his lady friend. I had no idea what their reputations were around town. I made a mental note to ask Roy.

I googled Tucker's name and various combinations of words: lawyer, legal, witness, bridge, boat crash, accident. Nothing came up about my case. Plenty of other sordid details had made it into the press, but not that one. I supposed Tucker was the kind of man whose connections could make problems go away.

A calendar alert popped up. It was time for me to go meet Ms. LaSalle down at the county jail. I swiped another bottled coffee and headed out.

The sense of Southern rightness I'd felt when I drove into town evaporated soon after I crossed the railroad tracks and returned to the main drag. After passing the DMV, a gas station, and some kind of agricultural supply place, I took a wrong turn and hit poverty: a half-collapsed house overgrown by weeds, disemboweled cars rusting out in people's yards, a tiny storefront church.

My impression of Ms. LaSalle, from her jailhouse Zoom call, was that she'd come up in this part of town or something like it. The tree-lined avenue barely a mile away was not her world.

I found my way to the jail, grabbed my briefcase from the passenger seat, and went in. I surrendered my cell phone to the older White lady at the desk, who had a fan pointed at herself to supplement the freezing AC.

As she went through the necessary paperwork, pausing to lick her finger a couple of times to make the pages easier to flip, she told me, "I ain't seen a lot of city lawyers up this way."

"Oh, I ain't city. I'm from over in Basking Rock."

From the way she looked at me, I might as well have said Philadelphia.

"Well, anyway," she said. "I guess that girl thinks she's special."

A guard brought Ms. LaSalle to the room I was waiting in and locked the door behind her. She was a wiry, impatient-looking woman, thin and pale and shorter than I'd imagined when we talked on Zoom, hardly any bigger than most twelve-year-olds. For the self-defense argument, that was a good thing.

"I want to thank you so much for coming up here," she said, "and I hope this don't sound rude, but I want to get straight to the point. I got kids. I got a job, for now, anyways. I cannot spend any more time in jail."

I flipped my notebook open and asked, "Where are they now?"

"My kids? They're with my momma. But she's not well. The couple of weeks she's had them have been real hard on her."

"Okay," I said, writing that down. "And is there anybody else who could help her out?"

"Why are you asking me that?" She was alarmed. "I paid you everything I had. Do you not think you can get me out of jail?"

"Ms. LaSalle, I would not have taken your money if I didn't think I could help you. I'm just trying to get a backup plan squared away, since there's no guarantees."

"I don't want no backup plan. To me, that's a *failure* plan. I got to stay positive."

I gave her a nod to say I understood. "Okay. You want me to map out what I'm fixing to do in court? And how I think it might go?"

"Yes, I do."

"Okay. So, tomorrow is your preliminary hearing. That's our first shot at getting this kicked out—which, as I told you on our call, is not likely to happen—or at least knocked down from murder to manslaughter. On *that* charge, you'd get bail."

She'd been denied bail on the murder charge before she'd hired me. No lawyer could've done much to change that; courts in our fair state almost never let murder defendants out on bond.

"I don't know how I'd afford bail, anyway," she said. "All the money I was saving is in your pocket now."

"Well, affording it is what bail bondsmen are for. And we'll cross that bridge if we come to it. But either way, whether it's murder or manslaughter, under South Carolina law, you have the right to a hearing on self-defense. And I've already filed the motion for that."

"And that's what we're doing tomorrow?"

"Unfortunately not," I said. "The court set that hearing for the end of May—"

"Do these people not understand?" She looked at me, wide-eyed. "How long is an innocent person supposed to sit in jail for? I got three kids under eight years old! And I got a good job, but I already used up my vacation days and almost all my sick days on this!"

"I know," I said.

She'd told me she was a licensed electrician, working for the local utility company. I doubted she'd easily find another job like that if she lost this one for being in jail on a murder charge.

"My momma has rheumatoid arthritis," she said. "She just— Her body don't *work* in the morning, simple as that. I got a truancy letter already for my two kids that are school-age, 'cause she can't get them there. She's barely hanging on, and I got no one else, so—"

That was bad. Kids missing school, with their mom in jail, were probably a hair's breadth away from being taken into foster care.

I asked, "Nobody at all? Family? Friends?"

She looked at me, shaking her head a little, with an expression like the story was too big to fit into words.

"Maybe a neighbor?" I suggested.

"Mr. Munroe," she said, "the thing is, I don't come from good folk. Apart from my mom, when she tries." She looked out the barred window, squinting as the sun hit her face.

"I got through high school," she said, almost to herself. "Nobody else did. And I got into the apprenticeship, for the electrical. That took a real long time. But I got through."

"Seems like you did a hell of a job."

"For all the good that's worth now," she said, shrugging. "Randy always said I wasn't ever going to get nowhere."

Randy was the husband she'd killed.

When she looked back at me, I saw her desperation. "My kids got nobody else but me. Nobody who'd take them anywhere but down. I hired you to get me out of jail, not to tell me to sit here until the end of May!"

I nodded to say I understood and I was sorry.

Her voice rose almost to yelling as she said, "I called the police on him, more than once! I filed for divorce! I don't know what else I was supposed to do! And you're telling me I'm staying in jail another, what, two months almost? Because *he* broke into *my* house?"

I recognized the look in her eyes. Disbelief, betrayal. It was the look my clients always got when they started realizing that what was going wrong in their lives was not a bad dream, or a mistake that would quickly be corrected.

It wasn't even remotely fair, but it was how the system worked.

3

APRIL 6, 2021

The next morning, I showed up at the courthouse at 10 a.m., fifteen minutes earlier than I normally would. With the fever checks and social distancing, lines went a lot slower these days. The building was an architectural Frankenstein, a quaint Victorian with a two-story cement box hitched to the back of it to contain, I supposed, the folks caught up in the county's rising crime rate.

Since it was a preliminary hearing, Ms. LaSalle wasn't required to be there. But I wanted the judge to see how tiny she was, and I wanted her to hear what law enforcement said about the incident. That way she could set me straight on any details they got wrong.

So I'd arranged for the jail staff to bring her over, but I had not been able to arrange an outfit other than prison dress. She'd told me all she owned were T-shirts and jeans, and the couple of local stores I'd visited did not carry women's clothes in anything close to her size.

She sat beside me at the defense table in an orange jumpsuit, handcuffs, and the only feminine-looking thing I'd been able to find for her, a mask made of pink floral material. I could see it was taking everything she had to keep calm. I didn't blame her. A courtroom was a terrifying place when your liberty was at stake.

The bailiff called out, "All rise," and I got my first look at the judge. It was a woman at least a decade older than me, with a motherly physique, wire-rimmed glasses, and a slightly sour look on her face. Her mask was black, matching her robe.

"Court is now in session. The Honorable Anne Merriweather, presiding."

She perched up on the bench, framed by the state and national flags, and looked from the local solicitor to me as her clerk announced the case. To the solicitor, she said, "Morning, Mr. Fletcher. I see you came down here yourself today. Because this is a murder case, correct?"

Fletcher, a heavyset man in a gray suit, was the circuit solicitor. His office was in Columbia, nearly an hour away. I knew that because he'd recently been assigned to step in as prosecutor on my boat-crash case, after Ludlow's office was recused.

"Yes, Your Honor," he said. "It didn't seem right to send one of my assistants down."

She nodded and turned to me.

"May it please the Court," I said, "Leland Munroe, counsel for the defense."

"Morning, Mr. Munroe. I understand you're from out of town?"

"Yes, Your Honor. Basking Rock, small town about an hour south of Charleston."

"And has our town given you a good welcome so far?"

"Yes, Your Honor. A Southern welcome, through and through."

She nodded in what looked like approval.

"Okay, then. Mr. Fletcher, please proceed."

"Well, Your Honor, as I'm sure you're aware, last month, on the night of March 18, a gentleman by the name of Randy LaSalle was the victim of a homicide."

"I'm familiar with Mr. LaSalle," she said. "He had graced my court-room with his presence once or twice."

As a native speaker of Southern, I could tell that she had an opinion of Randy that could not politely be shared. He didn't have that much of a criminal record, but in a town with only a handful of judges, it wasn't surprising that he'd appeared before her.

"Well, Your Honor," Fletcher said, "I am not here to claim that Mr. LaSalle was a pillar of the community. But it is my sworn duty to do right by every American, so I'm here to do right by him. And that means to make sure that Your Honor understands that the evidence shows the defendant here, Mr. LaSalle's wife, has rightly and properly been charged with his murder."

After asking him to spell both parties' names for the record, Judge Merriweather said, "For the avoidance of confusion, since they share the same last name, I'm going to ask y'all to refer to them as Britney and Randy. Now, Mr. Fletcher, what is the State's case?"

"Uh, as the investigating officer will testify, Your Honor, Mrs. LaSalle —I mean, Britney—does not deny that she shot her husband. She so stated on the 9-1-1 call, which we have a recording of if Your Honor cares to listen to it. The weapon was recovered at the scene and proved to have her fingerprints on it. So that much is entirely undisputed."

"And what's your evidence on malice aforethought?"

"Well, Your Honor, this was a lying-in-wait situation. Britney was aware of her husband's presence, so she stated, for some moments prior to the shooting. She armed herself at that time, and she waited. Under *State v. Belcher*, that is sufficient to show implied malice. And as Your Honor knows, even a single second can suffice for the intent to murder to arise in a person's heart. And I'm sure"—he turned to me with a courteous sweep of the arm—"Mr. Munroe here will not dispute that."

I nodded and said, "Mr. Fletcher and I are in disagreement as to whether that applies here, but I don't dispute that that is the law."

"And in this case, Your Honor," he went on, "we're not talking about just a single second. Britney waited for her husband to approach for a good moment longer than that."

Judge Merriweather nodded. "All right. Well, Mr. Munroe, assuming that Mr. Fletcher puts on evidence to confirm what he's just stated, he does appear to have the requisite elements for a murder charge. But I don't suppose you drove all the way up here to agree with me on that?"

I stood up. "Your Honor, I don't make a practice of disagreeing with judges."

I heard a chuckle from her clerk. With a hint of a smile, the judge said, "That's probably wise."

"So what I drove up here to disagree with," I said, "as I alluded to just now, was Mr. Fletcher's characterization of the evidence. The incident of March 18 took place in Britney's apartment, not in the marital home. She and Randy lived separately, due to her having moved out in January and filed for divorce."

Her Honor was nodding. She looked like she already knew all this. I was well aware that in a small town, judges heard the local news and gossip just like everybody else.

"Now, for the record, Randy was not on the lease of this new apartment. And that was because after several years of physical abuse, Britney had finally saved up enough money to leave and, as I said, file for divorce. She'd also filed for a restraining order, which was still pending at the time of his death. On the night in question, he broke into her home. It was shortly after midnight, while the children were sleeping, and Britney had gone to bed too."

I paused for effect, then gestured to her beside me.

"Britney was aware," I said, "that someone had entered her home, without permission, late at night. She thought it was either her estranged husband, whose history of abuse I trust Your Honor is aware of, or a stranger. Either way, she feared for her life. As we can all see, this young lady is about five foot two with shoes on, and at most a little ways north of a hundred pounds. She's alone in bed, in the dark, and she heard a man's footsteps in the hallway. This was not a lying-in-wait situation, Your Honor. There was no malice. This was a mother knowing that somebody had broken into the home where her children were sleeping. Matter of fact, as she was lying there, she sent a desperate text message—"

Judge Merriweather said, "Mr. Munroe, let me stop you right there. I hear what you're saying, but it's not appropriate at this juncture to start getting into any evidence that there may be in favor of your client. All we're here for today is to test the sufficiency of Mr. Fletcher's case."

"Thank you, Your Honor," Fletcher said.

"Understood, Your Honor." I was glad she'd let me paint as much of a picture as she had. "But I do just want to mention one procedural issue, if I may." She signaled that I could, so I said, "Our position is that this case falls squarely under Section 16-11-440 of the Protection of Persons and Property Act, under which my client, Britney LaSalle, is immune from prosecution for this incident. I filed a motion to that effect, and I believe the evidentiary hearing is scheduled for Friday, May 28?"

One thing I did appreciate about South Carolina law, in terms of efficiency and fairness, was that self-defense wasn't something you had to wait until trial to raise. If it had been, Britney might have had to sit in jail for a year or more before I could argue it. Instead, it was a legal immunity that you could raise at any point after arrest. I'd filed that motion the day after she hired me.

Judge Merriweather looked at her clerk, who nodded.

"Okay, then," she said. "We can get into your client's self-defense evidence at that hearing."

I could feel Britney deflating next to me. Despite my explanations of how this all worked, and despite the fact that my motion had a good chance of setting her free for good in less than two months' time, it seemed she'd still held out some hope that her problems would be solved today.

"Now, Mr. Fletcher," the judge said, "is there any dispute that the apartment where this homicide occurred was leased to Britney in her name only?"

"Uh, no, Your Honor—"

"And does the State agree that the parties were living separately at the time?"

"That— Well, in the sense that he continued to maintain the marital home, yes."

"Was there any sense in which they were *not* living separately?"

He didn't have an answer, so I spoke up to say, "If I may add, Your Honor, my client filed for divorce on February 10 of this year."

She looked at Fletcher. He said, "The State is aware of that, Your Honor."

She asked him, "And do you have any evidence that on the night in question, the deceased was an invitee?"

Had Britney invited him in, she meant. Despite her warning that now was not the time to get into self-defense, she was asking questions that pertained to exactly that. Under state law, a person who shot an intruder was immune from prosecution; the same was not true if the victim had been invited into the home.

"That, Your Honor, we—the State— We don't feel it's appropriate at this juncture to make a factual determination, Your Honor. At the preliminary hearing stage, I mean."

"I agree completely, Mr. Fletcher." She smiled, or at least that's what it looked like, with her cheeks rising behind the mask. I had always had the sense that among middle-aged Southern ladies, it was not permissible to allow more than a certain number of minutes to go by without smiling. "But," she continued, "that's not what I was asking for. You are absolutely right that we're not to weigh competing facts at this point. All we're inquiring into at this hearing is the sufficiency of the State's evidence. And the questions I've asked pertain, in my view, to malice."

In other words, they went to whether the State had probable cause to believe this death was murder, as opposed to some lesser type of homicide. Without malice, there was no murder.

"Your Honor," he said, "we have the investigating officer, as well as the other officer who was involved in Mrs.—in Britney's interrogation. And we have, as I mentioned, the legal presumption that given the deadly weapon and the lying in wait, that the requisite malice was in Britney's heart. But above all, Your Honor, if I may, the State does not feel that this hearing is the appropriate venue for considering any

21

aspect of any alleged self-defense immunity. That is scheduled, as Mr. Munroe noted, for May 28."

Up on the bench, Judge Merriweather was nodding. She didn't look happy. I sensed that if the self-defense hearing were today, and the evidence was consistent with what I'd said so far, she'd find in our favor and set Britney free. But the rules of criminal procedure tied her hands.

I spoke up. "Your Honor, may I have a moment to confer with my client and then with the solicitor? If we might step outside?"

She glanced at the clock. "If that's agreeable to you, Mr. Fletcher, we'll take a ten-minute recess."

———

Fletcher and I stepped into the hallway outside the courtroom. I tried the door of the nearest office, which traditionally was available for litigants to use, but it was locked. We were going to have to negotiate out in the open and keep our voices down.

"Morning." I held my hand out to shake. "Haven't had the pleasure of a proper meeting yet."

"Yep, that's the other reason I came down. Thought we ought to meet before we try that other case."

We shook. He didn't have the country-club soft hands I expected from a man of his age and position. There was something more solid to him, more down-to-earth.

"I understand your position here," I said. "I truly do. I spent most of my career with the solicitor's office myself."

His brows flickered in surprise, and he said, "That so?"

"Yep." I was surprised he hadn't looked me up already, but since he hadn't, I chose not to mention that I'd worked in Charleston. I didn't want to come off as a city slicker who thought too highly of himself, and it could be useful to let a man underestimate me. I just said, "So I hear where you're coming from on this. And I think we can both see this hearing could go either way."

"Maybe so," he said a little stiffly. He wasn't going to grant me that point.

"What I was thinking," I said, "was that if you were to propose dropping this to manslaughter, and if we could see eye to eye on a bond amount, I'd be willing to waive any preliminary hearing on that charge and just sit tight until May."

That way, he could walk out of here without losing, without any public finding by the court that he'd brought a case he couldn't support. And I could get my client out on bond.

It would mean throwing away the chance to get the case dismissed today. It would also mean giving up the possibility of having manslaughter charges dismissed at the preliminary hearing stage. The chances of that were slim, but I'd had it happen up in Charleston. Sometimes the investigating officer or another important witness wouldn't show up, and without their testimony to support the prosecution's case, the charges would have to be tossed.

So it would cost us something. But those outcomes were long shots, and I knew what my client cared about most.

Fletcher said, "You're willing to wrap up this hearing before Her Honor makes a ruling, and waive your right to be heard on manslaughter? Why?"

"Well, we might win," I said, "and I believe we ought to. But if we didn't? For a mother with little kids, seven or eight more weeks is a long time to sit in jail."

He nodded. That made sense. "What were you thinking as bond?"

"With her ties to the community, not to mention the fact that he broke into her house, I was thinking it ought to be on the low end. Say, five thousand?"

He screwed his face up. "For manslaughter? That's an insult. A man lost his life here."

"I understand that, but a bond my client can't afford is no bond at all. And is it that unreasonable to say a woman who shoots an intruder in the middle of the night ought not to lose her job and her home while she's awaiting trial?"

He gave an angry sigh and said, after a second, "Thirty thousand."

I paused to give that some thought. Whatever number we came up with, the judge would need to go along with it—and Britney would need to pay 10 percent in cash. I figured a bail bondsman might give her a grand or two for her car.

I said, "Fifteen?"

He hesitated. I knew that pride and negotiating tactics did not permit an immediate answer.

But then he said, "Deal."

4

APRIL 9, 2021

A s Terri pulled the last few take-out boxes from her bag, I said, "My goodness. I don't think my office has ever smelled this good." I pulled my shrimp gumbo closer and opened one of the bowls of rice. This lunch was a welcome break from brainstorming with her about the boat-crash case.

"Charleston turned you into a real city boy," she said. "You still don't know where to eat down here."

"Yeah. I mean, in high school, if lunch cost more than three dollars, I wasn't eating. And what did I know about soul food?"

"Well, you're not in high school anymore. And this is Gullah. But I guess that's a kind of soul food."

I tried to express interest—I knew almost nothing about her heritage, and I liked learning more—but my mouth was too full to talk.

She settled into her ribs and red rice. The receipt was stapled to one of the restaurant bags. I did the mental math and tossed thirty bucks onto the table by her purse.

As I sipped the sweet tea she'd brought, I sat back and gazed at the photos, maps, and documents pinned up on my corkboard. I'd turned a whole wall of my home office into a work surface; it helped me think. On one side of it was a photo of my client, Clay Carlson, in his varsity jacket.

A few weeks earlier, after his first lawyer suffered a stroke, Clay had come to me and told me with absolute earnestness that he had not been driving the boat when it crashed. He had every reason to lie, of course, but so did the other survivors. Even without factoring in that all three of them were drunk and underage, vehicular manslaughter could get you ten years in state prison.

But I'd seen no evidence, and nothing in the boy himself, to make me think Clay was the liar here.

His trial was set for July.

From the other side of my board, the dead boy, Hayden Parker, stared out at me. He'd been a good-looking kid: wavy brown hair worn a little long, a strong jaw, and a smile that looked genuine, if a bit uncertain.

He'd have been twenty years old by now, like Noah, if he'd lived.

On the corkboard, pushpins held pieces of string radiating out around Hayden's picture. One went to each of his parents, another to his sister, another to his strikingly beautiful girlfriend, who'd been on the boat that night. A few more strings went farther afield. Seeing the networks connecting people helped clarify things. It was like an aerial view of a community, making things visible that you wouldn't notice from down on the ground.

Terri wiped her hands on a napkin and said, "I wish I knew whose idea it was to have the DNR handle a case like this."

"Right?" I shook my head. "Since when do the folks who regulate duck hunting have the skills to investigate a boy's death?" The state's Department of Natural Resources was in charge of all waterways, so they'd been tasked with the initial investigation into the crash.

Twenty-four hours afterward, as it became clear something criminal had likely occurred, the DNR had handed the case over to the county sheriff. By that point, most of the evidence had been contaminated or just disappeared. One of the DNR officers working to remove the wrecked boat from the water had left his own fingerprints on the wheel, smearing prints that were already there. Two of the kids' cell phones were gone. Jimmy Ludlow, the solicitor's son, claimed in his statement to investigators that his phone had fallen in the water. I'd had no trouble believing that... until I saw the GPS records showing that it went from the accident scene to the hospital before shutting off.

And his clothes—all the clothes the survivors had been wearing—were taken home and washed.

This case was somehow more depressing than the last two big cases I'd had. More than the teenage boy charged with beating his father to death or the influencer whose house party had ended with a young woman dead.

What made it worse was the fact that tragedies didn't require any evil at all. This boy's death, and the fact that one of his surviving friends was looking at a ten-year prison sentence, had happened without any apparent malice. All it took was teenage foolishness.

Terri said, "Have you watched the news footage yet?"

I shook my head.

"We might as well see what they were saying on the night."

I leaned over and pulled one of the three plastic file boxes out from under my folding table. The front half of it held several clearly labeled Redweld files, and the back half had a bunch of color-coded boxes in different sizes. I flipped the plastic lid over to read the list taped to the underside.

Terri said, "Is that a list of what's in there? Oh my Lord. You *know* Laura deserves a raise."

"Yeah, I've told Roy that more than once."

Laura had been Roy's secretary for at least the twenty years I'd known him, and due to his generosity and her unusual enthusiasm for criminal law, she'd become mine too.

Terri said, "I wish somebody like her had been in charge of collecting the evidence at the scene."

"If only."

Laura had sent me a photo of the file boxes we received from Clay's old lawyer, just to share with me her outrage at the shape they were in. I never saw the fiasco myself, because by the time I got to the office to pick them up, she had reorganized every scrap of paper, thumb drive, and photo by topic and chronology, and banished the original packaging to the trash.

I opened the green box, which I knew contained a dozen CDs and DVDs in their own plastic envelopes, and pulled out the DVD labeled *News Footage 3/18/2020*. Laura had burned each audiovisual file onto a disc, as well as copying all the video and audio scattered across various USB keys onto a portable hard drive, with backup in the cloud.

As I was poking a paper clip into my DVD player, trying to make it open, Terri asked, "How'd that case go, up in Elkin Springs? She manage to make bail?"

"Yeah, she and her mom pledged their cars as collateral. She's home with her kids now."

"Thank God."

"Yeah. They got a fair-minded solicitor up there. Very reasonable guy."

"I wish we could say the same down here."

"Uh-huh." I popped the disc in. "Oh, if you got time, I might need a little of your detective work in advance of her self-defense hearing."

"How much?"

"I don't know. Five, six hours?"

"Sounds fine."

As I clicked play, she scooted her chair over to turn off the light, then slid back to get close to the screen.

The footage was shot outside the local hospital on the night of the crash. One of the young women newscasters from our local station said, "After a motorboat collided tonight with a piling on the Sea Island Bridge, unconfirmed reports tell us that one person may have died."

She went on, but we weren't watching her. Terri pointed to someone in the background, and I hit pause.

"I don't know who else that could be," she said. "I mean, the hair."

We had some running jokes about Pat Ludlow's fluffy silver curls, mostly relating to the 1980s soap opera stars or lounge musicians he resembled.

"So, he goes into the hospital at 2:13 a.m.," she said, copying into her notebook the time stamp on the news banner running across the bottom of the screen. "Thirty-two minutes after the first 9-1-1 call."

"Well, his son was in an accident—"

"Oh, of course, I'm not saying it's weird for him to be there. I just want to finish putting together the timeline. What did that nurse say?"

"She wasn't specific about the time," I said, reaching for the Redweld marked *Hospital*. Behind it was a folder labeled *News Stories*. I pulled that one out and handed it to her. "There might be some timeline stuff in here too."

While she flipped through it, I skimmed the statement the nurse had given Clay's old lawyer.

Terri said, "Have you looked through this? I can't tell if it's news or Ludlow's reelection campaign."

She splayed the folder open so I could see the headlines: "Ludlow Urges Unity on Boat Tragedy." "Ludlow Son Released from Hospital." "Solicitor Ludlow Stays Strong."

I grimaced. "You'd almost think his family was the only one the crash affected."

"Well, you know. He and Dabney the Fourth go way back."

"Do they?"

"Oh yeah. They pledged the same fraternity at USC. And so did their daddies."

"Huh. That's not exactly a win for independent journalism."

"You didn't know that about them?"

"I didn't run in those circles, did I? Those boys wouldn't have let me fetch water for them back in the day."

She said, "I'm not sure they would even now."

I laughed. Then I said, "Oh, about the timeline, let's keep an eye out for the earliest point when anybody alleged that Clay was at the wheel. If they breathalyzed him before they had reason to believe he was the one driving, I might be able to get the proof that he was drunk thrown out for lack of probable cause."

"That would help."

"Yup." I went back to perusing the nurse's statement. After a minute, I said, "So, she says Ludlow went to see his own kid first, of course. Says he got there within about ten minutes after the ambulance brought the kids in."

Terri shrugged. "That's fast, but it's understandable he wanted to make sure his son was okay."

"Yeah, but… She says she wasn't really paying attention to him until she noticed him in Emma's room. Then Clay's. Says he asked medical staff to leave so he could talk with the kids in private. And they did so. She couldn't swear to the exact timeline, but she thinks he was in with each of them for a good fifteen minutes or so."

I looked up from the statement. Terri was shaking her head, like the world had once again confirmed to her its corruption.

"I just want to say," I said, "although you must know already, that is not normal. As a prosecutor—as a father—leaving your kid alone after an accident so you can go have some kind of private tête-à-tête with injured teenage *witnesses*, for God's sake, as they're lying in their hospital beds, is not what you do. You don't talk to them before the sheriff does."

"*You* wouldn't," she said. "But…"

"Are you saying everyone in small-town law enforcement—"

"Who said small town? Where's your Tony Rosa right now?"

"Uh… yeah. Fair point."

Rosa, my former colleague at the solicitor's office up in Charleston, had recently embarked on a twenty-year sentence in federal prison. Unethical interrogation techniques like Ludlow's would've been the very least of his sins.

5

APRIL 14, 2021

I walked past palm trees into the bungalow near the causeway that served as Roy's law office. And mine, too, I supposed, though my title was still just "of counsel," and my name was not on the sign.

The reception desk was empty. I hoped Laura was there, so the donut I'd brought her from the bakery wouldn't go to waste. I also wanted to ask for some background info on the meeting she'd arranged for me, which was the reason I'd come in.

"Morning, Leland!" She came around the corner—from the pantry, I assumed, since she was carrying a discount-sized bag of ground coffee. With her black-rimmed glasses and her gray hair up in its usual bun, she looked like a cheerful older librarian.

"Morning. Roy in?"

"No, he's out golfing with a client."

"Tough life," I said. "But someone's got to live it."

She laughed. "You're a little earlier than I expected," she said, putting a coffee filter into the machine.

"Yeah, I had a couple of questions about this guy I'm meeting." I noticed she was wearing a cardigan. "Are you cold? You ought to put the thermostat up where you like it."

"Oh, me? No, I just need a cup of coffee. I'll be fine."

I set the donut on her immaculately organized desk, and she said thanks.

"So this guy," I began. "Victor Guerrero. He's not the actual client?"

"No, he's paying, but he called about his mother. She's been in the women's prison over by Columbia for nearly twenty years now."

"What was the crime?"

She looked at me with a flicker of surprise. "Oh," she said. "I forget, sometimes, how long you were away. Here in town, we all remember. It was murder." She hit the button on the coffee machine and went back to her desk. "I'll see if I can find you some articles on it," she said, wiggling her mouse to get the computer to wake up. "Although it was such a long time ago. I don't really recall how much news made it onto the internet back then."

"Who was the victim?"

"My goodness," she said. My ignorance had apparently shocked her so much that her hands froze a few inches above the keyboard. "You know what, why don't you pull up that chair there."

I did as I was told.

"All right," she said. "I'm going to explain this to the best of my recollection, and then I'll send you whatever articles I find. I don't want to get into a whole Google search when Mr. Guerrero's probably only ten or fifteen minutes away."

"Good call. But before I waste your time, this isn't a child-abuse case or anything like that, is it? Because unless we've got some total

34

miscarriage of justice, with a one hundred percent innocent client, that's not what I—"

"No, I understand. I wouldn't have taken the meeting if it were. Even if you were interested in defending that sort of person, Roy wouldn't want the firm's name on anything like that."

"Makes sense."

I got my first whiff of coffee and heard the machine burbling.

"So let me try to sum it all up real quick," she said, "if I can. Around 2000, I think it was, Mr. Guerrero's mother was working as a nanny for Pat and Peggy Ludlow—"

"This truly is the smallest of small towns," I said. "Everybody knows everybody. Wait, did you say Peggy? Isn't his wife named—what is it —Catherine? Or Cathleen?"

"Peggy was his first wife."

"Huh. Didn't know he'd been divorced."

"Oh, he wasn't. Peggy was murdered."

I didn't have time to answer; the bells jangled on the front door.

Laura looked past my shoulder and gave a big smile. "Good morning! Come on in! You must be Mr. Guerrero."

———

A few minutes later I was in my office, inviting him to take a seat, with cups of coffee on my desk for both of us. Victor was a short but strong-looking Mexican guy, about thirty, who'd dressed up for our meeting and didn't seem comfortable in a suit. He was too intense for it, and too powerfully built; he looked about as natural as a big old tomcat in a necktie.

He sat with his knees about two feet apart, leaning forward, like a football player. "Mr. Munroe," he said, "I want to thank you for taking this meeting. And I want to assure you that I have the money for whatever it is that you need to do."

"Well, you're welcome. Why don't you tell me what all you're hoping we can do?" I raised my coffee cup to him and took a sip.

"It's about my mother," he said. "Maria. Now, she came here over thirty years ago, before I was born. From Mexico. She was sixteen years old, and she worked herself to the *bone* to give us kids a better life. She's the best mother a man could have. Even from jail, she's kept right on doing what she could to take care of us. It wasn't much, but she tried. She learned to read and write there, just so she could send us letters and read what we sent her. She's always put us first."

He gave me a piercing look, checking to see if I was really listening. I nodded and said to go on.

"I know you must've heard about her case," he said, "since everybody has. My mother's been in state prison since I was twelve years old, for a crime that she did *not* commit. And I've been working ever since then to get to a place where I had enough money to help her out. Which I finally do."

"Well, you know what," I said, "I salute you. That's a hell of a challenge to rise to."

For a second, I wondered if I should ask about the details of the case or how he was so certain of his mother's innocence. I decided against it.

"So, Mr. Guerrero, I don't know that we need to discuss the actual crime right off the bat. What I would need to do, though, to avoid wasting your time, is figure out what the options are, legally speaking, for your mom. Now, first off, what type of sentence was she given?"

"Life. No parole."

"Uh-huh. And, uh, I trust she already appealed her conviction, and lost?"

"Oh yeah, right away. Her public defender did that a long time ago."

"Okay, and did he ever do anything else? Or any other lawyer?"

"There was one of those innocence things. It was called, uh, Found Innocent. You heard of it? Up in Charleston?"

"I have, yes." It was a nonprofit that specialized in exonerating wrongfully convicted prisoners. "And what did they do?"

"They, uh… I mean, I'm not exactly sure. I found them in 2018, and they tried a few things, but, you know, I'm in landscaping. I got four companies doing landscaping and masonry across three counties. I don't know about all the, uh, legal moves or whatever you'd call it." He shrugged, looking a little embarrassed, and took a swig of his coffee.

For a moment we were both so quiet that I could hear the palmetto frond outside brushing against my office window. I kept my expression attentive and sympathetic, but I was a little annoyed with Laura. I could not believe that when I was working on a case that might implicate Ludlow's son in a felony—and already suffering some slings and arrows shot by Ludlow's media-magnate friend—she would set up a meeting to see if I wanted to metaphorically dig up the corpse of Ludlow's murdered wife. What possible benefit could there be to me or my clients in turning the local solicitor into my sworn enemy?

"Mr. Munroe," Guerrero said, "I don't know if you can understand what it's like to grow up without a mother."

I gave him a nod. My son knew. And I could imagine what it might've been like for him to lose her at twelve, like Guerrero had, instead of eighteen.

He was shaking his head, looking off to the side, like he couldn't find the words. "Or what it's like for *her*, you know? It's a three-hour drive, one way, so we didn't get much chance to visit her. She didn't get to watch us grow up."

I said, "I do have some sense of that."

"I saw what you did for those kids," he said. "The one who they said killed his dad, and that girl whose friend died. Mr. Munroe, I talk to a lot of people every day. And I did not know *one*, not one soul, who thought those kids would ever go free. I mean, a lot of people said they were guilty, but people said that about my mom too. I don't listen to that. I make up my own mind."

I nodded and said, "Small-town gossip can be a terrible thing."

"I got no time for it. I want to see for myself. So I was there, you know? Your trial with that boy, right before the pandemic? Not the whole thing, but I took a day off and sat where they let people sit. I *saw* what you did. I saw you fighting for him. And I thought, if this Found Innocent lawyer can't help my mother, maybe this is the one guy who can."

———

I concluded our meeting without a commitment, telling him I'd need to reach out to Found Innocent to see what legal options might be left. He nodded hard, saying, "Yeah, that's fair, that's fair." He stood up, clapped my palm with a powerful handshake, and left. I looked out the window and saw his battered pickup leave the lot, rattling with its load of landscaping tools.

I had a soft spot for working people. And for anybody that the deck was stacked against.

6

APRIL 15, 2021

When I called Terri the next morning to see what she could tell me about Maria Guerrero's case and the death of Peggy Ludlow, she suggested I swing by. It wasn't something to discuss in front of Noah.

We sat out on her deck. It was still the time of year when you could be outside without sweltering, and we weren't going to miss out on that. Her fenced backyard was festooned with every type of spring flower I knew the name of—azaleas, tulips, lilacs, a magnolia, and the last few daffodils of the season—plus at least half a dozen I didn't.

I poured myself a glass of sweet tea from the pitcher she'd set out and said, "I don't know how you have *time* to keep a garden like this. Or how you keep Buster from digging it all up."

Her rottweiler was racing back and forth across the grass.

"Oh, he keeps the squirrels away," she said. "And the rabbits, and the deer. He's this garden's bodyguard."

"I like that," I said. "That's a great excuse! I'm going to start telling people the reason my backyard's nothing but dead grass and busted cement is because all I've got is a Yorkie."

She laughed. "Maybe you should hire Victor Guerrero to fix it up. I hear he's good."

"Yeah, he must be. He's been really successful for a man his age. Hell, any age."

She nodded, took a sip of tea, and said, "I sure don't envy him his motivation, though."

"No. Did he really have to help take care of all those kids? At twelve?"

"Yeah, he was the oldest. And his aunt worked double shifts."

She'd told me social services had placed the five Guerrero kids with their paternal aunt, since their dad was long gone by that point.

"And you think the mom is innocent?"

"I never thought she was guilty. That never made sense to me. And I heard… I mean, nobody on the force disagreed with the verdict, that I knew of, but—"

"Oh, right," I said. "I hadn't done the mental timeline yet. I forgot you would've already been an officer then."

"Yeah, I became a detective a little before her trial. So I wasn't on the case myself, but I heard about it. And it was one of those things where the word was that the verdict was right, but there was more to the story."

"Facts that didn't make it into the courtroom?"

"Exactly. But nobody let on to me what those facts were."

"You were too new on the force, I guess."

She gave me one of her looks. "That was part of it, I'm sure. At any rate, I wasn't in the circle that got that information."

She stood up to yell to Buster. He reluctantly stopped digging in a flower bed.

After she tossed him a tennis ball and sat back down, she added, "I get *different* information. Like, women tell me stuff—I mean female crime victims, witnesses, arrestees, anybody—that they wouldn't tell a man."

"Anything about Guerrero? Or his mom?"

"Not specifically. But just… the difference between the word on the street and the word on the force, about that case, made me wonder. And I never understood her motive."

"What, covering up a theft?" I'd read the articles Laura had sent me, so I knew the basic outline of the case. "Shooting your employer is pretty extreme, but when your family's hanging by a thread, economically, and you know you're done for if they catch you…"

I shrugged, set my tea down, and leaned back in my chair. A bird flew over us, dark against a perfect blue sky. I'd had my own brush with desperate economic straits, and I could imagine what that could do to a woman in her situation.

"I mean," I said, "with five young kids to raise, and her barely speaking English? I've never hired a housekeeper, but I imagine all they've got to go on is the good word of the previous employer. So if you steal something and get caught, you're done. Even if they let you go without calling the cops, nobody's hiring you after that. You're as good as homeless."

She didn't say anything. I looked over and saw her looking out into her yard, shaking her head. After a second, she said, "It's sure easier to think of it that way. But you know Found Innocent doesn't take a case if they don't think the person was innocent. That's their whole mission, isn't it? Helping people who shouldn't have been convicted at all."

I sighed. "Yeah, but they didn't keep pursuing her case, did they."

"Do you know why?"

I didn't.

She looked at me. "You still haven't called them, have you?"

I shook my head. "I don't want to get too deep into this without thinking it through. I mean, Ludlow must not think there was any miscarriage of justice, or he would've done something to get it fixed. And you don't go reopening the murder of the solicitor's wife without a damn good reason."

"Yeah. He's already pretty hard to deal with, so…"

"Exactly. And I've got to deal with him on almost every single case, at least the ones in this circuit. It's not fair to my other clients to give him a grudge against me."

"Oh, he already has one. Remember how hard he pushed Ruiz in Jackson's case?"

"Well, that's true." In my first big case after moving home, defending a friend of Noah's who'd been accused of murdering his father, Ludlow had operated as a very aggressive backseat driver for Ruiz, the assistant solicitor handling the prosecution. "Oh, speaking of Ruiz, I saw him in town the other day. He asked how you were."

"Oh, tell him hi." She chuckled and added, "And if Ludlow makes life hard for you, make sure you tell him. You know he'd go out of his way to undermine Ludlow."

I laughed. Ruiz, to say the least, did not get along with his boss.

"Still," I said, "getting in his crosshairs is a bad idea. Even when his office isn't involved, he's still got Fourth in his pocket."

"Mm-hmm. I can't believe the strings that man is trying to pull on the boat-crash case."

Ludlow had recused himself from the case, of course, since his son was directly involved. I'd gone further, getting his whole office conflicted out and persuading the court to bring in an outside prosecutor. But it was pretty clear that even so, Ludlow was still trying the case—he was just doing it through his media friend, in the court of public opinion.

"And chances are," I said, "there's not even anything I could do for her. You can't retry a murder case from twenty years ago just because you think it was wrongly decided."

I could hear the smile in her voice when she said, "You're trying to talk yourself out of this. But you know, if she's innocent, then she's the ultimate little guy. It's David and Goliath, and you love that kind of case."

I laughed. "I guess I should at least ask them why they took the case," I said. "And why they didn't keep going."

"Mm-hmm."

"But this kind of thing, I mean, to be able to bring it, you need new evidence. And if there was evidence that got overlooked, even if it could've proven her innocent back then, would it still exist now?"

"Yeah. I mean, I doubt this is a DNA case."

I nodded. "Right? I don't even know what DNA they would've tried to collect at the scene."

"They might do fingernail scrapings, in case Mrs. Ludlow fought back. But that type of hand-to-hand self-defense is unusual in a simple firearm murder, and I don't recall anything about that at the time."

We both knew that with current technology, it was easy to prove that the guy sitting in jail did or did not commit the rape he was charged with, as long as the original evidence still existed. But the vast majority of other cases didn't involve any DNA evidence at all.

"If I start digging around," I said, "and find out there's nothing I can do, Ludlow's going to hear about it, and he isn't going to like it. Or if I take the case and somehow show it was an accident, not murder, so I get his wife's killer out of jail, I'm his sworn enemy for the rest of his life. And apart from that, I mean…"

I stopped talking. The flowers in Terri's yard reminded me of the ones my own wife used to plant up in Charleston. Some birds were tweeting. I tried to listen to them.

She said, "You thinking about Elise? And what you went through?"

I nodded.

"I got a sense of what it does to you," I said. "Even if it wasn't someone else's fault at all. So I wouldn't blame him for hating me if I open this back up."

———

That afternoon, I drove Clay to Columbia so we could watch the videos of the witness interviews after the boat crash. Fletcher had to let us see them, but he didn't have to make it convenient, and he didn't. We'd made arrangements for Fletcher to provide a laptop, with the videos on its hard drive but no internet connection and no USB ports, in the conference room of a local law firm.

As a prosecutor, I'd done the same thing myself; you didn't want a defendant copying evidence like that and potentially posting it on the web.

On the way there, I explained to Clay that I wanted him to hear everything his friends, or former friends, had told investigators about that night. If there were holes in their stories, he might be the only person capable of spotting them.

Clay was a gawky kid with brown hair, dressed in chinos and a blue polo shirt. A secretary from the law firm brought us in and offered both of us coffee, which he accepted with a "Yes, please, ma'am!" He sat with his back straight and his hands on his thighs, attentive, polite. He was good-looking in a boy band kind of way, and if I had to guess, I'd have said he weighed at most 140 pounds.

Every time I saw him in person, I was hit with the knowledge that this kid, if he went to prison, would be absolutely brutalized.

That was why we'd already rejected a two-year plea deal. That, and the fact that Fletcher was only offering a recommended sentence, not a negotiated one, which meant that the judge was free to impose a longer sentence.

While we waited for our coffees, I asked, "How's school? You pick a major yet?"

"Well, I was thinking business originally." He sounded hesitant. "To go work with my daddy, you know." His father, one of Roy's clients, owned a few car dealerships in and around Basking Rock.

"Something else starting to interest you now?"

"Well, this whole, you know… situation. It's got me thinking I might want to be a lawyer."

I nodded. "That's understandable. And after this you'll know a whole lot more than most law students do. Although this is a damn hard way to learn it."

The secretary came in with our coffees. I thanked her and teed up the computer.

"So what we've got here," I said, "is video of the officers' body-cam footage from the crash site, and then the interviews with Jimmy and Emma. And by the way, I'm sorry if it gets tedious to hear me saying this all the time, but I've got to remind you not to talk about anything we say with your daddy or anybody else."

"Oh yeah," he said, nodding. "Attorney-client privilege, I know. I had to explain that to my dad. He wasn't too happy, but he understood."

"Okay, good. So, take a look at this. We can watch it through, or you can stop me anytime to point out something. Whatever makes sense to you."

I hit play, and on the screen, the image of Emma Twain began to shiver and cry. The body-cam footage showed her standing beside an ambulance, soaking wet, with a blanket around her.

I hit pause and wrote down the time stamp on the video. The high-security process Fletcher and I had agreed to was for me to request copies of any clips or stills I thought I might need, which he would provide ten days before trial. It went without saying that I wanted pictures of where everybody was and how they looked after the crash.

When the video started again, Emma's face turned from blue to red and back again as the lights flashed on a nearby police car.

"Where is he?" she asked, sounding terrified. "Did you find him? You need to get him out!"

"Miss, we got men out there looking right now." The officer speaking —the one whose body-cam footage we were watching—was Deputy McDonald. "Was it just the four of y'all on the boat?"

"Yes!"

"Okay, and where was he when the impact occurred?"

"He was right—" She gestured with one arm. "Right next to me, but…" She turned toward the water and shouted Hayden's name a couple of times.

We heard a man's voice say, "Emma!"

She screamed, "Go away!"

The officer turned. His body cam brought Jimmy Ludlow into the frame. The kid was soaking wet, and he said, "Emma, I'm sorry."

The officer yelled, "Okay, listen to me. I am trying to find your friend, and I need your help. Miss, whereabouts were you on the vehicle?"

She looked confused. "The vehicle?"

"The boat, miss. If you tell me where he was sitting, it might help us locate where he would've got thrown."

"He was standing up. Next to me. I was sitting, uh… facing the side, I guess? I didn't see anything coming."

"And was he closer to the front or to the back?"

"He was— He was—" She held out her right arm. "I guess closer to the front?"

"Was he close to the— Which of them two boys was driving?"

"I— Why does— You have to look for him! Please! I don't know!"

"We're looking, miss."

The view swung around as Deputy McDonald headed down toward the beach, and a second later it stopped on Clay. The deputy asked if he needed a blanket, and he said, "No, help my friend! He went into the water!"

I hit pause and said, "What's that on your shirt?"

His white T-shirt was soaking wet, with a brownish stain across the front.

"Oh, that must be— Hayden got sick on the boat. He was drunk."

"He threw up on you?"

"He threw up everywhere."

I hit play. The deputy shined his flashlight toward the DNR guys out on the water. In the background, Emma was screaming Hayden's name.

Clay looked shaken.

I hit pause again. "I'm sorry. I know it's hard." He nodded.

He said, "Jimmy told her he was sorry. He knew it was his fault."

"Uh-huh. And we'll bring that up. As for what she said, did you hear anything that didn't match your recollection?"

"Doesn't it matter that she said she didn't know, but now she's changed her mind?"

"Yeah, that's part of our defense, of course. But apart from that, is what she said pretty much how you recall things happening?"

He screwed his brows up like he wanted to make sure he said the right thing. "I mean... it depends which part you're talking about."

I kept my face expressionless. I didn't want him to see I was dismayed. Someday this kid might make a good lawyer, or he might fend off questions well in a civil deposition. Right now, though, it was not the right approach. His way of thinking things through and hedging his answers did not play well with juries.

"Well," I said, "which part of what she said is something you remember, and which part isn't?"

"I wasn't looking at them, so I don't remember exactly where they were or who was closer to the front." He looked at me like he wanted a cookie for doing such a precise analysis.

"Well, do you recall roughly where they were sitting?"

"Oh, behind me. Like she said."

"Okay—"

"Or I mean, they were back where the seats are. Not up by the wheel. I don't know for a fact that they were sitting down, because I wasn't looking at them."

"Uh-huh."

Clay had said, to me and from the very start—in his statement to a DNR officer at the crash site, and to the sheriff less than forty-eight hours later—that he'd been standing near the wheel, yelling at Jimmy to slow the hell down. He hadn't mentioned where the others were, but since it was a motorboat, there was only one other place to be.

"Okay, and now here comes the part of her interview that I really want you to see."

The next video was from Emma's statement two days later at the sheriff's office. I scooted forward to about the nine-minute mark.

Her eyes were red, and her blonde hair was in a limp ponytail. By this point, thirty-plus hours after the crash, she knew her boyfriend was dead.

The deputy pushed a Kleenex box across the table and said, "Here you go."

She dabbed her eyes and blew her nose. I noticed she was still wearing her white plastic hospital bracelet.

The deputy said, "So Clay was up at the wheel?"

She nodded. "I was with Hayden by the seats. Clay wasn't with us."

"And who was actually driving the boat?"

"Well, it wouldn't have been Jimmy. He was—honestly, he was way too drunk."

She was looking off to one side as she spoke. At the nearest wall, apparently. I got a sense of shame off her.

"And where had y'all procured the liquor?"

The shame was palpable. She was looking at her lap. "I brought it," she said, so quiet you could barely hear. "I drove us all over to Beaufort for it. I had a fake ID."

Her ID was at the bottom of St. Helena Sound, but she could hardly lie. She must've known the liquor store's security camera had recorded the transaction.

"And what was it that you brought?"

"Just beer."

The deputy wrote that down.

"And they all got drunk?"

"Jimmy and Hayden did. I don't know about Clay."

"So that's why he was driving the boat?"

"Uh-huh."

50

I hit pause again and asked him, "What about that?"

"She's right: he was drunk. But he wouldn't let anybody else drive. I was up there shouting at him, trying to pull him off, but—I mean, he's a wrestler, he's got a grip like you wouldn't believe. And I'm—you know." He gestured to his own skinny body.

"So what'd you do?"

"I gave up. I just tried to navigate, you know? Shouting at him to turn around when he was heading for the ocean, trying to get him to take us back to land. And I was *trying* to steer him around the bridge. I was shouting to pull left, but he wouldn't listen."

"I know. Here, take a second. Have a sip of coffee."

He did so.

When he'd calmed back down, I said, "So the thing we've got to confront for the jury is, why would she say that? Why would Hayden's girlfriend, who of all people ought to want to see the right man in jail, say you were driving if you weren't?"

He looked stricken. "Do *you* not believe me either?"

"No, that's not what I'm saying. I believe you. I'm just trying to understand why she would point the finger at you."

"How'd she even know? She said Hayden was next to her, between her and us. And she didn't see the bridge coming. So how'd she see who was at the wheel?"

As I nodded, I couldn't help but smile. "That's a good observation, exactly what a lawyer ought to pay attention to." I shifted in my chair, getting back to business. "And we'll point that out to the jury, but I don't want to rely on that alone. Because she could've just said she didn't see. What I want to know is, why didn't she say that? Do you know of any reason she might want to make things hard for you?"

"She's not making it *hard*," he said. "She's trying to put me in **prison**. For years! I never did anything to *anyone*, much less her, that deserves that." He was upset, which was understandable, **but** I couldn't help but notice he hadn't answered my question.

"Oh, I'm sure," I said. "But what I'm asking is, was there any **type of** **bad** blood between the two of you? Ever?"

"I don't know. Maybe? We met in ninth grade, and all kinds of **dumb** things happen at that age. Just stupid kid stuff." He was gesticulating, still upset. "But I don't remember one single thing that could **make** a person lie and send somebody to jail!"

For the first time since I'd met him, I knew he was hiding something from me.

To come right out and say so didn't seem like a useful approach. **I had** to let him know without accusing him.

"Listen, Clay," I said, looking him dead in the eye. "Do you **want** to stay out of prison?"

"Of course I do! What kind of question is that?"

"Well, then, you're going to have to remember."

I don't know if it was my look or my tone, but something **subdued** him. He went back to his attentive, polite posture, with an expression on his face like he was trying to understand or come to terms **with** what I'd said.

"Sir, are you saying... you want a *list* of everything I ever... **I don't** know, anything I can remember that could've possibly upset **her** in some way?"

I nodded and said, "Yeah, that'd work."

7

APRIL 21, 2021

At the highway rest stop, which wasn't much more than a roof on stilts with a few vending machines underneath it, I fed another dollar bill into the slot and hit the button for a Coke. I was heading a few hours north to the women's correctional facility outside Columbia to meet Maria, and I needed some caffeine.

A few days earlier, I'd spoken to a woman at Found Innocent. All she could tell me was that, right before the pandemic, the lawyer in charge of Maria's case had filed a motion for habeas corpus based on ineffective assistance of counsel at her original trial; then more recently, she'd filed another motion based on a Brady violation, meaning a failure by the prosecution to turn over evidence that might have shown Maria was innocent. The person I spoke with didn't know what that evidence was. Like most habeas motions, both of them had been denied, and then Maria's lawyer had moved on to a different job.

"I don't know much about this case," my contact had said. "I'm real sorry, but we're kind of a skeleton crew here. Not nearly enough funding for all the work that needs to be done. I'm happy to send you the file."

I'd hesitated for a second, then told her to send it on over.

I wanted to know what the evidence was.

I told myself I ought to at least find out if Maria had a shot. If she didn't, I could tell Guerrero that and save him his money.

I stood under the shelter, looking off into the trees, and drank my Coke. I wasn't about to risk spilling a drink in Roy's Malibu. Especially when I hadn't even mentioned this trip to him, or the possibility that I might take this case. Fighting for the convicted murderer of the circuit solicitor's first wife was about as far from Roy's genteel brand as could be. He'd probably prefer that I park both the Malibu and his own BMW in the path of an oncoming freight train.

If I turned around and drove home, nothing would happen. My life and career would proceed normally.

Of course, then I'd have to explain to Terri why I'd chickened out.

I finished the Coke, got in the car, and headed back onto northbound I-95.

———

The women's prison was a two-story brick building behind several rows of barbed-wire fence. I showed my ID at two different sets of security doors and then put my briefcase on the X-ray belt, promptly set off the metal detector with my belt buckle, and suffered the indignity of having to walk through again in drooping pants while my belt was screened for contraband.

I wasn't the only visitor. More folks came in behind me, and a few yards ahead, by some tables, a little boy watched me curiously while a woman I took to be his grandmother transferred keys, a phone, and other items from a plastic tray back into her purse.

I figured the kid was visiting his mom. I wondered if he lived nearby or if, like the Guerrero kids, this was a rare visit.

As a lawyer coming to speak with a potential client, I was escorted to a private room instead of the visiting area. The room was bare except for a table, which held a bottle of water and a stack of plastic cups, and two chairs. The small window had wires in the glass and was set too high to see anything but the clouds.

A few minutes later, a guard brought Maria in. She was short, built like a very feminine fire hydrant, with a gray braid down her back. She was wearing a turquoise-blue prison uniform that made me think of a nurse's scrubs.

She looked irritated. That was not the attitude I'd been expecting.

But then, if you'd been sitting in prison for as long as she had, it was reasonable that there'd come a point when you stopped believing in lawyers anymore.

"Afternoon, Mrs. Guerrero," I said. "I'm Leland Munroe. Would you like a glass of water?"

She shrugged.

I poured for both of us.

"So, I spoke with your son, Victor. He cares about you very much, of course, and he asked me if there's anything I could do to help you. So—"

"You don't *touch* his money," she said.

"Excuse me?"

"He works hard." She pointed at me, giving a warning. "He don't need somebody taking it for nothing." Her accent was strong, considering she'd been in America for more than thirty years, but there was no mistaking the angry tone.

"Well, Mrs. Guerrero, I hear you on that. I haven't taken one dime from him, and I'm not going to unless I believe that I have a solid chance of getting you out of here."

"A what?"

"A good chance." I slowed my speech down a little and tried to choose my phrasing more carefully. "What I mean is, I have not asked Victor for even one dollar yet, and I will not take any money unless I truly believe that I can get you out of prison."

She sat back in her chair, crossed her arms over her ample belly, and cocked her head as if to say she'd believe it when she saw it.

I took a sip of my water.

"Oh," I said. "Victor asked me to bring this to you."

I reached into my briefcase and pulled out a plastic envelope containing an eight-by-ten photo of Victor with his brother and sisters and the several children they had between them. He'd suggested the envelope as a way to protect it, since frames, even without glass, weren't allowed in prison.

She took it, gazed at it with a bittersweet smile, and blinked fast like she was trying to keep back tears. "So big," she said.

I didn't know if she meant the grandkids had gotten big, or if she was referring to the photo itself. Victor had told me that families weren't allowed to bring any type of photos or documents on prison visits, and pictures sent by mail had to be four-by-six or smaller. But lawyers visiting clients operated under different rules.

I said, "It's a real shame that you can't see them more often."

She nodded. After a second, she looked up from the photo and said, "You know, they try to break you here. A lot of the women are broken already. After a lot less years than me."

I took that in. I was starting to see how her anger might have served her well. "But you're not?"

She dismissed that idea with a quick shake of the head. "No. Why? The one who deserves to break is not me. It's the procurador, the judge, the…" She waved one hand to indicate everyone else in that category.

Prosecutor, she'd said. Apparently, at least one of my brain cells had picked up that Spanish word somewhere.

"Not you."

"Not me, no. A mother can't break. Because then what happens to the children?"

"Uh-huh. Yeah, I get that."

She dropped her gaze to the photograph again, tracing her finger over it. I couldn't see from where I was sitting, but I figured she was caressing the faces of her kids.

"He's the same age," she said, almost to herself.

"Who?"

"Carlito, Victor's son." She looked up from the photo. "The same age as their little boy, Brandon, back then."

"Oh, is he?" I remembered that when Peggy Ludlow died, her child—Pat Ludlow's first son—had been about three years old.

"Yes. Brandon was such a good boy. Do you see him? I wonder many times how he's doing."

The sympathy and concern in her voice were unmistakable.

I said, "Did you spend much time with Brandon? When you were working there?"

"Oh, yes. I was—she didn't like to say nanny, Mrs. Ludlow, she called me 'mother's helper.' Yes, I spent a lot of time with him."

"Why didn't she like to say nanny?"

"Oh, because for her, a nanny is for a mother who is not there. She was there, you know. She did not work outside of the home."

"Uh-huh. And what was she like as a person? Or as a boss?"

"Oh, she was pretty nice, you know? Never yelled at me, and at Christmas, she gave me presents for my kids. Maybe I could have used money instead, but she wanted to pick the presents herself. And she was a good mother. That's why I worry, you know, about how he's doing."

"Yeah, I understand. It sounds like you got along pretty well."

She shrugged.

"And I can see why you would've preferred money, with five kids to feed. So, can you tell me, one thing they said at your trial was that you'd taken some jewelry from—"

"Never. I never did that." She stared me right in the eyes as she shook her head. She was smoldering with rage. "I never steal nothing in my life. And even if someone doesn't know me, doesn't believe me, I ask them this: What am I going to do with those things she wore? It was like for a queen, what she had. Her big gold necklace that weighs a whole pound, am I going to walk into a jewelry store and say, hello, this is mine, can you pay me thousands of dollars for it? They would call the police!"

I had to laugh. I apologized for it and said, "You have a point, absolutely. That makes sense."

"I never did that! And I never even heard that they were stolen until after, from the police. If they were stolen, I don't know that, but I can tell you she never accused me. *She* knew I would not do that."

"Uh-huh. Well, were there ever any problems between you and her?"

"Oh, you know." She shrugged. "Sometimes, if she's in a bad mood, everybody knows about it."

"Did that happen a lot?"

She squinted, looking up toward the ceiling, like she was trying to remember.

"I mean… not too much, you know? Just sometimes, like anyone. Mostly, she had a beautiful little boy, a beautiful house—she was happy. She really loved that boy. As a mother, she was happy. As a wife, maybe not as much."

That got my attention, but I kept my expression unchanged. "Oh? How so?"

"Just, you know, there was fighting sometimes, and the way she looked at him, or complained… I don't know."

"Huh," I said. "That's interesting." After a second I asked, "And what did you think of Mr. Ludlow?"

"Oh, he…" She shook her head and looked away. Her opinion clearly was not positive.

When she didn't go on, I said, "Uh-huh?"

"He just, he liked things *his* way. Even when I'm putting away his wife's clothes, not even *his* clothes, if he's there on the weekend and he sees me, he has *his* way he wants me to do it. For that, and for everything."

That was odd, but knowing Ludlow, not surprising.

She didn't seem inclined to keep talking, so I switched gears. "Okay, Mrs. Guerrero," I said. "I know your kids want you home. But I can't make you any promises—except, like I said before, I won't take Victor's money unless I think I can win. Right now, I don't know enough about your case to know if there is any way to get you out. Your old lawyer is sending the file over, but it hasn't arrived yet."

She winced when I mentioned her old lawyer. Whatever had happened there, maybe that's why she'd come into the room mad at me. "So how do you know?" she asked. "How you find out if there is a way?"

"Well…" I sat back, looking at the little square of blue and white sky that was visible through the window before turning my attention back to her. "Here's the thing. You exhausted your appeals a long time ago —" Her face was blank, so I switched from legalese to normal English. "What I mean is, you already appealed and lost, right after your trial."

She nodded.

"And your last lawyer tried to get you out by saying that there was some evidence you were innocent. Right?"

"Yes."

"But that failed. It's still the right approach, though. What I mean is that at this point, right now, the only way to get you out would be to come up with some evidence that you're innocent. Evidence that wasn't heard, or, you know, presented, in court at your trial."

She was nodding like that made sense.

"Now, if your trial was tomorrow, if it hadn't happened yet, I wouldn't need to ask you about your innocence. Because it's up to the, uh, procurador to prove that you're guilty. That's *his* job. It wouldn't be *my* job to prove that you're innocent. I'd only have to convince the jury that they couldn't be sure." I was gesturing, off to the side and then toward myself, trying to illustrate where the burden was and who had to prove what.

"Okay. But now it's different?"

"Right. Exactly. Since the trial already happened and you were convicted, and the appeals and everything failed, the only thing left would be to find some way of showing that you were actually innocent. That's—"

I stopped myself before saying it was a whole different ball game, since I didn't want to complicate things with any idioms that might not translate well.

"That's a real different job, for me," I said. "It means, for instance, that I need to ask you if you're innocent."

"Of course. I never killed *anyone*. I told everyone this from the very first day."

I nodded as she spoke. My inner lie detector didn't go off, but her tone had changed: for the first time in our conversation, she sounded beaten down. I supposed if you'd been saying the same thing for twenty years and nobody ever listened, that would take something out of you.

"Uh-huh. Now, remind me, since I haven't gotten your file yet, did you testify at trial?"

"Yes! I told them everything. But nobody believed me!"

"Okay. Why don't you tell me, then. What happened on the day Mrs. Ludlow died?"

"I heard a gun. I was with Brandon in his room, and I went to do the laundry because he was napping, he'd just fell asleep. And I heard— Her dressing room was at the corner of the hallway, and from there I heard her. Not scream, but like start to scream or to say something, and then I heard the gun. So I don't move, I keep the door closed. Then there was no sound. So I decided to go to the phone. My purse was downstairs. I didn't have it." She stopped, staring at nothing—or at what she was remembering, I supposed.

"So you went out?"

She nodded. "I looked down the hallway. And her door was open, and I saw her hand on the floor." She shook her head slowly. "Her hand *moved*. It moved, so I go to her, instead of going to get my phone. And she was— There was blood—" She touched her chest, as if recalling where the blood had been. "I tried to help her. I tried to stop the blood. And then Mr. Ludlow came in."

8

APRIL 23, 2021

Terri, sitting on the far side of my office desk with what was at least her second coffee of the morning, said, "I don't even want to imagine what old Fourth is going to say about you when things start heating up on Maria's case."

"Yep, that'll be fun."

"What'd Roy say?"

"Not a lot. He was heading out to meet a client for golf when I told him."

"Huh. Is he really okay with bringing the wrath of Ludlow down, or was he not paying attention?"

"I don't know. I probably ought to sit him down and explain it more, but I had to get the engagement letter out, and that week he was in and out so much that there just wasn't time."

"I suppose he must realize that if he's got you on board doing criminal defense, his firm and Ludlow are never going to be on the same side."

"Yeah. And with the other lawyers in Ludlow's family tree, it's not as if anybody that guy's even slightly related to has ever given Roy one dime's worth of business."

"Mm-hmm." Terri's phone dinged, and she looked at it. "Oh, in two hours I'm talking to Britney LaSalle's cell provider. Call me when you're out of the hearing, and I'll let you know what they say."

"Okay. If I have to get a subpoena, I will, but I'd rather not deal with that."

Britney had changed her number after leaving her husband because he'd bombarded her with dozens of messages a day, but unfortunately, she hadn't kept any screenshots. I needed to see what he'd sent her, in case it included threats of violence; those would be helpful at her next hearing.

"Good Lord," I said. "In forty minutes I have to be in my car heading for the courthouse." We were preparing for my 10 a.m. hearing in Clay's case. Court-imposed deadlines ruled my life. "Was there anything else you thought I ought to see?"

"Well, that, to start with." She'd printed out the article that had appeared in March on the local news website—the one Noah had mentioned to me—and tossed it on my desk to make me finally get around to reading it.

"God, that photo," I said. "You think Fourth really believes people want that good a view of my nostrils?"

She laughed and said, "You know how he is. If he doesn't like you, he goes out of his way to get a bad picture."

"This one's enough to give me a complex."

I started reading. The article talked about my "legal sleight of hand" and referred to what it called "damning evidence" against Clay, which, if it existed, I hadn't seen yet. That was the topic of the 10 a.m. hearing: I'd filed a Rule 5 motion to compel the State to turn over all the information they were planning to use against Clay at trial. I needed it to prepare the defense, and I knew there was more than what they'd provided so far.

"So why was it you said Fletcher must have leaked something? I thought he was more of a straight shooter."

"Look at the date. And then these other two."

"Huh." The other articles were illustrated with photos of Clay that brought to mind a movie I hadn't seen in years: *American Psycho.* "These all came out the same week they offered Clay that plea deal?"

She nodded. "Kind of turns the heat up on him, doesn't it."

"I mean, it did bother him." Clay had wavered in his resolve, wondering if he ought to take the deal. "And, man, that fingerprint thing! It drives me up the wall."

One headline said, "Fingerprints Show Carlson Drove." It wasn't until the fourth paragraph that you found out Jimmy Ludlow's prints were also on the wheel.

"The plea offer before that was in November, right?"

"I think so."

As Terri tapped away at her laptop, I rummaged through the plastic box containing the files from Clay's previous lawyer, who had rejected a deal offering a five-year sentence. Five was far better than the potential twenty-five years that Clay could get for vehicular manslaughter under the influence, but in my view, he'd been wise to reject it. Since then, we'd rejected a far better deal, and I stood by that decision. Even if Clay could be bubble-wrapped to protect him from the brutality of other prisoners, which of course wasn't possible, a manslaughter conviction would likely torch any chance of his becoming a lawyer.

I found the timeline. "Yeah. November 10, they offered, and November 16, he refused."

I saw her brows raise at something on her screen. "Look at this." She turned her laptop around.

She had a page up with all the articles on Clay's case that had appeared on our local news site. Last fall there'd been nothing until two days before the five-year deal was offered. One article had come out right before the offer, and another two came out during the week he took to think it over.

"Nice headlines," I said, shaking my head. The first one was "Boat Crash Teen 'Felt Guilty,' Friends Say." The so-called friends quoted in the article had remained anonymous. The next headline, over a photo of Clay's dad smiling outside one of the car dealerships he owned, said, "Business as Usual While Boat Tragedy Parents Grieve."

"And then look at the offer you handled."

I'd rejected a two-year plea offer in March. Her screen showed another flurry of negative press right before that offer and right after it. The period between those two deals, from December to February, had no articles on Clay's case at all.

I said, "I know I'm more paranoid than most people…"

She smiled. "Nothing you could say would sound paranoid to me."

I laughed. Her years as a cop, and subsequently as a private investigator, had given her an unflattering view of humanity. "Yeah, I guess not. But on top of poisoning the jury pool, doesn't the timing almost seem like a warning to him? 'Take that deal, or we'll make everybody think you're a monster,' that kind of thing? Not to mention destroying his daddy's business."

"Mm-hmm. I guess if you're a prosecutor, it helps to have a friend who owns newspapers."

"Right. But as you say, for the second leak, if there was one, it'd have to be Fletcher. Once Ludlow's office was off the case, nobody there should've known about the plea offer. Not unless Clay accepted it."

"Yeah, well… You know that down here—for some people, anyway—'should' is more of a suggestion. Not so much a command."

"That rings true for Ludlow. And maybe I was too quick to think Fletcher was more on the up-and-up."

"Actually," she said, cocking her head like she'd just thought of something, "that might explain the paramours too." We'd taken to calling that pair of witnesses "the paramours," partly so we could talk about them without it being obvious who we meant, and partly because we were entertained by the ridiculous word.

I laughed. "As in, they paid no heed to the rule that if you're going to get it on with someone other than your spouse, you shouldn't do it outside where folks might see you?"

"If there was a thought process at all," she said, "that must've been it."

"Speaking of, did you find out anything about them that I ought to know before the hearing?"

"Maybe. I don't know how relevant it is for today, but Mr. Paramour is no friend of Ludlow's. He purged his social media last year, or thought he did, but I dug up some old posts about how Ludlow is corrupt and un-Christian and…" She spread her hands out to encompass every other bad thing there could be. "Matter of fact, I have it on good authority he was planning to file papers to challenge him in the primary next spring."

"To run against him? For circuit solicitor?"

"Mm-hmm."

"He kicks off his political career by going at it under a bridge, with someone else's wife?"

She shrugged as if to say it takes all kinds. Then she added, "It's funny how that didn't make it into the papers."

"The bridge thing? Yeah, I don't remember hearing about it before we took the case."

"You didn't. I searched the web for it. I found not one word."

———

As I drove to the courthouse, I thought about leaks. I knew that defense attorneys normally liked to get as much press coverage as possible; if the client had a solid chance of getting off, defense counsel would want the reasons for that to be repeated over and over in the media. So anything that got in the way of sharing information with reporters was anathema to them.

Or anathema to *us*, I realized: I was one of them now.

We liked talking to the press. We wanted the opportunity to get the public on our side.

But with the local press in Ludlow's pocket, and Clay's case not being sensational or outrageous enough to attract attention from the national media, maybe the usual rule didn't apply. I didn't want my client to keep getting smeared, and I certainly didn't want witnesses reluctant to talk to us out of fear that they might get dragged through the press themselves.

But I couldn't get up in front of the judge and accuse Fletcher or Ludlow of being in cahoots with Fourth. The fact that a few hit pieces got published on suspiciously convenient dates wasn't nearly enough to go on, and the last thing I wanted to do was make the judge think I was paranoid or drama-prone. If he got that impression, he'd factor it into everything I said or did from now through the end of trial, and I'd have to argue twice as hard to convince him of anything.

Sitting at a traffic light, I recalled that the brief Fletcher had filed in opposition to my motion to compel had an interesting point buried in it—something I might be able to use. In the first few pages, Fletcher had expressed indignation at my accusation that the State had improperly withheld evidence, and he set forth a laundry list of what the State *had* provided: this many gigabytes of digital data, that many thousands of documents, ten or twelve bullet points itemizing the types of evidence they'd disclosed. The State, he argued, had bent over backward to give us what we were entitled to.

But halfway through page four, he'd acknowledged that there were a few things they'd withheld. His explanation was that it was "highly sensitive personal information" about certain witnesses, and he indicated he would happily share that information if I agreed to come view it on a computer at his office instead of receiving copies, as I'd done for the body-cam footage and interviews.

I parked outside the courthouse, fed the meter, and headed in. He didn't know it, but Fletcher had given me what I needed.

———

"All rise." The bailiff's deep baritone called us to attention. Along with the courtroom staff and us lawyers, half a dozen spectators stood up too. On my way into the courtroom, I'd recognized one of them as the local reporter who'd been in the courtroom for every hearing in the case so far.

The white-haired judge walked briskly to the bench.

"Court is now in session," the bailiff said. "The Honorable George Chambliss presiding."

I'd been before Judge Chambliss several times. He liked a low-key, civilized approach, and I suspected the umbrage with which Fletcher had responded to my motion had not sat too well with him.

After greeting the courtroom and outlining his rules for decorum, Chambliss said, "Morning, counsel. Okay, Mr. Munroe, you're the movant, so why don't you go ahead and tell me where things stand. Are we still where we were when you filed last Friday, or have you and Mr. Fletcher worked anything out?"

"Unfortunately, we have not, Your Honor. And I want to stress, that's not due to any failings on Mr. Fletcher's part. I had to travel out of town on another case, and we weren't able to make our schedules align."

"Okay, well, I appreciate the collegiality. Are you suggesting you might have been able to come to some type of agreement otherwise?"

"I am, Your Honor. If I could just draw Your Honor's attention to page four of the State's brief, Mr. Fletcher indicated he was willing to provide some of the requested evidence, under what I would characterize as extremely stringent conditions."

"Uh-huh," he said, flipping to the page and scanning it.

"And after we submitted our respective briefs, I complied with those conditions. I was obliged to travel to his office up in Columbia and review the evidence on a laptop, under supervision, but I am not permitted to obtain a copy of the evidence until ten days before trial."

"Uh-huh. What's the reason for those conditions? I'm starting to feel like we've got an international espionage case going on right here in Basking Rock."

With the exception of the bailiff, who remained expressionless, everyone laughed. You had to, when you were before a judge who liked to crack the occasional joke. Fletcher shook his head like that was a real good one.

"If I may, Your Honor," I said, "the evidence he imposed those conditions on is videos of certain witness interviews—"

"Oh, okay," Chambliss said. "Mr. Fletcher, is it the case that you've agreed to turn over witness interviews?"

"Not necessarily turn over, Your Honor, but share, yes. As I'm sure we're all aware here, under Rule 5(a)(2) we're not obligated to turn over pretrial statements made by our witnesses until after they've testified on direct at trial—"

"Right, of course."

"—but we're going that extra mile, Your Honor, in the interest of ensuring that Mr. Munroe's client has a full and fair opportunity to defend himself, and we're sharing witness statements, some on paper and some recorded. Some of them we've already provided paper copies of, but for a few that raise very sensitive issues, we asked that defense counsel come view them at our office."

Chambliss turned to me. "Is that the case, Mr. Munroe? Is that all we're here about?"

"That's the primary issue, Your Honor, but not the only one. As for the two other categories of evidence that I mentioned in my brief, which Mr. Fletcher doesn't contest that we're owed, all I'm asking for is a deadline by which he has to provide them. But the larger dispute remains the videos. Mr. Fletcher stated in his brief that his concern is the privacy of the witnesses. I fully appreciate that sensitivity, and I have a suggestion that I think might resolve our differences."

"And what is that?"

"Well, as Your Honor surely knows, this case has attracted a lot of attention ever since it started. We've got a veteran reporter there, who I believe has been at every hearing thus far..."

I gestured to the spectator area. The reporter, with a deer-in-the-headlights look, gave the judge a quick nod.

"And I've got printouts here of several articles published about the case in just the past month, if Your Honor would care to look through them."

I held up the sheaf of paper, but Chambliss waved me off. "No need, counsel. I'm aware."

"Certainly." I set them down. "What I'd like to propose, if I may, is an arrangement similar to what Mr. Fletcher had suggested, in terms of protecting witnesses from potentially having their private business aired in public, but reciprocal. Because while I don't mind the inconvenience of having to review evidence at his office, I do very much object to the one-sidedness of his initial proposal."

It was Fletcher's only proposal, not his initial one, but I wanted to make it sound like a mere suggestion designed to kick off negotiations.

Chambliss said, "Well, I can see the sense in that. But I'm not following what you mean by making discovery reciprocal."

I could see why he was confused. Since this was a criminal case, not a civil suit, there couldn't be reciprocal discovery obligations. As defense counsel, I had no duty to turn evidence over to the prosecution.

"I apologize, Your Honor. I was unclear. What I meant by reciprocity is that *both* sides ought to abide by the principle of not disclosing private facts that we learn of during this case. Both of us ought to protect personal information about witnesses, for instance."

"Oh, I see."

"So what I think might resolve that issue is to have an order entered to prohibit both parties and their witnesses from disclosing any facts or allegations or evidence whatsoever to third parties or the press. With the obvious exception of whatever needs to be disclosed in open court to resolve a given issue or try the case. And then there ought to be no obstacle to providing me with copies of the videos so that I don't have to drive two and a half hours just to view them."

Chambliss nodded. "Well, that sounds fair. Mr. Fletcher? You have any objection to that?"

Fletcher stood up. Like any good lawyer, he could read the room. He wasn't going to win by objecting to my suggestion. The only way to go was to reframe it as something else—or, as a last resort, to narrow the order down to something he could tolerate.

"Your Honor," he said, "I, of course, have no objection to reasonable measures to protect witnesses from harassment. That's why I proposed what I did in the first place. But my concern here is that what Mr. Munroe is proposing is a gag order. And we surely all know that gag orders are strongly disfavored and subject to the closest possible scrutiny."

"Indeed they are," Chambliss said.

Fletcher leaned forward for emphasis, resting his fingertips on his table. "Yes, because it is a fundamental American value that justice is to be transparent. The public *must* have access to the pertinent facts and the proceedings, in order to maintain public faith in the integrity of our judicial system. I am not saying this to gain any tactical advantage. This is not about me or my office or any individual involved in this case. This is a *constitutional* issue."

While he took a breath, I said, "Your Honor, if I may?"

Chambliss nodded, so I continued.

"As Mr. Fletcher points out, the public has a constitutional right to access these proceedings. That's what I was alluding to when I specified that any issue we need a court filing or hearing to resolve would, of course, be open and accessible, and we'd both be able to present what evidence we needed. What I'm referring to is just two things. First, this is a big case in a small town. We've only got one local news site, and most folks read it. I'm sure we all want to avoid tainting the jury pool with pretrial disclosures of facts that may not be admissible or may not even be accurate."

"Of course," Chambliss said.

"And second, I'm referring to the… morass, the vast body of evidence that both sides have that we *don't* need to use in our case. For instance, in his brief, Mr. Fletcher referred to several hundred gigabytes and several thousand pages of materials that he's already disclosed—that's the proverbial haystack that both sides have to sift through in search of the needles we actually need. And—"

"Yeah, as for that, Mr. Munroe," Chambliss said, waving his hands, "you don't need to explain discovery to me. Looking at this," he said, picking up Fletcher's brief, "I do not want to go through all these bullet points one by one to figure out what all ought to be disclosed or not."

Fletcher said, "Your Honor, if I might suggest—"

"Yes?"

"This is no doubt something that counsel can resolve in a meet and confer. I see no need to take up Your Honor's valuable time with the details of what the parties can or can't disclose."

"You read my mind, Mr. Fletcher. How long will you two need?"

Fletcher and I looked at each other. He asked, "Three days? Business days?"

That was tight, but it wouldn't be good for me to look uncooperative. I nodded.

Chambliss said, "So, Wednesday? The twenty-eighth?" He gestured to his clerk to make a note of that. "Okay, Wednesday, let's say by noon, I want to see a joint motion for entry of a protective order. You two come up with reasonable terms."

I said, "Your Honor, in the meantime, would it be inappropriate to enter just a temporary order precluding any and all disclosures for the time being?"

"No, that's fine. I can do that," he said, gesturing again to his clerk.

———

Chambliss took a recess after the hearing, and I stepped over to Fletcher's table to confer about when I could view the interviews.

"Monday's fine," he said, "any time after 10:30 a.m."

"Great. I'll come by with my assistant at 10:30. And I can send you a draft order over the weekend."

He gave me a cold smile. "Sounds good. I'm very interested in seeing what all you want to keep under wraps."

"Well, my vote would be for a blanket order," I said. "Just protect everything. Makes it easier on both of us, since we don't have to figure out which facts can be disclosed and which can't."

"Based on what Chambliss was saying," he said in a voice so low I doubted even his paralegal could hear it, "you won't get everything covered, so you're going to have to pick what you care about most.

And you know what? It's not every day a defense counsel lets me know specifically what he's trying to hide."

He stepped back, held out his hand to shake, and said, "See you Monday."

9

APRIL 26, 2021

"That poor girl," I said. Terri and I were in a conference room at Fletcher's office in Columbia, watching the video of Miss Paramour's interview. Kayla Bennett—that was her name—had raccoon eyes from crying her mascara off, and she was so humiliated about her escapade under the bridge that she kept apologizing to the sheriff's deputy.

"She clearly doesn't know any law enforcement officers," Terri said.

"Oh, you mean because she thinks he was offended?"

"Yeah! If we had to choose between responding to a murder scene or some domestic abuser waving a gun, and *that*? Catching a couple doing— My goodness, I wish I could let her know that was the best part of his day. That kind of thing is hilarious. He's going to be telling that story for *years*."

With a smile, I pointed out, "You said 'we.'"

"Oh. Well, once a cop…"

"I know what you mean. It's hard to switch hats."

"Yeah."

I'd hit pause while we chatted, so I pressed play again. Kayla, weeping, said, "I never did anything like that before, I swear. He got me drunk. I didn't know what I was doing. I'm so sorry."

"Drunk is good," said Terri.

"Yup." I paused the video, noted the time stamp, and added it to my notes. Anything that interfered with a prosecution witness's perception or memory was good for us.

Terri asked, "Do we have a breathalyzer on her?"

"I don't think so." I made a note to check.

On the screen, Deputy McDonald said, "Okay, miss, calm down. Whereabouts did you consume the alcohol?"

She explained that they'd originally parked at an overlook nearby, where she swigged from a flask he'd brought, but they were spooked by another car and decided to continue their tryst down by the bridge.

"You consumed the alcohol in his vehicle? Okay."

"He brought it." She was nodding hard. "He opened it and handed it to me."

Terri said, "In a car? That's a misdemeanor. Nice to see her throwing Tucker under the bus."

Kayla was sobbing, saying, "I'm not like this! I didn't mean to do it! Is there anything—is there, like, just a warning you could give? Or a first-offense type of thing, or—"

"Miss, I just need to gather the facts here. If you could please just walk me through this step by step, I'd appreciate that. A young man lost his life last night, and I need to understand what you saw."

"Okay. I'm sorry." She blew her nose. "Yes, sir, okay."

"At the moment that's what I'm focusing on. Okay? Not your, uh, your personal... whatever was going on there. Just the boat. So, where were you and Mr. Tucker?"

"Uh, we were—you know—under one of the—" She started coughing, from nervousness, it looked like. To finish her sentence, she traced an arch in the air.

I sat back in my chair and watched her try to catch her breath. I'd been under the vast concrete arches of that bridge myself, and I knew the lay of the land on either side. Scrub, spartina grass, trees, not a lot of light... How hard would it have been to get away? I was starting to wonder why a woman who was this panicked about getting caught had remained on the scene at all.

I paused the video and said, "Wasn't it seven or eight minutes between the first 9-1-1 call and when the sheriffs arrived?"

"Mm-hmm. You wondering why the two of them didn't run back toward the crab shack, or somewhere?"

"Yup." I wrote that down on my list of questions to ask her, if McDonald didn't ask in the video, and if she was willing to talk. Prosecution witnesses had no legal duty to talk to me at all before trial, but they were allowed to if they wanted to. The trick was getting them to want to.

Terri, clearly thinking along those same lines, said, "She might tell *me*. I'm sure she'd rather tell me a lot of things in private than wait for you to ask her all about this on the stand at trial, in front of the world."

"Good thought."

When I hit play again, Kayla was blowing her nose, and then she looked up as we heard somebody enter the room.

"Afternoon, Sheriff Gaillard," McDonald said.

I looked at Terri. "What's he doing there?" It seemed unusual for the county sheriff himself to show up at a witness interrogation.

"I guess it was a bigger case by then. Hayden was dead, and they knew Ludlow's son was involved."

Gaillard said, "Miss, we are talking about the death of a young man here. A boy even younger than you."

I hit pause. "Wait, how old is she?"

"Twenty-four," Terri said, looking at her notes. "She got married when she was still an undergrad, and her husband filed for divorce last year."

"After all this?"

"No, before. So I guess Tucker was kind of her rebound thing."

"Huh."

I hit play again, and Sheriff Gaillard continued, "I realize the circumstances are a little unfortunate for you, but you have got to set aside your embarrassment and do the right thing. You've got to help us out. Okay?"

Looking up at him, she nodded hard, apologized, and blew her nose again.

"Okay, so tell my deputy what all you saw."

She told the whole story in a barely coherent rush. Hearing the boat, looking up, noticing how fast it was going: "The masthead light was coming at us, almost straight on, real bright, real close, and, um, and the boat was listing, I think, but that might've just been because it was turning?"

McDonald said, "You were able to see the watercraft that well? That it was listing?"

"What I— It was dark, but when the boat was coming at us almost straight on, I could see the red sidelight was higher than the green one. That's what I mean. And I could see the people on it, in the mast-head light. And then it turned starboard, so we—Mr. Tucker and myself, we weren't lit up anymore, and then a second after it went out of sight, I heard the crash, the— It was awful."

She shuddered, staring into the memory and shaking her head.

Deputy McDonald said, "And then what did you do? The two of you?"

"We— Okay, um, I want to be real clear about this. I wanted to— I tried to— I stepped forward and went to see what I could do. I wanted to help, but then the officer, you know, intercepted me. Stopped me. He'd seen us when the boat's light was on us, I guess, and that's what he—that's where his priority was."

Terri and I looked at each other. What officer was she talking about? How could one have been there before the crash even happened?

McDonald hadn't noticed the timeline problem. He moved on with his questions, and she told her story up to the point where she'd been placed in the back of a police car and driven away.

Terri pulled something up on her laptop, read it, and said, "The arresting officer, for her, was Chad Waring. He was driving the first vehicle on the scene, four minutes after the 9-1-1 call."

"How many vehicles responded?"

"Eventually, three, and four ambulances."

"So, six officers responding?"

"Mm-hmm, between seven and ten minutes after the call." She pointed to the list of their names and arrival times on her screen.

"Then who is she talking about?"

"I'll find out."

———

After leaving Fletcher's office, I called the women's prison and made an appointment to see Maria later that afternoon. In the meantime, Terri and I drove to get lunch near the USC campus.

Heading up Blossom Street, I said, "Emma lives right in there."

The university's Greek Village, home to twenty-odd fraternities and sororities, was coming up on the right. Hayden's girlfriend, Emma, was at USC on scholarship.

"Can you turn in there? I want to see the house."

"It's Chi Theta Tau," I said, swinging between brick-and-stone gateposts onto the neatly landscaped street. Every yard looked the same—a vast putting green of a lawn—and most of the fraternity and sorority houses were big red-brick affairs whose porches supported white columns two stories tall, like somebody had tacked a Greek temple onto the front of a house.

Chi Theta Tau looked like the rejected stepchild of the lot, half the size of the other ones, with no columns. Lacy wrought-iron pillars held up the roof of its deep Southern-style porch, and white roses grew all along the front.

"So apparently," Terri said, looking at her phone, "their motto is 'Wisdom through Knowledge.' And that's their official flower, the white rose."

"Huh. What is it, more of an academic type of sorority?"

She scrolled. "This review says, 'The sorority for nerds. No cheer-leaders allowed.'"

I chuckled and said, "Huh. Interesting."

I turned the corner, and we continued past more Greek temples.

"And that," I said, "is Ludlow and Fourth's fraternity, Delta Alpha Chi." It was enormous, with the largest and most perfect lawn we'd seen yet.

"No surprise there," Terri said. "Did I tell you, Fletcher pledged that frat too?"

"Are you serious?"

"Yeah. Not in the same year as Dabney and Ludlow. He's five or six years older."

"Huh."

As we cruised by their enormous frat house, she added, "Emma's Insta is full of anatomy charts and pictures of her in some laboratory. She wants to be a PA."

"A personal assistant?"

"No, physician assistant. It's kind of like a nurse practitioner or a basic family practice type of doctor. Someone who does routine health care."

"Huh. Wonder why she doesn't just go to med school."

"Have you even read my notes on her background? In her family, just graduating from high school was an accomplishment. Lot of dropouts, and more than a few addicts."

"Wow. That's hard. She's come a long way."

"Yeah. She's a real smart girl, obviously. And from her Insta, it sounds like she's very family-oriented. She posted a few times about wanting to finish her education and get established early, so she'd still have time to have several kids. As a PA, she'd be done with school at twenty-three or twenty-four, and probably starting at eighty or ninety grand a year."

"Wow. Maybe I ought to point Noah in that direction."

"He have any interest in health care?"

"Uh… No, I don't believe he's ever said one word in that direction. Dammit."

As I turned another corner and headed back to the main road, she said, "Everything Emma was posting about that was before Hayden died. She's hardly been on social media since."

"Poor kid." After a second, I added, "That's got to be pretty weird for her, socially. Coming from a family like that, and hanging out with the Ludlow and Carlson kids? How'd she manage that?"

Terri laughed—at me, not with me, but there was nothing mean about it. I got that indulgent reaction from her on occasion, when I said something particularly ignorant. "My goodness, Leland. Have you not seen that girl? You tell me what boy wouldn't want to date her!"

"Yeah, okay. I think I was identifying with her a little too much. You know, coming from the wrong side of the tracks and then moving up into a different class." I stopped at a stop sign. "I forgot how that can work, since I obviously have zero experience with my looks helping me get ahead."

"Yeah, I don't think either of us got any head starts there."

"What?" I smiled as I put my foot on the gas.

"Wait, that came out wrong. I'm sorry!"

"I mean, I know I'm no George Clooney, but come on!"

"I swear," she said, grinning, "I did *not* mean it that way! I was just trying to say, you know, there are people like Emma: models, Hollywood stars, that type of looks. And then there's people like us. Normal folks."

"Huh. I don't know." At the next stop sign, I smiled at her and said, "When Oprah was younger and looking her best, she did look like you, and *she* counts as a Hollywood star."

She looked down. As I started driving again, I thought I saw a smile on her face.

"And maybe I've got movie-star looks too," I said. "I mean, that guy from *Seinfeld* counts as a movie star, right? George what's-his-name, Costanza? And Danny DeVito?"

She cracked up. "You do *not* look like those men! Oh my God. You have hair! And you're in decent shape!"

"Uh-huh." I smiled up at the traffic light; we were waiting to turn back onto the main road. I was glad to get a little better sense of where I stood. If she ranked me higher in looks than two pretty normal-looking famous guys, that was not a bad thing.

The car behind us honked its horn, so I stopped daydreaming and got back to driving.

"*Anyway*," she said. "We've got crimes to solve here. Right?"

"Right."

"So, what else do you want to know about Emma?"

"Well, I was wondering how far back you can go in her posts. And whether you can see her friends. I want to know if there's ever been any bad blood between her and Clay."

"I'll see what I can find." After a second, she added, "Do you remember, in high school, what happened to her mom?"

85

"Her *mom*? No. I couldn't even tell you who her mom is. Apart from saying I assume she's a Mrs. Twain."

"No, that's Emma's father's name. He wasn't from the Lowcountry, and he didn't stick around long. Her mom never did get married. She's called Crystal Smalls. Remember her? Wrong side of the tracks, but really pretty? Not as pretty as her daughter, but still. Long, wavy hair, strawberry blonde?"

No bells rang in my mind. "Nope," I said. "I just… not at all." I stopped at a red light and looked at her. "How do you *do* that? I mean, notice so much, and remember it?"

She shook her head and shrugged.

"You're— I mean, that's astonishing to me."

I was sitting almost sideways in my seat, marveling at her. She was looking straight ahead, smiling. "The light's green," she said.

"Thanks." I turned my focus back to the road. "When you do that," I said, "I wonder… I'd really like to know how the world looks to you, when your mind works that way."

She gave a little laugh and said, "Complicated."

———

After lunch, we headed to the prison to meet with Maria. As we crept through the wretched traffic along Interstate 26, I said, "What I'd like you to do is ask her questions as if you were the investigating officer back at the time. If you were starting from square one, trying to solve this case, what would you want to know? Where should we dig if we're looking for evidence that she was innocent?"

"Mm-hmm. And since she's the defendant, I'm guessing no memo?"

"Yup, no memo. Just verbal. I'll take notes off of your amazing memory."

In principle, my private investigator could talk to my defendant without waiving attorney-client privilege. Anything she and Maria said to each other that was for the purpose of helping me give Maria legal advice was covered. Photos or written notes that Terri gave me would fall under work-product protection as well. In short, the law protected the confidentiality of Terri's work… but figuring out exactly where that protection stopped was not a battle I cared to have with Fletcher or any other prosecutor. So the simplest approach was for Terri to not write anything down.

When we walked into the prison meeting room, I saw Maria's shoulders relax as soon as she laid eyes on Terri. As I watched them dive right into a conversation, I reflected for about the hundredth time on how useful it was to have a female PI—especially one with Terri's gift of rapport.

She'd told me, back when we first started working together, that people told her things that they'd never say otherwise, because nobody found her intimidating. She was five foot four with shoes on and had, as she called it, a baby face. I disagreed—to me her face was simply pretty, although I didn't say that out loud—but to prove her point, she'd shown me a photo of herself at the age of twenty, and if it hadn't been for the police academy uniform she was wearing, I would've thought she was about fourteen.

I'd forgotten that either of us had ever looked that young. It seemed so long ago that it was another world.

I snapped back to the present time, to Maria in her turquoise uniform, telling Terri all about the private life of Peggy Ludlow. I'd asked questions about that myself, but Maria hadn't been nearly so forthcoming with me. Now I could just sit back and watch.

Terri asked, "Do you happen to remember the gardener's name?"

"Yes, yes. Angelo. She called him Angel, you know, 'my Angel'"—Maria looked skyward and put one hand to her heart, imitating a love-struck Mrs. Ludlow. Then she rolled her eyes.

Terri chuckled, shaking her head. "Oh my goodness. Well, with her husband being Mr. Ludlow, I sure don't blame her."

Maria laughed and said something about Dios.

"Do you happen to recall Angelo's last name?"

"Oh, I don't know. But I don't think he did this, you know? I didn't see him there that day, when it happened."

"Did he ever come inside? To, I don't know, get a glass of water? Or—"

"Oh, maybe. Sometimes. But mostly, Mrs. Ludlow, she would go outside to him."

"*To* him? Was there someplace on the property that they could meet?"

Maria squinted like she was peering back into the past. "It was a big place," she said. "What was there? A pool house, a big garage... I don't remember exactly."

In a confidential, girlfriendy voice, Terri said, "Do you know if they had an affair?"

Maria rolled her eyes and shrugged. "Mrs. Ludlow did a lot of things," she said. "I watched her son, the maid service came once or twice a week to clean the house... She had no work. She was beautiful, and she did whatever she wanted."

From reading the file on Maria's case, I already didn't have the highest opinion of her public defender. But watching Terri get this information in five minutes made him drop farther down in my rankings of local lawyers. As a rule of thumb, any man who was dating, sleeping with, or married to a woman at the time she was murdered was a suspect until proven otherwise, and the more of them there were, the better for the defense. Her original lawyer had had a year to investigate the case before trial, and not one word on Peggy's private life appeared in his files.

10

APRIL 29, 2021

At home on a Thursday morning, in the laundry room, it was no challenge to my detective skills to figure out why Noah had started doing his own laundry all of a sudden. When I opened the dryer, a pair of white, lacy panties was sitting right on top. His new laundry routine, I realized, had started a few weeks earlier, when I went out of town overnight.

I didn't know how to react. For a second I was offended that he was sneaking someone into my home without telling me, but that dissipated when I realized how awkward it would've been—especially for the girl—to introduce her and let me know she was staying over.

That would not have been gentlemanly of him. It felt strange to me, but if it spared the girl embarrassment, then he'd made the right call.

And he was twenty years old, I reminded myself. He was in school, vaccinated, and finally back to in-person classes after the lockdowns, and he was making up for lost time. Not just the time lost to the pandemic, but before that, too: the months of hospitalization and recovery from his accident.

I closed the dryer. Then I opened it again—I still needed to dry my own laundry—and carefully put his in a basket, making sure not to touch the panties.

A minute later, in the kitchen pouring my third cup of coffee, I had another thought. I went back into the laundry room, pulled out a few T-shirts from the side of Noah's basket, and tossed them over the panties in a crumpled pile. I didn't want to leave his girlfriend's underthings on top like a triumphant announcement that I knew his secret.

I figured he ought to be able to tell me in his own time. Although I did hope that time came quick.

When he finally peeled himself out of bed and came to the fridge for sustenance, I was looking through the mail. It was junk and bills, except for a sparkly purple greeting-card-sized envelope, which for a second I thought might be a clue as to who his girlfriend was.

That went out the window when I saw it was addressed to both of us. I ripped it open and said, as Noah put a cup of cold coffee in the microwave, "Oh, hey! I forgot about this. You remember Cardozo's daughter, Rachael?"

"Yeah," he said.

"I remember you liked her big sister back in middle school." I was determined to use this piece of mail to create an opening for Noah to tell me who he was dating.

He moved on to struggle with the toaster, which was broken and didn't always stay down. "Yeah, she was cute."

"Well, I guess we're going to see them soon. This is an invite to her bat mitzvah in June."

"Huh."

He wasn't taking my bait. I was going to have to wait until he felt like talking.

———

That afternoon I met Terri at my office to start going through Maria's case file, which had finally arrived, and look over the protective order. It included a confidentiality agreement for us to sign.

"Lord," she said. "I hate signing things that go on the record. You know how I like to pretend I'm invisible."

"If it's any consolation, everybody that so much as stands near a file box on this case has to sign."

She signed. "Did you get what you needed, though? Without giving too much away?"

"Yeah, Fletcher fought hard to get me to lay out specific things I wanted kept confidential, but I drafted it more broadly. And Chambliss eventually saw it my way."

"Good."

I pulled a box of Maria's documents out from under my desk. Her trial had lasted nearly three weeks, so the transcripts ran to nearly four thousand pages. To avoid getting bogged down, we didn't start there. We went for the police files instead, to see what they'd investigated and what they hadn't.

We had the place to ourselves, since Roy was out golfing and Laura had gone home. I'd hung corkboards along the one remaining bare wall of my office, and we put documents that seemed important in a stack to hang up later.

As we read statements and looked through crime scene photos, we pushed a piece of paper back and forth across the desk between us to write down a title or description of each document we touched. If it had a Bates number or an exhibit number on it, we wrote that down too. Laura would type up an inventory of everything these boxes contained. One of the first things I'd learned as a lawyer—and one of the most alarming things to me, since I was not naturally all that organized—was how often winning your case depended on simply knowing what you had and how to find it fast later on.

"So, Ludlow said he came in," Terri said, reading a statement from an officer who responded to the scene, "and found Maria with blood literally on her hands, standing over his wife's body."

"Which is basically consistent with what Maria told us."

"Mm-hmm. And Ludlow's the one who called 9-1-1."

We didn't have a recording of the call. According to the cover letter that the prosecutor had sent to Maria's original lawyer along with some discovery, even back then the recording could not be found. I added that to my list of things to look for. There wasn't much hope of finding it, but you still had to try.

While Terri read the officer's statement, I looked through a folder that contained a copy of an insurance claim form listing the jewelry Maria was accused of having stolen. It described a missing cookie tin containing a gold necklace, two ruby-and-diamond rings, a "vintage Cartier cuff," whatever that was, and a pair of emerald earrings, with a total value of nearly $40,000.

"Look at this," I said, chuckling in disbelief. I handed her the claim form. "The next time somebody asks me why I think rich people are different from you and me, I'm telling them about this lady who kept forty grand worth of jewelry in a cookie tin."

"Oh my God." She shook her head, smiling. "If I had a tenth of that, it'd be in a safe-deposit box."

I laughed. "Right? And occasionally you'd go down to the bank, open up the box, and then stand in the bank vault wearing your jewelry for a little while before putting it all right back."

She cracked up. "Exactly. I don't know how women can even enjoy an evening out with that much money hanging around their neck."

"Uh-huh. I'm right with you, there."

I returned the claim form to the folder. Right under it were a few receipts and three photos of Peggy wearing some of the pieces. It looked like her tastes ran to the chunky and colorful.

There was also a police report for the theft, but although it said the loss had been discovered just over a week prior to Peggy's death, the report was dated a couple of days after the shooting. I figured there might be any number of reasons that Mrs. Ludlow hadn't reported the theft. Maybe she'd suspected Maria but didn't have the heart to put her son's nanny in jail. Still, I made a note to check the trial transcript and any statements Ludlow had made for an explanation.

I asked, "Is there anything in there about where Ludlow was when his wife was shot?"

"In his office," she said. "On the phone."

"With whom?"

"Doesn't say."

I wrote down, *Phone records?*

The next thing I found was the coroner's report. Flipping through it, I asked, "When you were on the force, in a case like this, you'd want to exclude suicide, right?"

"You should. I mean, shooting yourself in the chest is unusual, but the weapon was a handgun, so it's obviously possible."

"Uh-huh. If you see anything about them talking to friends of hers, or her doctor or shrink if she had one, flag that, okay?"

"Mm-hmm."

A little later I came across Maria's statement to the police. It was dated the day after the murder, and her signature had the same almost childish script that I'd noticed on the copy of her driver's license that I'd seen elsewhere in the file.

I read through it.

"This is not good," I said, sliding it across the desk to Terri and tapping the paragraph where Maria confessed to stealing the jewelry right before she took a one-week vacation. The day she came back to work was the day Mrs. Ludlow had been killed.

"Oh my."

I had already recapped for Terri what Maria had told me about the jewelry when I had first met her. And I'd told her that I believed Maria.

"Yeah, it's pretty bizarre for her to confess that right there in writing and then be so adamant when I talked to her about it."

She gave me a look. "Yeah, well, '*confess*,'" she said, putting air quotes around the word.

I looked at the statement again and remembered something. "Did I tell you that Victor said Maria didn't learn to read and write until after she went to prison?"

"No." She looked at the statement again and nodded. "But I can believe it, with the way she signed this. I've worked with some women at the halfway house who were barely literate. Nearly all of them could sign their names, though, and it usually did look kind of…

childish, like it took them a long time to write out their signature. So she wouldn't have been able to understand—"

"What this statement said? Yeah. That was my thought. I don't know if he meant she was literate in Spanish but learned to read English in jail, or if she wasn't literate at all—"

"But either way, she couldn't have read through this and confirmed that it said whatever she'd told the police."

"Right."

I reached for the manila folder that contained a case docket, a list of all the filings made in the case. The second page listed some motions in limine filed before trial to try to kick evidence out. One of them was called "Motion to Exclude Alleged 7/21/2000 Signed Statement of Mrs. Guerrero."

That was the date printed on her statement. A few lines down, I saw the order denying it. I sighed.

Terri said, "They already try getting it thrown out?"

"Yeah. It got denied. And any halfway competent attorney would've raised that in the appeal." I started making a note to double-check that, then stopped midway through, annoyed with myself. "I don't know why I'm even thinking about this. It's not evidence that she's actually innocent, and it sure as heck isn't *new* evidence."

"Mm-hmm. It's a different job, isn't it, trying to get someone out years after they were convicted?"

"Yeah, but man, I have got to quit getting lost in the weeds here." I slapped my hands on the desk and stood up. Maybe a walk around the office would clear my brain a little. "You want another coffee?"

She glanced up, smiling. "Oh, Lord, no. I'm already going to be up way too late just from this one."

When she looked back down, the sunlight filtering through the palm tree outside hit her hair. Her locs, as she'd told me they were called, were longer now, and she had them twisted up on top of her head in a shiny black spiral that made me think of waves or certain kinds of seashells. In this light her face glowed a deep, coppery brown, and one of her earrings flashed gold—it was shaped like a sand dollar. Everything about her felt like the beach.

She looked up at me again like she was about to say something, but I saw her expression change at the sight of me. She smiled again, said nothing, and looked back down at her notes.

"Sorry," I said. "I just, I think I need some coffee."

I went out to the reception area and poured myself a cup.

I stood there wondering if I was imagining things. When she saw my face and her expression changed, had she looked pleasantly embarrassed, the way you look when you're about to blush?

I had no idea. That look was all of a quarter second long, and I was in an agitated state of mind. I couldn't even remember the next step in making my coffee. Had I added sugar or not?

I tasted it: no.

After stirring in a spoonful, I got back to business.

"So," I said, walking into my office. "Any mention of the gardener in that officer's statement? Or on their lists?"

"Not so far. But we should ask Victor—"

"Oh, yeah, of course! Since they're in the same line of work—"

"If Angelo kept on being a gardener, right. And from his name, they might both be Mexican, and it's not a big community."

With barely ten thousand people in Basking Rock, every community other than Black or White was a statistical blip.

I set my coffee down and stooped to scribble a note about asking him. "Yeah, that's a great idea," I said. "Because the alternative... I mean, I am not about to ask Ludlow about this gardener."

She laughed and then said, "You know what, this is honestly a relief. I mean, it's not ideal to be getting on Ludlow's bad side, but compared to being on the bad side of a freaking *drug* cartel, this feels a lot better, doesn't it?"

"Oh, man," I said. "Thanks for giving me a flashback to almost getting killed."

"Which time are you referring to? I'm starting to lose count."

I shook my head. "Yeah, I mean... thanks for saying that, actually. It's good to get some perspective on this."

She nodded. Then she said, "Listen, I didn't need a coffee, but a walk might do me some good. Would Roy be okay if we walked around his... uh, his property? I'm not sure if I should call it a yard."

Roy's bungalow, which he'd long ago converted into offices, was set well back from the road, on about half an acre of palm trees and meandering stone walkways that nobody ever walked on.

"Yard probably works. And I don't see why he'd mind, although the lizards might."

————

We walked around for half an hour or so, talking about Maria, pointing out a couple of striped lizards skittering between rocks.

"I can see why her case went the way it did," she said. "It is *not* a good thing to be found right next to a dead person with their blood on your hands."

"Yeah," I said. "That's not generally a situation that I would recommend."

"Juries can be a little judgmental about that kind of thing."

We both laughed. It was good to work with someone who understood the occasional need to use dark humor to get some relief from life's horrors.

On the armrest of the cast-iron bench Roy had installed, which nobody ever sat on, an apple-green lizard was sunning itself.

"Will you look at *that*," I said. "How does a thing that brightly colored sit right out in the open without something swooping in to eat it?"

She cocked her head and thought for a second. "It's about the color of a palm frond this time of year," she said. "And with that palmetto right next to it, I guess it can hide in plain sight."

"Hmm," I said. "I guess that's how a lot of things work." She'd brought my mind back to the case, so I started thinking out loud: "Okay, Maria's in the room with Peggy's body, and Peggy's gun is on the floor. So we've got means and opportunity right there, and the jewelry theft adds the motive."

"Mm-hmm. Pretty much any officer would look at that and figure, case closed. Right?"

"But you don't?"

She screwed up her face. "I just know that there was more to it. I remember some of the other officers saying it, or insinuating it, on the down-low. And… I'm not saying I'm infallible or anything, at all, but I *believed* what Maria said."

After a minute of walking in silence, I said, "I guess we ought to get back. There's, what, about nine thousand more documents to get through?"

She sighed, resigned. "My goodness. I hope it counts as exercise to push myself around in that little wheelie chair of yours. I don't know why I thought being a PI would let me avoid a desk job."

———

By early evening the new corkboards on my wall had started to bring Maria's case to life. Pieces of string connected the photos of the people involved: Peggy smiling in a red dress and a gold necklace only a little less flashy than the stuff out of King Tut's tomb. Maria looking tired but happy with a couple of her kids. Terri had printed out a map of the Ludlows' neighborhood, which we'd labeled with the names of all the neighbors we'd identified so far. Most of them were familiar to one or both of us; Basking Rock was not a big town.

With some social media sleuthing, she'd gotten her hands on a few more things. Nothing on Angelo, but she had found a recent photo of the Ludlow kid who'd been napping when his mother was killed.

As she pinned it up on the corkboard, she said quietly, "That boy is not okay."

I didn't need to ask how she knew. She had a whole mental library of the people in our town, but I doubted she even needed that. You could see the wrongness in his eyes.

11

MAY 4, 2021

I stopped at a traffic light behind a Mercedes—we were on the more upscale side of town—and asked Terri, "So what is it that these people do, again?"

"Mr. Pennington's the CFO at a defense contractor up in Charleston. And his wife was in marketing at a hotel chain, but as far as I can tell, she stopped working last year. They're both in their fifties."

We were heading to the house where Peggy Ludlow had lived and died. I'd reached out to the current owners, drawing on every ounce of tact and persuasion I had, and they had very graciously agreed to let us pay them a visit and look around.

The light turned green, and we cruised on, curving past trees on one side and a gated community on the other. I said, "I think the turn's about a mile up this way."

"Oh, Lord," she said, shaking her head. "Are you *ever* going to join us in the twenty-first century?"

"If by that you mean am I going to spend a hundred dollars a month on a computer to carry in my pocket," I said, "the answer is no. My flip phone is all I need."

She cracked up. When she got ahold of herself, she said, "Except you also need a map. A big old paper map that you have to pull over to read. Or, I have an idea: maybe you should learn how to get around your own hometown!"

"Oh, very funny," I said. "I would not call this side of Basking Rock my hometown. I mean, didn't I tell you that the road we're looking for is called Devonshire Grove? You can tell just from the name that it's not somewhere I ever go. Those folks probably have fox hunts in their yards."

We were still laughing when she pointed out the turn. As I took it, she said, "Did I tell you Kayla lives on this side of town? Or her parents do. She's back living with them."

"Miss Paramour? Really? Didn't know she was rich. You visit her?"

"I tried. They're about a mile downhill, so not, like, fox-hunt rich." She flashed me a smile. "I cruised by, just to get a sense of how she lives, and then I called her, but she flat-out refused to talk."

"That's too bad. I'm glad these folks were more welcoming."

The Penningtons' house, formerly the Ludlows', was a grand old Victorian with a huge sycamore to one side and palmettos down the driveway. The neighborhood looked to have been built at two different times: the houses on either side were of similar vintage and charm, but across the street was a development of McMansions, each on its own half-acre lot.

It was coming up on suppertime, so folks were home, and all down Devonshire Grove, the driveways displayed fine European vehicles.

To avoid having my Malibu look like a child's toy beside our hosts' midnight-blue Bentley, I parked on the street.

Mr. Pennington swung the door wide to greet us and gave me exactly the kind of firm, practiced handshake that his conservative looks and CFO title led me to expect. Behind him, his wife smiled and exclaimed her pleasure to see us. Her hair was the color of caramel and so full that it brought to mind the old phrase "the higher the hair, the closer to God."

She stepped forward, took Terri's hand in both of hers, and said, "Call me Shannon. I am *so* honored to meet y'all, and I truly do hope we can be of some help."

For a few minutes, they walked us around the large, wood-paneled living room and the open-plan kitchen with its acres of granite, explaining that they'd bought the place eight years earlier, after relocating from Raleigh.

"Now, you just let me know what you'd like to drink," Shannon said, throwing open the French door fridge to show us what was on offer. "Or the wine fridge is over there," she said, "if you want something a little more exciting."

We made our choices, and when we'd all been served, Terri said, "I love this kitchen remodel. Did you folks do it?"

"She insisted," Mr. Pennington said with a smile.

"It was just *dark*," Shannon said.

"And you know what they say: happy wife, happy life."

He laughed, so I did too.

Shannon said, "But we did not *touch* anything else. I am such a fan of historic architecture."

"Oh, I hear you," I said. Apart from the updated paint and decor, the house still looked much as it had in the photos I'd seen in Maria's case file. After taking us to the dining room to admire the inlaid parquet floor, Mr. Pennington excused himself for a work call, and we followed Shannon upstairs.

"I just love this mezzanine," she said. We were standing at a railing that overlooked the foyer, with a crystal chandelier at eye level in front of us. While I tried to imagine what level of supervision the Ludlow boy would've needed to safely navigate a mezzanine perched twelve feet above a marble-tiled floor, Shannon said, "This is where I stand on New Year's Eve—we always throw a big party—raising my glass of champagne to all our guests."

Terri said, "It's so important that you're able to bring joy and life back to this house after what happened here."

"Oh, I'm glad you said that. I think so too."

"Indeed," I said. "And I'm real sorry we're having to remind you of such unpleasant things."

"Oh, not at all. And let me tell you—this isn't something I'd share with just anybody, but given the line of work you two are in, I'm thinking y'all might understand." Leaning closer, lowering her voice like she was letting us in on a secret, she said, "I actually really wanted this place *because* of what had happened here."

"Is that so," I said, with mild curiosity. I wasn't about to let her see how revolting I thought that was.

"Yes! I cannot get enough of those true-crime stories. I got furloughed last year, with the pandemic, and you know what I did? I took it as an opportunity. I started a true-crime podcast."

"Did you really!" Terri said. Despite her smile, I could tell she was annoyed with herself for not having dug that fact up when she'd researched the Penningtons that afternoon.

"Yes! I don't dare put it under my own name, though. You will not see one single picture of me anywhere on the site! I am not that brave. But I love doing it. I call it *Carolina True Crime*. It's strictly North and South Carolina—that's my niche."

"That is so interesting," Terri said.

"Why, thank you! Anyway, let me show you around. So, starting from the end, there's Doug's office, and that one in the middle would've been the little boy's room. It's a guest bedroom now. And then right at the corner here is what used to be Mrs. Ludlow's dressing room, which is where it happened."

She led us to it and pushed the door open. It was a good-sized bedroom, with two windows on the front wall overlooking the driveway and another two across the room from us, on the side of the house. It was set up as an office, but next to the computer was a big microphone on a tripod.

"Oh," Shannon said, noticing what I was looking at. "Yes, this is my office. It's where I do my podcast from."

"Huh." I wondered whether she told her listeners that she was broadcasting from a room where a woman had been killed. "Looks like a nice setup there."

"It sure is."

Terri asked, "Isn't it a little noisy, though, facing the street?"

"Oh, around here there is just about *nobody* home during the day. I don't record on the weekends, that's for sure. But even so, you know, this old architecture, it's surprising how little sound carries."

I said, "They don't build them like they used to."

"No, they sure don't."

Terri asked, "Wait, did Mrs. Ludlow's dressing room have *two* closets?"

I saw what she meant: one of the interior walls had two doors.

"No, that one goes to a Jack-and-Jill bathroom. I think both my office and the little boy's room were meant to be children's rooms. I don't know that for sure; I'm just assuming because they share the one bathroom."

Terri said, "Oh, that makes sense."

"If you don't mind my asking," I said, "where would the main bedroom have been?"

"Oh, everything else is down there," she said, pointing to a hallway that led away from the other side of the staircase. "That's more the private area, versus the mezzanine."

"Okay, thank you. And I apologize for the intrusive question. I'm just trying to get oriented in here."

"Oh, of course. I sure do hope this is helpful to you."

"It truly is. Nothing like being on the scene in person, is there."

"I *so* agree."

"Well, thank you again," I said. "And now I'm sure I need to let you get back to getting dinner together, so—"

"Oh, not at all! Doug's on his call until probably eight o'clock, and as for me, who needs dinner? Just pour me another glass of white wine and I am good to *go*!"

She threw her head back and laughed, hiding her mouth with a manicured hand, so I laughed too.

"My goodness," she said, quieting down but still smiling. "Anyway, if y'all ever want to stop by and take another look, or take pictures or something, you just let me know. If you've got any questions about the history of the house, I will track down my realtor or whoever else, and I will find out."

Terri said, "You know what, I did have one question. That development across the street went up not too long ago, didn't it? Ten or twelve years?"

"Oh, yes. The folks we bought this place from told us it went in while they were here. The family between the Ludlows and us, I mean."

"I thought so. And do you happen to know what was there before?"

"I do! Now, let me see. I have photos of the area over the years, but I don't recall if it was the previous owners who gave them to us, or the realtor. I mean real, printed photos, not digital. And as I recall, there were just a few grand old homes, not nearly as many as are out there now."

"On the big old lots?"

"Real big, yeah. And right across the street from us was a beautiful old place with a double porch—a fine old plantation-style house. But it had been turned into apartments. I think at that point, you know, before all of this gentrification, several of them had. And then they got torn down."

"That is such a shame," Terri said.

"It *is*. This type of architecture is a dying breed."

"My goodness, yes. You know what, if it's not too much trouble, do you think you could find those old photos? You never know—it might be helpful to look at them."

"To get the lay of the land? Of course! I tell you what, if I find them, I'll give you a call, and you can come on over and we'll scan them together. Whatever you need."

"Well, that is just above and beyond! Thank you so much."

I said, "True Southern hospitality. Thank you again. We'll just get on out of your way now."

Terri said, "I'm so sorry we'll miss Doug, but could you tell him we said goodbye and thank you?"

"Oh, of course."

Shannon walked us downstairs and stood at the door waving as we walked down the driveway.

We got into the Malibu, slammed the doors, and put the AC on max. I turned around and drove back up Devonshire Grove. At the first stop sign, Terri and I looked at each other. We both cracked up.

As I turned left, I said, "That woman is absolutely desperate to get us onto her podcast."

"One hundred percent," she said. With a grin, she added, "And, ideally, to get into your pants."

"Oh, good Lord, no. My God. Why would you even—"

"I'm just saying. I mean, you heard how much she loves true crime. Really, *really* loves it."

"That is so bizarre. It's just— It—"

"Creeps you out a little bit?"

"More than a little bit."

"I do think we have to talk to her again, though. I want to see those photos. I want to see what the landscaping and nearby houses were like. If there was any way to sneak in or anywhere good to hide."

"Uh-huh. But you know," I said, "if we go back, she's going to dig like hell for salacious details."

"Mm-hmm. So we apologize and tell her there's a gag order."

"She might interpret that as meaning that as soon as the case is over and the order's dissolved, we'll give her the scoop."

"She can interpret it however she wants."

12

MAY 9, 2021

"I'm glad we got the old menu back," Noah said. "This town isn't fancy enough for what they were selling last year."

We were sitting in a booth at the truck stop, about to order lunch. We'd arrived around one thirty to give the lunch rush time to disperse.

I took a sip of coffee. "Yeah, I bet the grilled cheese sandwiches are selling a lot faster than... What was that? Smoked salmon and avocado on house-made focaccia?"

"Yeah. Give me a grilled cheese any day." He looked up and smiled at someone over my shoulder. "Hey there, Ms. Grant. Thank you."

Our waitress, Mazie Grant, stopped by to top up my coffee. Terri and I had gone to high school with her, and I'd gotten her son out of a trumped-up murder charge the year before the pandemic.

She brushed a lock of blonde-going-gray hair out of her eyes and said, "You ready to order?"

"If you're not too run off your feet," I said. "If you need a break, we can keep nursing the coffee and Coke until you're ready."

"Naw, I'm good. You know I like to keep busy."

After we ordered our sandwiches and fries, I looked behind me to make sure nobody was close enough to eavesdrop. Then I asked, "So how's the new management? They treating you well?"

"Oh yeah. Your boss put in some pretty good folks."

After the truck stop had imploded the previous year, Roy had gotten together with a few guys from the chamber of commerce to take it over.

Noah laughed. "I don't dare call Roy his boss myself. He hates that."

"Oh, I'm sorry!"

"I don't *hate* it," I said.

Noah, with a smile, told her, "Yeah, my father is an independent professional now. He's won some cases, so he's getting a little big for his britches."

I swatted his menu with mine and said, "Big enough to buy you lunch, *if* you're polite."

Mazie said, "You know what, it is so good to see you two again."

"Yeah, it's been a while. Glad you stopped working at out-of-the-way restaurants I never go to."

"I'm glad a better place would have me. And that pandemic, my goodness. It is such a relief to be getting back to normal. Noah, you should come over again! I wish Jackson was still hanging out with you instead of with that Ludlow kid."

I kept my voice relaxed as I asked, "What, Jimmy? Really?"

"Oh, no. You know that boy wouldn't give folks like us the time of day. I meant his big brother, Brandon."

Peggy's son.

I said, "So he's less of a snob than the rest of the Ludlows?"

"I guess you could say that," she said grudgingly. I got the sense that might be the one good thing she could say about him. She glanced behind her and then said, "I got to go help that table. And I'll put this order in for you."

After she headed off, I said, "Do you know that Ludlow kid?"

"Oh, kind of. Why?"

"Well..." I debated what to tell him.

"Is he in trouble or something? Is he part of some case you're on now?"

"No, he's not in trouble, that I know of. But... look." I leaned forward so I could speak more quietly. "You're probably going to start seeing some more nasty articles about me. I should tell you that right now. And it's because of a case that relates to him. Not anything he did, but he's connected to it."

"Oh, man. You liked that article last month?" he teased. "You want to go for more?"

"I can't say I do." I took a sip of coffee and sat back in my seat. "But unfortunately, with the way things run in this town, it comes with the territory."

"Nice," he said, in a tone that meant not nice at all.

"Yup. But anyway, because of the connection with him, I'm curious what he's like. How well do you know him?"

"Oh, hardly at all. You know how me and Jackson played OtherWorld a lot during the lockdowns?"

He was referring to one of the more popular online games. "Yeah, I know there wasn't a whole lot else for kids to do."

"So, he started bringing Brandon in on some raids, too. And then after that we all hung out once, at Jackson's place, but… I don't know. That guy is like twenty-three or twenty-four and just…" He winced like something was off but he couldn't quite find the words to say why.

I asked, "Does he have a job? Or go to school?"

"I mean, is smoking weed a job? Because he does that pretty much full time."

"Man," I said, shaking my head. "That's sad." Then, worried for Mazie, I asked, "Does Jackson smoke it too? Is he in trouble?"

"Naw, like usual, only at parties or whatever. As far as I know, anyway. It's been a while since I've hung out with him."

I nodded. I didn't quite know how to ask what I wanted to ask, so I tore open a sugar packet, dumped it in my coffee, and then twisted the paper up until it couldn't twist anymore. Tapping it on the table, I said, "You'd let me know, wouldn't you, if you ever needed any help with that kind of thing again?"

"Aw, hell, that ain't going to happen. I know I can't get my PI license if I get in that kind of trouble. And besides, I'm not into that scene at all anymore. Not even cigarettes—look at this." He pulled up the sleeve of his T-shirt. Stuck to his deltoid was a plastic patch about the size of a matchbook.

"What is that, a nicotine patch?"

"Sure is." He let his sleeve drop back down and picked up his coffee cup. He looked proud. "I decided to kick my last real vice."

I said, "That's great. I'm proud of you. What made you take the leap?"

"Honestly, you watch somebody who's still caught up in all that, like Brandon, and it just..." He shook his head. "Addiction makes a person like a rat in a cage, pressing the button for their fix. There's zero appeal. I mean, I know I had my own problems for a while, but I think I'm more of a straight-edge at heart."

"A what?"

"Jeez. Uh..." He leaned back, putting his hands behind his head and his elbows out. "I don't know how to... Okay, you know the punks, right? As in punk music, from England, back in the day?"

"Oh, uh-huh. Like with the spiky hair and whatnot?"

"Wow. Yeah." He smiled like it was truly entertaining how little I knew.

I smiled and said, "Don't roll your eyes too hard. You don't want them to get stuck."

He laughed. "Okay, so anyway, yeah, spiky hair. It's more about, like, an attitude toward the world, right? And there's different kinds of punks. Some are like, just wanting to tear everything down. But the straight-edge punks are more... Like, they have a *code*. They're all about justice and doing what's right even if everyone's against it. Even if doing right's not even legal."

I gave him a slow nod, considering that. "I guess there's situations where that makes sense. Like what, hiding Jewish people in World War II? That kind of thing?"

"Yeah, exactly. Or whatever's happening in your day and age. But anyway, the other thing is, they don't do drugs. They don't steal. It's... I don't know. A lot of it makes sense to me."

I kept going with the slow nod, like I could just about see where he was coming from. With a shrug, I said, "Huh. Interesting. I mean, I never heard of it, but you know me—pop culture is not my thing."

He laughed out loud. "Yeah, not at *all*."

I glanced up and saw Mazie with our plates in her hand. "Here you go," she said. "Ham and cheese for you, Leland, and chicken salad for Noah. The fries just came out of the fryer. They are the *best*."

"Thank you muchly," I said.

We dug into our lunches. I was glad to break eye contact with Noah. I didn't want him to know it, but what he'd said made me want to stand up and cheer like he'd just hit a home run. He had somehow found a cool, rebellious reason to behave exactly how I had always wanted him to. I knew better than to tell him that I thought it was cool too.

———

Later that afternoon, while I was standing on a corner in my neighborhood watching Squatter nose around the base of a yucca plant, Terri called.

"Hey there," I said. "How you doing?"

"Pretty good. You have a minute?"

"You caught me in the middle of walking my dog," I said, "so if he gets in a fight or something, I'll have to go, but otherwise, yeah."

"Aw." I could hear the smile in her voice. "If he does, you pick him up and put him in your pocket."

"Poor thing'll die of embarrassment if I do. But what's up?"

"Britney's phone company finally sent me what I asked for."

"Oh, her text messages? Hang on a second. Squatter went under this yucca plant and— Dang it! I forgot how sharp these things are."

"Yeah, yucca is nasty. Listen, come on by when he's done with his walk. You should take a look at some of these messages."

"Will do. But I'm actually meeting Victor at six thirty. He was old enough when everything went down that I want to hear what all he remembers. You free?"

"Are you kidding? Absolutely."

———

Half an hour later, Squatter was snoozing under a chair on Terri's deck while I scrolled through the texts on her laptop. I said, "I sure hope the State hasn't got a copy of these."

"I know." She was standing up, adjusting the umbrella shading our table to put it at a better angle to the sun. "But with murder or manslaughter charges, and a perp who knew the victim, you have to assume they asked for them."

"I wonder if they have the manpower to review them all."

She laughed. "Yeah, you wouldn't know this, but folks who have smartphones send a lot of texts."

"Two hundred and sixteen pages, though? In a month?"

She shrugged, turned the umbrella crank a couple more times, and sat back down.

"Thanks for getting these, though," I said.

"No problem. At least now you won't be blindsided at the hearing."

Britney, it turned out, had remained very much in touch with her estranged husband after moving out. The texts showed the two of them riding an emotional roller coaster: resentful accusations on one side or both, denials and outrage and ultimatums, a storm of verbal abuse, and then quieter emails that showed failed attempts at reconciliation: *I never should of let u come over*, from her. Then from him: *Baby I'm sorry we can still make this work.*

I asked, "Is there time to get the texts from her new phone before the hearing?"

"Maybe, depending who the carrier is. But I thought she'd shown you the more recent texts."

"She didn't show me two hundred pages worth."

"Yeah. And whatever the State's got, you need to see it too."

Britney had shown me a half dozen texts from her ex, all filled with enough rage to scare any woman. A few contained physical threats. My concern was that the texts she hadn't shown me might include the reconciliation part of their cycle of abuse. If there were any showing she'd allowed him to come over on the night he was killed, we could not win at the self-defense hearing. And in that case, the State would send her back to jail and most likely take her kids into care.

I sighed and looked out at the flowers in Terri's backyard.

"You wondering why the world's so full of messed-up people?" she asked.

"Oh, man, I… no. I can't even think about that anymore."

"Mm-hmm. It wears you out after a while, doesn't it?"

I nodded. The sky was bright blue, and her yard was so quiet I could hear the bumblebees on the rosebush a few yards away. "Man," I said, "this retreat you've made here, it's really something. I don't know how you ever bring yourself to leave it."

She smiled. "I wish I didn't have to."

"Yeah."

The silence was broken by a sound that I recognized.

"Is that Buster? Where is he?" His collar was jangling, and it sounded like he was scratching himself.

"He likes to sleep under the deck."

"That's where I'd be, too, if you didn't have this umbrella."

She laughed.

I said, "That's really it, though, isn't it. I mean, the reason you can even have this oasis, the reason we can relax in this Garden of Eden with fluffy clouds overhead, is because you've got an attack dog under the porch."

"Yeah," she said, nodding. "I've got my dog, and I've got my gun."

———

A few minutes later, she put a bowl of water in her fenced yard for Buster, and we headed over to Victor's place after stopping by mine to drop Squatter off with Noah.

Victor's house wasn't big, as far as I could tell; it was hard to see behind the spectacular profusion of flowering shrubs, intricate brick paths winding between fruit trees, and the rest of the landscaping. Beside the house, on a big stone patio with a firepit at one end, two little boys were shooting cars around a plastic track. At the other end, three girls were playing under a pergola covered with red climbing roses.

As we headed toward the porch, I said, "Man, does he know how to design a yard!"

"And a porch too, apparently."

His little yellow Victorian had a wraparound porch with wrought-iron railings and hanging baskets of flowers. Both the deck and the porch ceiling were hardwood planks stained nut brown.

"When this is all over," Terri said, "you have got to hire this man."

I laughed. "Well, first I've got to buy myself a house. I'm not paying to fix up my landlord's yard."

"Oh, true."

I was coming up the steps, looking at yet another outdoor living room to our right and a porch swing in the far corner, when Victor swung the front door open and said, "Hey there, Mr. Munroe! And, uh…"

"Terri," I said. "This is Ms. Terri Washington, the private investigator that I told you about."

"Yeah, yeah!" He stepped forward and shook her hand. "So, come on in—it's nicer with the AC."

We went in, past a stairway whose intricate railings testified to the skills of old-time woodworkers. The front room was comfortable, with kids' artwork and toys scattered around. We got situated on the couch, with lemonade brought by Victor's wife before she disappeared back into the kitchen.

"We got family coming tonight for Sunday dinner," he explained. "Seven thirty. So she's real busy."

"It sure smells good," Terri said.

I said, "Yeah. You know what, though, I don't want to get in the way of a family event. If this isn't a good time to talk about… what happened… I mean, I'd completely understand."

"No, no. My whole life is a family event." He laughed. "It's either this or I'm working in somebody's yard, right? There's no great time to talk, so, it is what it is."

"Okay. Well, I guess what I'd like to know first is just what you recall from that day. For instance, where were you when it happened, or when you heard?"

"Oof." He leaned back on the sofa opposite me and looked at the ceiling, shaking his head, like he was sifting through his memory.

Then he sat forward, elbows on his knees, and said, "You know, I was there that day. It was spring break, right, at my middle school, but my brothers and sisters' school was out the week before. My mom took her vacation to watch them, but she couldn't take two weeks off. She took me to work. She did that a lot—I had to keep out of the way. And I've thought about this over the years, but it's hard to remember, like, a *story*, you know? It's just a few details that don't connect to anything, and... a feeling. A bad feeling, right, because I went to work with my mom, and then I never went home with her again. That was it."

"Yeah, I'm sure," Terri said in a soothing voice. "That's traumatic. You were, what, twelve?"

"Yeah, and there's—it's total chaos, and there's police, and they won't let me get to my mom. And they took her away, and—I don't know, I remember being in the back of a police car, worrying about who was going to get my brothers and sisters from school." He was shaking his head, his eyes closed.

"Can I ask you this?" Terri said. "Do you remember a man called Angelo?"

He opened his eyes. "Yeah. Yeah, the handyman, grounds guy?"

For a fraction of a second, I thought I'd seen him wince. Because of that, I said, "Yeah. He ever do something that made you uncomfortable?"

He caught my eye and then looked away. Then he glanced over his shoulder—checking where his wife was, I thought—and said, more quietly than before, "He, uh... he never *did* anything, to me I mean, but... I couldn't tell you which day it was or, like, the details, but I was once messing around the house while my mom worked upstairs, and I came around the corner and he was there with, uh, with his pants off."

"His pants off?"

"Yeah, or down, anyway—I mean, what I remember is that his, uh…" He gestured to his crotch. "He was… uncovered, just… hanging right out. And he pulled me into the room and said, you know, you tell anybody about this, I'll fucking kill you." He looked at Terri and added, "Sorry for the language."

She said, "No problem."

I asked, "Do you recall who else was home? Mrs. Ludlow, or—"

"No, and I don't even… Like, I can't remember the house well enough to say what room it was."

Terri asked, "Did you ever tell your mom? Or anyone?"

"Oh, no. No, I was… I took it literally, what he said."

"Wow. Did he— You mentioned he was a handyman. Was he in the house much?"

"No, mostly he did the landscaping and stuff. But yeah, I didn't know how things worked as a kid, but now I would think the inside stuff was mostly little repairs it wasn't worth calling somebody for."

"That makes sense," Terri said.

"What else do you remember about him?" I asked.

"I mean, this is going to sound weird, but he also kind of… mentored me? I mean, like, he's the reason I got into landscaping. He used to take me around sometimes, show me how to do stuff, when I was at work with my mom. As long as I kept my head down and did what he said, I learned a lot."

"Do you happen to recall his last name?"

"No, uh…" He thought about it. "You know what, I'm not sure I ever knew it. I was a kid—I just called him Mr. Angelo."

"Can I ask, was he— Did he speak Spanish with you? Or English?"

"English. Real good English. With my mom, though, he spoke Spanish. And with my aunt, too—he tracked us down somehow, after we got out of foster care and went to my aunt's."

"Tracked you down?"

"Yeah, uh, he—this sounds weird, as an adult, but he, like, brought us candy, and toys. Nothing like that other thing ever happened again. But he… I don't know, with my mom in jail, I thought he felt sorry for us."

"Mm-hmm. Did you—it sounds like you lost touch with him at some point?"

"Oh yeah, years ago. Before I finished high school. He just disappeared. Didn't say he was leaving or anything, he just… was gone, you know? Never came over, and I never saw him around anymore."

She was nodding. "Do you know a lot of people in landscaping now?"

"Oh yeah, everybody. I work in three counties, right?" He cocked his head as if he'd just realized what her point was. "Yeah, it's funny, isn't it. If he was still in landscaping around here, I'd know him. I started doing that as soon as I could drive, man, the day I got my license. I was sixteen: I borrowed my aunt's car and started doing lawns. Been working in the same business ever since. But I never ran into him again."

13

MAY 14, 2021

A few minutes before three in the afternoon, I parked a couple of blocks from the courthouse and walked over, stopping on the way to get a latte for Ruiz and a regular for myself.

He'd called that morning to let me know that Ludlow was leaving for a conference after lunch and wouldn't be back in the office until Monday. The upbeat tone in his voice had made me think he was suggesting that I should drop by once Ludlow was gone. I didn't ask why. Instead, in a similar tone, I'd told him that it so happened I was planning to be downtown after lunch myself, so maybe I'd swing by.

I didn't have any such plans, but if there was something Ruiz had been waiting to tell me until he was sure his boss wasn't around, I was interested.

When I got to the courthouse, the sun was blazing down. The palm trees looked like they were wilting, and I was glad to get inside where there was air-conditioning.

I was the only person in the elevator, and when I stepped out onto Ruiz's floor, it was unnaturally quiet. The heels of my shoes clacked as I walked down the hall. I tapped on his door and said hi.

Seeing the coffee in my hands, he said, "Aw, you didn't have to do that! Come on in."

"You the only one here? I almost expected to see tumbleweeds blowing across the hallway."

"Well, you know. When the cat is away on a Friday afternoon, the mice will get the hell out of the office. Sit on down."

I sat, and we both took good long sips of our coffees.

He set his down. "Sorry I can't offer you any cookies. Marisol's too busy with the garden right now."

His wife was a domestic goddess, constantly producing incredible food. "She harvesting stuff already?"

"Oh yeah. Beans, corn, carrots—it's been so hot, we've even got zucchini coming in."

I smiled. "I remember when I was a kid, the first time my mom planted zucchinis, I guess she didn't read the instructions, because out of nowhere we had about nine hundred of them."

"Uh-huh. I remember your mom. She was a good woman."

"Yeah, she was." She'd died when Noah was a toddler.

"I bet you had more zucchini than you had grass. Those things are like weeds. We always end up giving away at least thirty loaves of zucchini bread."

"Oh, sign me up, if you've got extra."

"I will. And you can have whatever I was going to give Ludlow, since last year I found the ones I gave him in the break-room trash."

I shook my head. "He doesn't exactly have the human touch, does he."

"No. Hey, you mind shutting that door?"

I leaned back and pushed his door closed.

When the latch clicked, he leaned back in his chair, crossed his arms, and said, with a little smile, "Tell me, are you *trying* to mess with Ludlow? Or should I not believe what the papers say?"

"Man," I said, "I tell you what, never get on the wrong side of Dabney the Fourth."

Despite the fact that I hadn't spoken publicly about Maria's case or filed anything to try to reopen it, Fourth had found out that I'd visited her in prison. I suspected one of the guards had tipped him off. The headline in the Sunday paper—the only print edition that Dabney still published; everything else was online—had been "Disgraced Ex-Solicitor Befriends Convicted Murderer."

"Oh, I know," Ruiz said. "Nobody wants to get in his crosshairs. Why do you think I invited you here? I can't be seen meeting you at the diner or wherever. But nobody's going to bat an eye at seeing you walk into the courthouse."

"Damn," I said.

"Ludlow's pissed."

"I'm sure he is."

"You really think you've got something on that case?" He sounded genuinely curious.

I didn't think we ought to talk about that, but I didn't want to be rude. Instead, I said, "You were here back then, weren't you—I mean, when the case was originally going on?"

"Yeah, fresh out of law school. We were conflicted out, obviously, so the office wasn't involved in the prosecution, but I certainly remember it."

"Uh-huh. I was up in Charleston with a toddler, so I don't recall much at all. I was actually trying to figure something out: do you recollect, back then, how it worked when we or the police had somebody whose English wasn't that great? Was that before or after the State started providing certified, or whatever they're called, qualified interpreters?"

"Oh, after. I was in law school, or maybe undergrad, when the new rules came in." He laughed and shook his head. "Yeah, I can't believe how it used to be. You know, I once interpreted for some guy in traffic court back when I was, like, a freshman?"

"You did?"

"Yeah, my qualification was 'warm body that knows some Spanish.' They'd never allow that these days."

"No, they wouldn't. Anyhow, one of the previous lawyers on this case filed a motion about language issues with my client's police statement, and lost. I thought there was probably some merit to it, but I couldn't remember how things worked back then."

"Oh, you're looking at her as an immigrant who got railroaded by the system? That article the other day could not have been farther from that, could it." He whistled, shaking his head.

"Old Dabney thinks I invite hardened killers to my home for Thanksgiving, doesn't he."

He laughed. "Or he'd like to make the public think so. But, look, I didn't suggest you come by so we could chat about Dabney's rumor mill. I wanted to let you know I heard something interesting last week. And since our office is no longer involved, I don't see a conflict in mentioning it to you."

"Makes sense," I said. He had to be talking about Clay's case.

"Especially not when I'm under an ethical duty to seek justice and protect the innocent, right?" He was paraphrasing the ethical rules for prosecutors.

"Right."

"So I decided I ought to tell you. It's hearsay, though. Double hearsay, actually. Nothing you can use directly."

"Yeah, that's fine." We both knew that evidence you couldn't use in court could still be useful; it might put you on the track of something that you *would* be able to use.

"Okay. But I do need your word that you're not going to disclose the source of this info in any way. Meaning both myself and my own source." He was staring at me in a way that made me feel like I was being x-rayed.

I nodded. "You got it." He looked like he wasn't quite convinced, so I continued. "Ruiz, you and I will be around a lot longer than any particular case. I'm not about to blow up a good working relationship over one piece of evidence."

He nodded. "Okay. So… one of my daughters happens to be friends with the little sister of that girl in your boat-crash case."

He had two daughters. From their ages, it was pretty easy to guess which one he must mean.

"Uh-*huh*. Emma's sister? That's interesting." I took a sip of coffee.

"Yeah. So, I don't know why she fessed up after all this time, but last week she told me that not too long after the crash, Emma was home for spring break and they hung out, all three of them. And—I've already dealt with this, I obviously don't approve, but there was some drinking going on."

I shook my head. I wasn't sure any of his kids were even eighteen, much less drinking age. "That's hard. Just, as a parent."

"Oh, I know. You understand. Anyway, I only mention the drinking because it might explain why they were speaking maybe a little more freely than usual. So, get ready for the double hearsay: she told *me* that Emma told *her* that Emma felt terrible because she wasn't sure your guy was driving the boat. He was up there at the front, and she heard him and Jimmy arguing, but she didn't know whose hands were on the wheel."

I took that in. "She say anything about why she told the cops a different story?"

"Not really. What she—my daughter—tells me is, she asked that question herself at the time, and Emma just said that she was scared, confused, et cetera."

"Confused I can understand. But scared? Of what?"

He gave a big rolling shrug as if to say, *I leave that to you.*

————

After that, I needed to debrief with Terri. We met on the causeway to let our dogs walk off-leash, keeping an eye on them sniffing seaweed and chasing each other as we strolled down the sand.

She said, "It's a little nebulous, isn't it. Emma's scared. Okay, of what? With her being off social media, she's real hard to track."

"Yeah, I'm sure." I watched a ship out near the horizon. The tang of the sea breeze was nice. I said, "Man, is it peaceful here."

"Mm-hmm."

After a moment, she said, "Oh, I've got a little update on Maria. And Shannon. I went to see her again."

"Mrs. Pennington? She grill you for information for her podcast?"

"Oh, of course. She raised all the possibilities: suicide, love triangle, the works. She even mentioned the gardener, although she doesn't know his name."

"You're kidding."

"No. For an amateur, she's a good investigator. Have you listened to her podcast?"

I shook my head.

"It's... I mean, it's morbid, like you'd expect of someone that sets up her office in a room where a woman was killed. But the level of detail is amazing. And she's got this whole forum where women across the country—people, I should say, but she tells me it's mostly women—trade all these theories and clues and whatnot about cold cases."

"Wow."

"Yeah. I'm going to read through it. Maybe Noah should, too—that's a pretty harmless way for him to help out and learn some skills."

"Hmm. I'll have to think about how to do that. I can't exactly hire my unlicensed son as a PI, so confidentiality's an issue."

"True. Oh, also, she scanned some old photos for me. Pictures of the property. Some of the shrubbery and trees out front weren't there at the time, and what was there was a whole lot shorter. So it makes you wonder who might've seen anything."

"We know who owned the places across the street?"

"Yeah, I went to the county tax assessor's and pulled the records. Those old mansions they knocked down had huge lots, and only two of them seem like they were close enough to the house to see much of anything. And one of them was already abandoned back then."

"Man, that's hard to imagine in a neighborhood like that." Devonshire Grove and the cul-de-sacs that branched off it were home to surgeons and CEOs who commuted to Charleston so they could raise their kids in a wholesome small town.

"I know. Gentrification happened fast and furious on the north side."

I jogged ahead to pull Squatter off a hunk of seaweed he was chewing. He growled at me. "So who was living in the place that wasn't abandoned?"

"Three different families. Each floor was its own separate apartment."

"Oh, renters? So their names weren't on the tax records, I guess."

"No, some LLC owned it. But I searched voter registrations, DMV records, that kind of thing. I got the tenants for two of the three apartments that way—and here's an interesting coincidence: the one on the second floor was Dunk McDonough and his wife."

"Are you serious?"

"Mm-hmm."

My thoughts went to a dark place when I thought of the man who'd aimed a sniper rifle at Noah. "I'm sure that apartment was a nicer place than where he lives now." McDonough had been in federal prison for a year and a half and, I hoped, would be there for the rest of his life.

"I thought it was strange," she said, "that none of the tenants were on the list of folks the police talked to in their investigation. Why would you not talk to the neighbors?"

"Huh. Yeah, that does seem pretty elementary."

"And the police didn't even get Ludlow's statement until the next day. One of the responding officers wrote that he was too quote, unquote 'distraught' to speak to them at the scene."

"What? Who *isn't* distraught at a murder scene? You still talk to them!"

"Right? And the other reason it said Ludlow couldn't talk was that he had no one to watch his son."

"He had Maria, didn't he? Or had they already arrested her?"

"Oh, she was in the back of a police car as soon as they got there. But at a scene where a parent of young kids has been killed, we would have a—typically a female officer to sit with them in another room. And we might try to get in touch with a grandparent. It shouldn't be a reason not to talk to the surviving parent." She sighed. "That poor little kid."

"Yeah. Oh, did I tell you Noah knows him, more or less?"

"He knows Brandon Ludlow? How?"

"Video games. That one you were playing last year, OtherWorld."

"Oh, I still play that. Sometimes you need to get out of your own head for a while. So does he just know him online, or… They don't hang out, do they?"

"Why that tone?"

She thought for a second. "The best way to put it is, the circles Brandon Ludlow runs in are not ones you want Noah in."

"Yeah, I got that impression. What do you know about him?"

"He was never right after his mama died. He went into a dark stage around junior high, start of high school, and as far as I know, he still hasn't come out of it. His daddy more or less bought him his diploma —had to send him to one of those boarding schools for wayward kids up in the mountains. His crowd is basically rich kids with nothing to do but drugs, and the not-rich ones who sell the drugs. And do the time."

131

"Yikes." I'd seen kids like him up in Charleston. Unlike the dealers, who went to prison, the rich-kid customers always got into diversion programs, doing community service and counseling so their records could be expunged. I said, "I guess that explains why Jimmy is Ludlow's heir apparent instead of Brandon."

————

On the way home, I stopped by the office to get my laptop and some files. I sat down at my desk to read a couple of new emails. One was from Noah, forwarding links to the smear piece on me that had run in the Sunday paper. He'd written, "Is this why you were asking me about Brandon L?"

I didn't hit reply. I was going to have to remind him to be a little more discreet about what he put in writing.

A movement at the corner of my eye made me look up. Roy had draped himself across my doorway.

"Afternoon," I said. "That's quite the outfit. Were you in court today?" He was wearing two pieces of a gray three-piece suit. Every button on his vest was done up.

"Oh, Lord, you know that's a place I try never to be. No, I've got a dinner tonight. Political fundraiser type of thing."

"Sounds like a good place to meet new clients."

"Exactly. Dang, you're catching on to the business end of things. Slowly but surely."

He smiled. I did, too; he liked ragging on me, purely for the entertainment. It was never malicious.

"Got a little issue, though," he said. His face had turned serious. "I'm sure you saw the Sunday paper?"

I sighed. "Yes. I probably should've anticipated something like that."

He nodded. "Yeah, and I've spoken to Laura already. I know you didn't bring this one in. And I admit, I wasn't paying much attention when you mentioned it to me—I didn't connect the dots, in terms of how it might play out."

"Well, I suppose I ought to have explained it in a little more depth."

"And I ought to have paid closer attention."

I could tell from his tone I'd gone down a notch or two in his esteem. He hadn't paid close attention at the time because he'd trusted me not to do anything that might reflect badly on the firm. Now I'd lost some of that trust.

"So, here's the thing," he said. "In my view, you don't stir the pot and turn someone like Ludlow against you unless you've got a really—I mean, an *extraordinarily* compelling case. And a lucrative one. I respect pro bono work as much as the next guy, but we're not one of those innocence-type nonprofits, right?"

"Course not. This is a business."

"That's right. We take cases for one of three reasons." He counted them off on his fingers: "One, money. Or two, favors that might bring in more money later. Or three, good PR—which also might bring in money later. And that's it, right?"

"That's it." It was his firm, so I could hardly disagree.

"And unlike some professions, in the law, there *is* such a thing as bad publicity."

"Yeah, there is."

"So that headline… I'm going to have some explaining to do about it tonight, and going forward. And I don't know what the proper explanation is." From the look he leveled at me, I had about a minute to solve this problem.

"Well, I take it with a grain of salt," I said, "since we all know Ludlow and Dabney go way back—"

"They do, but to most folks that doesn't mean what Dabney says is wrong or not to be taken seriously. Does it? I mean, he's a third-generation newspaper man, and his little media empire does not depend on Ludlow in any way."

I acknowledged that with a nod.

Roy went on. "Granted, he's got his opinions or his take on things, but —I mean, I'd look like a fool if I brushed this off with some sugges-tion that he's lying to keep himself in Ludlow's good graces. Espe-cially when he's not lying, is he? Apart from the slant he put on it, it's true: you've visited that woman in prison, and so forth."

"Of course. Dabney knows how to walk right up to the line between insinuation and defamation, and how to lean as far over it as he can without one toe ever actually crossing it."

"He does. He learned that at his daddy's knee. So it sounds like you see what I mean here: the problem isn't that he's lying. The problem is the facts we've given him to play with."

I appreciated the word "we." It was generous.

After thinking over the options for a second, I said, "Roy, I apologize, obviously, for putting you in an awkward spot. And I agree that this is a hornet's nest that's not worth kicking unless there's an extremely compelling case that Mrs. Guerrero is innocent. And I want to mention, that's exactly why I've made an effort to keep things discreet while I investigate."

"Yeah, I'm aware you haven't filed anything or announced that you'd taken the case. I grant you that. And that was the right call."

"I'm glad you feel that way. But I admit, I failed to anticipate how thoroughly Dabney would be sniffing around all of this, or that he'd break the story before I was even sure there was a story to break."

He was nodding, thinking it through. "That's a point I can make. You're just doing your due diligence. This isn't even a case yet, and it won't become one unless you uncover something that anybody could see is pretty monumental."

"Uh-huh."

"Okay. I can work with that. Thanks."

He left.

I wasn't sure how *I* was going to work with that. I still operated on the same code Ruiz had been talking about in his office: Seek justice. Protect the innocent. Telling me to drop Maria's case unless I found "monumental" evidence was setting the bar higher than it rightly ought to be.

But then, in practice, that was where the bar was set when you were trying to get a wrongly convicted person out of prison.

So that was the kind of evidence I was going to have to find.

14

MAY 15, 2021

On a hot Saturday afternoon, I found myself back near Devonshire Grove. I was at the other end of the neighborhood from the Penningtons' home, driving past less-grand lots with newer houses on them. I was running late for a meeting with Mr. Tucker, the paramour. He'd given me his address, but I'd failed to anticipate that every house was a brick McMansion and the streets all had country club names: Fox Hollow, Elk Ridge, Fawn Drive.

In his driveway, when I finally found it, was a red Mercedes convertible with the top down. To my mind, that car, plus his escapade under the bridge, put Tucker squarely in the "midlife crisis" category.

I parked on the street and walked to the door. Given the sensitive topic I was hoping to talk with him about, I hadn't brought Terri. I thought it might be easier to discuss man-to-man.

He answered while I was still knocking, let me into the foyer, and gave me a firm handshake. He looked like a politician ready for a casual photo op: salt-and-pepper hair, polo shirt, chinos. The house was quiet; he'd told me his wife and kids were spending the weekend with her parents.

"Care for a drink?" he asked as I followed him to what turned out to be a den. "I'm having a gin and tonic, but you can name your poison."

He picked up a half-full tumbler from a side table and took a sip.

"Wish I could," I said. "But I'm on medication. Doctor's orders." That was not the case, but I didn't want to get into my true reasons.

He gestured me to an armchair and set a bottle of water on the glass coffee table in front of me.

Then he stepped over to the front window, shut the curtains, came back, and sat facing me on the couch. "Do you mind turning off your phone? I'll turn mine off too. Don't want anything recorded."

"Uh… sure," I said.

While he was fussing with his iPhone, I pulled out my phone, looked it over, and said, "You know what, I'm not even sure this *has* an off switch."

He looked up, gave a laugh of surprise, and said, "My goodness, they still make those?"

"Oh, there it is," I said, switching it off. "I don't honestly know if they still make them. I must've bought this eight or nine years ago."

He laughed again. Then he set his phone on the coffee table and said lightly, "I'm curious: what's your opinion on Solicitor Ludlow?"

Despite the casual tone, the question felt like he was offering a secret handshake.

I knew from Terri's research that Tucker's Southern roots went deep, so I thought he'd understand the unspoken volumes of negativity in my answer: "Thus far," I said, "I have yet to be impressed by him."

"Uh-huh." He was sitting very still, looking at me. "Are you speaking of his work as solicitor? Or on a more personal level?"

"There is no level on which he's earned my respect."

A smile flickered on his face, but I sensed that I needed to put another card or two on the table before we could connect.

I said, "The man is a triple-A arrogant, aggressive ass. His daddy passed the mantle to him for a job he never deserved, and I'm not aware of anybody who considers him a friend. That about sums up my views." I picked up my water bottle and opened it. "How about yours?"

He relaxed, leaned back on the couch, and said, "Same. And then some. There's a level of... what I would call amorality in him that I personally find repellent, especially in a public servant."

"Oh?" I kept my tone light. I found it hard to reconcile his self-righteousness with the fact he'd dropped his drawers with his mistress under a bridge while campaigning for office, but the man seemed sincere.

"Yes," he said. "That's why I was going to run against him."

"Was? You're not anymore?"

He gave a humorless laugh. "My hands are a little tied on that. Ludlow is obviously aware of some, uh, circumstances that I don't care to make public."

"Uh-huh. Relating to the night of that boat crash?"

He winced.

I was getting the sense that Tucker was too ashamed to speak frankly about the subject. So I said, "I can imagine what a relief it would've been not to see any of that come up in the local news. In that regard, would it be unreasonable for me to suspect that Ludlow might've offered a little quid pro quo?"

He downed half his drink in one gulp and said, "Well, that's certainly his style."

"I wonder if he might've made a similar offer to the young lady."

"I wouldn't know. She and I haven't spoken since the week of the crash."

I nodded and took a sip of water. I knew Ludlow wouldn't have hesitated to require two favors, not just one, in exchange for keeping Tucker's transgression secret: first, don't run against him, and second, provide testimony to keep Ludlow's son out of jail. But nobody liked being accused of agreeing to lie. Especially not someone like Tucker, who apparently saw himself, at least for the most part, as a high-minded upholder of morality.

So I said, "I've gotten the impression before that Ludlow likes to put his finger on the scales. I mean, well beyond the normal sorts of plea deals and so forth. I've long suspected him of pressuring witnesses in ways that, ethically speaking, no lawyer ought to even think about doing."

He was nodding hard. "Yes, uh-huh. I understand you were up in Charleston a good long while, but I've been down here my whole career, and I've had occasion to see that's how he operates."

"With severe consequences for those who don't go along with it?"

"I fully believe there are folks in jail, not to mention folks who got dragged into divorce court, just because they got on his bad side."

"Uh-huh. And knowing that he operates that way would put the fear of God into you, wouldn't it. It could turn what might just be a regrettable mistake into... well, the word that comes to mind is blackmail, although maybe that's a little strong."

"No, that sounds about right." He sipped his drink. "It's certainly a tricky situation."

"Very. Although one thing I've found: sometimes confessing a sin is better than hiding it. People can be a lot more supportive than you might expect."

"Huh." He didn't look convinced.

I took a sip of my water. "One thing I'm curious about, if you don't mind my asking, is who it was that, uh, observed you there under the bridge. Do you recall the officer's name?"

"No, that's—I have to say, that question was not top of mind for me right then."

He wasn't trying to be funny, so I stifled my smile.

Tucker said, "He was a taller guy. Taller than me. He showed me his police badge. I should've memorized the number, but I didn't think to."

"Okay. I only asked because I didn't see it in the reports."

"No? Well, I assume that's part of some plan of Ludlow's."

"Yeah, that may be it. Uh, would you mind if I turned my laptop on? I've got some photos I'd like you to take a look at. Some of the officers involved in the case."

He thought about it a second before nodding. "I can do that," he said, "if you wouldn't mind just putting one of these over your laptop camera while we do it."

He pulled a shiny card out of his wallet and peeled off a piece of it. "This is a privacy sticker. It hangs on by static cling—it won't leave anything on your laptop after we're done."

"Huh. Okay, one second here."

I opened my laptop, and he leaned forward and applied the sticker to the spot where the camera was. If he'd been anywhere near this much of a privacy freak before the night of the boat crash, he never would've taken his hottie down to the bridge and he'd be in no trouble today.

He'd lived and learned, I supposed.

"So what I got here," I said, "is some screenshots I took of body-cam and interview footage. I doubt this is complete—there were almost certainly some officers there that I don't have photos of. But if you could just look through and tell me if any of them is the one who collared you and your friend?"

He clicked back and forth through the pictures with his brows knitted together. On a few photos, he zoomed in. Then he leaned back, shaking his head.

"Okay," I said. "Well, it's good to eliminate some, anyway."

He nodded. I handed back his privacy sticker and put my laptop away.

He sat there looking thoughtful, gazing off toward the corner of the room with his legs crossed and his fingers interlaced on his lap.

After a moment, he said, "I appreciate what you're trying to do on this case. It's important work. But you spent a long time away from here, up in the city. So I'm not sure whether you're aware that what's at issue is bigger than this one case. And I don't say that to minimize anything—the loss of that young man was tragic. What I mean is that for Mr. Ludlow, it's not about that."

"What is it about?"

"Oh, it's about him. His ability to maintain power and control. I don't know that he has so much as one brain cell dedicated to anything else."

I chuckled and said, "I've gotten that same impression."

He looked me straight in the eye and said, "And you're laughing about it?"

"Well..." I shrugged. "Sometimes it's a way to deal with things."

"Is making light of corruption the right way to deal with it?"

I realized I was dealing with a humorless zealot. "I guess it depends."

"'Be alert and of sober mind,'" he said, still staring at me. "Peter chapter five, verse eight. 'Because your enemy prowls, looking for someone to devour.'"

I nodded as if I was taking that in. I never knew what to say in response to Bible verses.

———

Toward evening, as the temperatures were sinking back to tolerable levels, Terri and I drove over to the trailer park where Emma lived. As we passed the marsh beside it, I glanced at the car's clock and said, "If this takes much longer than thirty minutes, it'll be mosquito time. They will eat us alive."

"Mm-hmm. I've got my DEET spray. Say the word, and I'll make us both smell like—wait a second." She pulled the plastic bottle halfway out of her purse and read the label. "Fresh citrus."

"That's fine. You can make me smell like wet sheep and gym socks if it stops those critters."

We were rolling up to the trailer park entrance, with its shabby old wooden sign. She read it and said, "Or a whole lodge full of sheep? I've never understood why this place is called Sheep's Lodge."

"If *you* don't know that, I doubt anybody does."

"Naw, my specialty is people. That's what I remember. Not real estate."

I headed right, toward the slightly uphill side of the park. We passed some trailers where kids were running around with dirty, bare feet. An old lady in a nightdress stood in a doorway watching them.

"I don't think I've been in here since before the pandemic," I said. "Nothing's changed."

"I haven't been here since I was a cop."

"Oof. Lot of domestics?"

"That or, a few times, somebody making meth."

I shook my head. "Either way, it's always the kids who suffer."

"And the women."

I turned up the last road, parked, and looked at the map again.

"Here we are," I said. "Third trailer up."

We walked up a dirt path between trailers, pausing a moment to make sure that a hound growling at us looked like he was properly chained, and went up the two steps of a rotting wooden porch. A wreath of fake flowers hung on the storm door. When I knocked, a pretty but haggard woman looked out the window of the inside door and asked, "Can I help you?"

"Yes, ma'am, I hope so. I'm Leland Munroe, and this is Terri Washington. I'm a lawyer, working on a case that your daughter's a witness in."

Beside me, Terri added, "And you know what, Ms. Smalls, we actually all went to high school together. I don't know if you remember—"

"Oh," the woman said, recognition dawning on her face. "Oh, yeah. My goodness! Hang on."

She unlocked the inside door—it sounded like she had three locks on it—and then the storm door too, and invited us in.

"I'm sorry," she said, grabbing the collar of a mutt who came to investigate us. "He just needs to smell you. Um, have a seat. You can go ahead and move whatever you need to."

After the dog checked us out, Terri and I moved some magazines and a TV remote out of the way so we could sit down.

"Now, I don't got a whole lot of time," Ms. Smalls said quietly. She was sitting in a chair facing us; I noticed she hadn't offered us any refreshments. "I asked you in because I don't want no neighbors hearing my business."

Terri said, lowering her voice to match the other woman's volume, "I completely understand."

I said, "If you'd like to turn the TV on, that's what I do when I don't want folks to overhear."

"Hm. If you could just hand me that?"

Terri handed her the remote. Ms. Smalls clicked it and then said, over the noise of an ad for a truck, "I don't mean to be rude, but if you're here about that boat accident, my daughter has said all she's got to say, more than once. She has had enough."

"Yes, ma'am," I said. "I can imagine."

Terri said, "She's been through a lot. And we're trying to get this all over with."

"Well, when is that boy going to take a plea? We did everything your Mr. Ludlow asked. He said it would all go away soon, and that was a long time ago. Does he know yet when it's going to stop?"

Ethical alarm bells went off in my head. I was, unfortunately, not allowed to let her go on thinking I was on the prosecution's side.

"I'm sorry," I said, "I ought to make clear, I'm not here on behalf of Mr. Ludlow. I represent Clay Carlson."

Her eyes went wide. She stood up and said, "I'm sorry, but I'm going to have to ask y'all to leave right now." Despite the aggressive tone, she just looked scared.

I stood to leave, but Terri didn't. She said, "Crystal, don't worry. Pat Ludlow will never know one word of what's said here."

"There's not going to *be* nothing said here. I need both of y'all to leave."

Behind her, the door from the next room was open a sliver, and I caught sight of Emma.

Realizing she'd been seen, she stepped in and said, "Would y'all please leave my mother alone?"

"Absolutely, Miss Twain," I said. "But is there any way you could speak to us—"

"No! You need to leave us be!" She looked like she might cry. Her hands, at her sides, were balled into fists.

Terri said, "Emma, I know you've been through a lot—"

"Don't act like you care about me! If you did, you'd leave us alone!"

"We will," I said. "We're leaving. But if there's any way that at some point you could talk to us about Clay—"

She yelled, "Clay Carlson belongs in jail! You think you know him? I thought that too!"

When she turned and ran back to the other room, her mom pointed to the door and said, "Out. I need you out right now."

We left.

15

MAY 24, 2021

Monday mornings were a slow time for car salesmen, which is why Clay's dad had suggested I swing by his showroom. I'd emailed to float the idea of hiring an expert witness to try to discredit the eyewitness testimony, and he wanted to talk it through face-to-face.

I walked in past a few sparkling BMWs with price tags in their windows roughly equal to my previous annual salary as a prosecutor. Mr. Carlson leaned out a doorway at the far end and boomed, "Hey there, Mr. Munroe! Come on in, we're both here."

Clay was sitting on the customer side of his dad's desk, in a corner office with plate-glass windows. He set down the car brochure he was reading and stood to shake my hand. Outside, the sun was shining on the thirty or forty brand-new Beemers that filled the new-car side of his lot.

Mr. Carlson plopped himself in his chair and said, "Okay, so what's this expert thing? What the heck kind of expertise is going to get my boy out from under these charges?" Before I could answer, he added, "Hang on, Clay. Can you shut that door?"

Clay complied.

"Well, Mr. Carlson," I said, "the point of an expert is to help a jury understand certain evidence or how they should interpret it. For instance, if this was a gunshot case, there might be an expert showing blown-up photos of bullet casings and explaining what the markings on them mean, or—"

"But that's not us, right? I mean, what's the rocket science here? Don't get me wrong—if we need an expert, I got no problem paying for that. Because that's extra, right?"

"Yeah, they're professionals. And their billing rates are typically as high as mine, if not higher."

"Hoo!" Mr. Carlson sat back, shaking his head at the prospect.

"The reason I think we may need one is that this is basically a he said, she said type of case, and we need to give the jury a reason to take what the prosecution's witness says with a grain of salt."

"Witness? Isn't there more than one?"

"Yeah, but it's Emma in particular I'm worried about. The jury won't have any trouble understanding that Jimmy Ludlow might lie to get himself off the hook, but there's no obvious motive for her."

Mr. Carlson, rocking his chair back and forth, said, "What about them two, uh, lovebirds?"

"They were forty-odd feet away, and you might say their attention was elsewhere."

He laughed out loud. "Yeah, you might."

"So the thing about Emma," I said, "is that she was in the crash herself, thrown into the water, and a boy she cared about very much was killed."

I heard Clay gulp, and I added, "I'm sorry. I know he was your friend too."

Clay nodded. His eyes were closed. This was hard for him.

"What I'm trying to say is, she was traumatized. And the thing is— well, first off, have you heard about the DNA exonerations that have been happening since the technology got good enough for that? I mean folks who were convicted of crimes, but then the DNA was tested and it proved some other guy did it?"

"Oh yeah," Mr. Carlson said.

"Okay, so there's people who study that kind of thing, and what they found is that in about seventy-five percent of those cases, what got the guy convicted was eyewitness testimony. The victim or somebody else who saw the crime with their own eyes identified the guy, right on the stand in the courtroom, but later the DNA proved that the witness was dead wrong."

"Is that so." Mr. Carlson's chair was squeaking as it rocked. "How's a thing like that happen?"

"Well, turns out, witnessing a crime or being the victim of one is a pretty traumatic thing—"

"Oh, it's got to be, yeah."

"Right, and that messes with how your brain processes things. It can get you confused, even when the people involved are folks you know."

"Ain't that something. And there's experts that can speak to that?"

"Yeah, certain kinds of neurologists or psychologists. So I was thinking we might want to give one or two of them a call, see what they think, see if they're available."

"Sounds good. And forget about the price. If they can do what you say, I don't care if they charge a million bucks. Because what do I have, if my boy's rotting in jail? And for a thing he didn't even do?"

"Okay, then." I stood, and we shook.

As they walked me to the door, I said, "Oh, actually, Clay, you got twenty or thirty minutes to spare? I wanted to talk to you, too, if that's okay."

He shrugged. "I'm home from college. I got all summer."

"Great. You want to go for a drive? Just to keep things confidential?"

"Oh, sure."

"Hang on a second." Mr. Carlson walked to a desk at the side of the floor, dug in the top drawer, and tossed me a set of keys. As I caught it, he pointed out the window and said, "Take that black X5 right there."

"Thanks much, but I've got my car."

"No, you've got a Malibu. That is not a car."

We laughed.

As Clay and I headed for the door, Mr. Carlson, shaking his head, said, "I mean, a lawyer in a Malibu! Bless your heart."

———

Clay and I drove to St. Helena Sound—or charged there, or shot over there; the X5 didn't stoop so low as to merely *drive*. We hadn't been to the accident site together yet, and I wanted to see if it brought any details of that night back to him.

On the way, I asked if he'd remembered anything that might ever have made Emma mad at him.

He said, "Not before the accident. We were friends until then."

"Okay, what happened after?"

"Nothing. I don't know what she—" He paused, drew in a breath. "I didn't do anything, but she thought I did. There was a rumor going around that I'd sent a nude of her to some guys."

"You had a nude of her?"

"By accident, I did. Like… two years ago? She meant to send it to Hayden, but she sent it to a chat we both were on."

"Oof."

"She was so embarrassed. She realized it, like, ten seconds after she sent it, and she called me, and she was so upset. I told her I'd delete the whole thread. I told her not to worry."

He stopped there. After a second, I asked, "And did you?"

He sighed hard. "I should have. I know that. Mr. Munroe, I did *not* send it to *anyone*. But I didn't keep my promise either. I should've deleted it, but…" He looked out the window, shaking his head. "But she's so beautiful. She's just…" He sighed again. "Yeah. I kept it."

"So why'd she think you shared it?"

"Because some other guys had it. After the accident, after Hayden was… dead."

"Huh." I thought on that for a second and then asked, "Any idea how that happened?"

"No. For all I know—I don't want to say anything bad about him, since he can't fight back anymore, but I had to wonder, how does she know Hayden didn't share it before he died?"

"That's a good question."

I could see the bridge we were going to cross rising in the distance above the flat Lowcountry landscape. As we cruised toward it, I said, "Speaking of questions, one thing I wanted to ask you was what you and Ludlow talked about when he came into your hospital room."

He screwed up his face, like he either couldn't quite remember or couldn't articulate it.

I said, "Is it hard to recall?"

"It was, yeah," he said, "but you saying that just brought it back a little! Because it was weird—although I have no idea what's normal for a lawyer to say in a situation like that."

"What'd he say?"

"Well, he came in—he sent the nurse out and he came in and closed the door, and he was all apologetic and checking if I was all right. And he kept saying, 'I know it might be hard to recall right now'— that's why what you said reminded me. He was saying that with what I'd been through, it was probably confusing and hard to remember, but I shouldn't worry, because that was normal."

"Huh." Ludlow wasn't wrong on that; traumatic experiences could scramble a person's memory. Still, it felt off. "Did he ask you what happened? Or did he just launch right into that?"

He thought for a second. "I don't think so. I actually don't remember him asking me what happened at all. And I don't know how we got there, but at some point, he said he *forgave* me. And I was, like, for what? He said everybody makes mistakes, and I shouldn't feel bad that I made a mistake, too, because nobody was going to hold it against me."

We glided up the arch of the bridge.

"Did you tell him it was his boy at the wheel?"

"I don't honestly recall. I don't think he asked me. Which... is that weird?"

"Yeah, it is."

I wished we had a recording of that conversation, and of Ludlow's conversation with Emma, which I thought it was safe to assume was along the same lines. But Ludlow had made sure there wouldn't be any recordings by talking to them in the hospital instead of at the sheriff's office. Still, Clay could testify as to what Ludlow had said to him, and the jury could infer from the strangeness of Ludlow's behavior at the hospital that he might've spoken the same way to Emma.

So getting an expert to testify that such coaching could actually change a traumatized person's memories could make a dent.

I turned onto the side road that went down beside the bridge toward the water and parked where the road ended. We walked alongside the bridge, squinting in the morning sunlight, and stood on the sand, the same deserted beach where rescuers had run into the dark water trying to save the kids.

Clay took a deep breath and looked at the ground.

The water was pale blue, full of light, peaceful. A couple of seagulls flew by, squawking.

I could still see the scar on the cement piling where the boat had hit.

"When did you start being friends with Emma and Hayden?"

He looked across the water. "Oh, I knew him from grade school. And then I met her in ninth grade."

"You ever try to go out with her?"

He laughed. "In my dreams. A girl like that isn't going to be interested in me. I don't play sports, I don't… I mean, since when does the dork get the girl?"

I thought of Elise and smiled. "You'd be surprised."

I watched a white ship moving slowly north, about halfway to the horizon.

He said, "She *is* really smart. We were in AP biology together. But, whatever. That's all over." He kicked a rock into the water.

"What's Jimmy Ludlow like?"

He shrugged. "He's okay. I mean, he was, or apart from what happened, he is. I met him in ninth grade, too. You know he's got a big brother, right?"

"Yep. You know him?"

"Yeah. The weird thing is, I don't think I even knew he existed until tenth or eleventh grade. I mean, he's older, right? He wasn't in school with us. But I still thought it was weird."

"Jimmy didn't talk about him before then?"

"No, not until one night. We were… Can I tell you something and you won't tell my dad?"

"Of course. I'm your lawyer, right?"

He nodded. "Okay. Right. So, a bunch of us were smoking weed down at the beach. Him and me and Hayden and one or two other guys. It must've been the summer between tenth and eleventh grade. And so he mentions his older brother, and I'm like, your *what*?"

"That must've been weird."

"Yeah, but he explained, and, like… it bothered him. He said his dad was real harsh with Brandon—that's his brother."

"Uh-huh."

"I mean, *real* harsh. It made him mad. He said it wasn't fair." He shrugged. "So I guess it wasn't something he liked to talk about."

"Makes sense." After a second, I asked, "Did Jimmy ever tell you what he thinks of his dad?"

"Oh, he hates him."

I nodded. "Can't fault him for that."

For a minute we stood there silently. The sea breeze was in our faces, and his hair was blowing around.

I asked, "So you were good friends with Hayden?"

He didn't say anything. I saw his eyes were closed, and his face looked like he was in pain.

I said, "Yeah. It's rough as hell, losing somebody who matters to you."

He nodded. After a bit, he said, "Mr. Munroe, I don't have a brother. So that's who he was to me."

"I'm sorry."

Another seagull squawked overhead.

"I was driving at first, because Jimmy was—he gets stupid when he's drunk. Not in a mean way, not like some guys. I never saw him get in a fight. He's a good guy, mostly. But he gets, like, reckless."

"Uh-huh."

"But then Hayden, he started throwing up. I didn't realize until then how much he'd drunk. And Emma was trying to help him to the side, but she's little, you know? So I went to help. I put it to idle so we were just floating, and I helped her get him to the side."

His eyes were wide, staring at the water, but I didn't think it was the water he was seeing. He was back in the memory, hands jammed in his pockets, shaking his head.

"And then I heard the motor, and I looked up, and Jimmy was driving. Man." He shook his head.

Everything he was saying was consistent with the evidence. Both his and Jimmy's prints were on the wheel. According to the prosecution, one of Clay's prints overlapped one of Jimmy's—in other words, Clay touched the wheel last. The science behind that was dubious at best. I needed to get it thrown out.

"So what happened then?"

"We started moving. I was yelling at him to stop and helping Emma get Hayden back on the seat. Jimmy was laughing. He kept looking back at me and laughing, like he was doing it to mess with me. I was yelling at him to stop, and I stepped up toward him, and—"

He flipped his right hand up toward his shoulder.

"It just exploded. I don't remember when we hit. I just— Jimmy was laughing, and I was yelling at him, and then *boom*, everything was wrong, and I was in the water."

16

MAY 28, 2021

As we waited in the prison's security line, Terri and I didn't speak. We didn't know who at the prison had leaked our visits to Dabney, and we didn't want to say anything that our anonymous snitch might overhear.

And in any case, we were in no mood to chat. We were not there with good news.

Soon after we got to the meeting room, a guard brought Maria, let her in, and locked the door.

She was happy to see us. After a little chitchat, I handed her a manila envelope containing a couple of hand-drawn Mother's Day cards from her grandchildren. She cooed over them and marveled at how good their handwriting was getting.

Then I got down to business. "Look, Maria, we've got a big problem."

Her smile disappeared. "What?"

"I finally got to the last part of the transcript," I said. "I mean the tran-script of your trial. It's nearly four thousand pages long, and with everything else we've had to look into, it took a while. But anyway, I wish you'd told me up front what you testified to in court."

"What do you mean?"

"Sorry. I mean the jewelry thing. The— And I'm not talking about what actually happened, okay? I'm not talking about what the truth is. What matters, in terms of what options I have for possibly getting you out of prison, is what evidence we have and what the record is. I mean the record of the case. So I'm just talking about what you said on the stand about taking Mrs. Ludlow's jewelry."

She shook her head slowly, looking bewildered. "I don't know what you mean."

"Uh, I guess it *was* twenty years ago. Hang on."

While I was pulling my laptop out of my bag and getting it fired up, Terri talked to Maria about prison life. Half listening, I overheard that she was friendly with a couple of the guards, disliked a few more, and didn't think much of her new cellmate, who was in for felony check fraud.

"I think they put her with me because she speaks Spanish too. But, you know, you speak English. That doesn't mean you like everyone else who speaks English."

Terri laughed and said, "Oh, no, it sure doesn't."

"Sorry to interrupt," I said, "but here's what I'm talking about." I had a PDF of the trial transcript up, day twenty-two of the trial, page 138. I turned my laptop so we could all see it.

I said, "This whole page is what I mean, starting with where the solicitor asks, 'Looking at Exhibit 387'—which I have in a different file; it's a photo of some earrings—anyway, he asked, 'Isn't it true that you stole this pair of emerald earrings from Mrs. Ludlow?' And you said, 'Yes, it's true.'"

The rest of the page went through the same Q&A about other pieces of jewelry.

"No, no." She was shaking her head. "This is not—I didn't say this."

"Uh, I mean… You know, this might sound weird, but one thing I've learned over the years is how much a person's memory can change. Memory is a lot less reliable than people think, so—"

"No. I never, never said this." Her eyes blazed with indignant rage. "Why would I lie like this? You think I would put myself in prison? I say that, I go to prison. Why?"

She was absolutely convinced. And convincing.

After a second, Terri asked, "Maria, did any of your other lawyers ever show you the transcript before?"

She looked down, shaking her head. If I was reading her correctly, she was ashamed.

"Oh," I said. "You couldn't read it?"

She sighed and said, "No. And even now it's not so easy for me. Not fast."

"Maria," I said, "at your trial, did you testify in English?"

"No."

"You had an interpreter?"

"Yes. He translate what they were saying to me, and then what I said back."

Terri and I looked at each other.

"Just a second." On my PDF, I tried to run a Control+F on the word "interpret," but it wasn't searchable. I skipped to the index at the back.

While I was looking, Terri said, "What do you remember about the interpreter?"

"Oh, he was…" Maria shrugged. "I don't know, a guy. Not too old? I'm sorry. Not Mexican, but native Spanish. I forget what country."

"Here he is," I said, pointing at my screen. "Ramón Perez. I am so sorry. I skipped over the parts where witnesses were sworn in because it's always the same. I didn't see that they swore in an interpreter for you, and I should have."

In trial transcripts, interpreters disappeared. Once they were sworn in, the words they said were attributed to the person they were translating for. In our case, Maria.

———

On the drive home, Terri had her laptop open with a copy of the transcript. She'd made it searchable and was highlighting every incriminating thing Maria had said.

"So, assuming she's telling the truth," she said, "it could still be a mistake if it only happened once or twice. She could've misspoken, right? Or the interpreter could've messed up. It happens. But there's just so *much* of it."

"Uh-huh. Although, if he was giving the wrong translation for what she said, wouldn't you think people in the courtroom would've noticed? At least for some of it? I mean, I don't speak Spanish at all, but I can hear the difference between sí and no."

"Mm-hmm." She highlighted a passage and looked at it for a second.

Then she asked, "Could he have mistranslated what the *prosecutor* was saying? Like, if you change 'Isn't it true that you stole' to 'Isn't it true that you *didn't* steal,' then her answer—"

"—incriminates her! She's saying yes to the wrong thing. My God."

"Yeah. That could actually work."

We were coming up behind a farm vehicle. I signaled and passed it.

I said, "But the problem is, it sounds ridiculous. I mean, how could... and *why*? It's at the level of a conspiracy theory, almost. And let's say it's the God's honest truth: the interpreter framed her. That really did happen. What do I do with that? Am I going to get up there in court and argue that this trial transcript is wrong, and these people didn't say what the official transcript records them as saying?"

"And on top of that, it was twenty years ago."

"Right: twenty years ago, these people didn't say what they're quoted as saying in the official trial transcript! How do I prove that? Based on what?"

"Mm-hmm." She shook her head. "Based on a convict claiming she's innocent."

"Exactly. I'd get laughed out of court."

We passed a vast, flat field dotted with cows. Ahead of us, the sky was turquoise blue and cloudless. The highway swooshed beneath our wheels.

Terri said, "Thing is, though... I believe her."

———

As we rolled into Basking Rock, Terri turned off the music we'd been listening to and asked, "What did y'all do to get court interpreters back then? Could you just use anyone you wanted?"

"No. I actually asked Ruiz about that, since I couldn't remember. Far as he recalls, at that point we already had the system that we've got now. The interpreters are certified, and some office at the Clerk of Court provides them if the lawyer asks."

"Huh. That sounds pretty legit. But I should probably still see what I can dig up on this Mr. Perez."

"Yeah. I guess we've got to do at least a little due diligence on that."

I drove us to my office.

While Terri sat at the table running searches to see if she could find Perez, I checked my email. The only one that wasn't spam was a notice that Britney's self-defense hearing was being continued to the third week of June because the judge had COVID. I forwarded that to Britney with a quick explanation and then started drafting a motion in limine to exclude Clay's breathalyzer results from trial evidence. All such motions were due in two weeks, and his trial was scheduled to start thirty days after that.

If I could knock felony DUI out of the case, getting the charge down to involuntary manslaughter, the maximum sentence would drop from twenty-five years to five. That would give me some leverage—hopefully enough to work toward a plea deal with no jail time and no more than a misdemeanor on his record. It wasn't ideal; if Clay truly was innocent, then it wasn't justice at all. But it was a far better outcome than what the prosecution wanted.

And I wasn't an idealist. I didn't think I ever had been. The world was what it was. If justice was out of reach, I saw no dishonor in making a little less injustice my goal.

When Terri had exhausted all her leads for the moment and we were getting hungry, we ordered takeout and brought it back. I still had Clay's case on my brain, so I said, "This might be overambitious, but it would change the whole game if I could find out why Emma's told two different stories. You got any ideas?"

"Just proving *that* she's told two different stories would go a long way."

"Yeah, but I promised Ruiz I wouldn't involve his daughter."

She nodded. Then she sighed, leaned back in her chair, and closed her eyes. After a minute, she said, "I know you don't remember her mom from high school, and I have no idea if this really is connected. But I keep thinking about what happened to her."

"Which was?"

She opened her eyes and pinned me with a look. "I don't want this coming out, okay? Not on the stand, not anywhere. Because it's not your business, and it's not evidence."

"Okay…"

"At best, it's a lead. It might point you somewhere."

I nodded. "Yeah. I got you. Off the record."

"Absolutely off. Because people have a right to their private lives, and a right to work through their problems and traumas in their own time. And I will hold you to that. Okay?"

"Understood."

She took a second to put her thoughts together, and then she said, "When we were in ninth grade—you, me, and Crystal—Ludlow was a senior, remember?"

"Uh, vaguely. Yeah."

"And Crystal was gorgeous. Probably the most beautiful girl who's ever set foot in Basking Rock, in our lifetimes anyway. You must've noticed, even if you don't recall. And Ludlow certainly did."

"Uh-huh." I had a sense where this was going.

"Ludlow was eighteen," she said. "And rich, and class president, debate champion, all of that. Drove a red Audi. Dated a cute cheerleader. And, of course, his daddy was the circuit solicitor."

"Yeah, you're really bringing back to me how much I disliked him even then."

She nodded somberly, then continued. "Crystal was fourteen. She lived in a trailer, right down by the marsh, with parents that were good for *nothing*. And Ludlow found her at a party one night—or he invited her, I don't know. I saw him come out of a bedroom looking kind of furtive, and when he left, I peeked in and found her. I know I don't have to spell out for you what state she was in."

"Jesus."

"She wouldn't let me call the cops or tell anyone. She was too ashamed. And, Leland," she said, "he didn't stop. I saw them a few times at school, in the stairwell—him standing way too close, her just cowering. Sometimes she'd have bruises on her arm. Once I walked into the girls' bathroom and he rushed out, zipping up his pants, and she was in a stall crying."

"God*dammit*," I said. "That poor girl."

"I asked if she wanted me to tell a teacher or somebody, but she said it would just make things worse. Her exact words. And it didn't even end when he went away to school. Remember, I was at the police academy, and then after that I was doing traffic stops, breaking things up at sleazy bars, you know—and I kept seeing them together, whenever he was home from school. I don't think it stopped until she met Emma's father and got pregnant."

She was looking me right in the eyes, intently. I realized why.

"Emma's the same age as Jimmy Ludlow," I said.

She gave a slow nod.

"So when Brandon was born—when Peggy was alive—"

"Mm-hmm."

I let that sink in. Then I asked, "Do you think Crystal thinks Ludlow had something to do with Peggy's death?"

She shrugged. "Who knows? She might think he's capable of it, at least. But even without that, she knows the power he has, and the fact that nobody's ever stopped him from doing anything he wanted to. And she knows his son is at the same school as her little girl, living in a high-end frat house practically around the corner from her."

"Oh, Jesus."

"Yeah."

She gave a deep sigh, lowering her chin to her chest until she was looking at her own lap. For a few seconds she sat there—composing herself, I thought.

Then she sat back up, shook her head, and wheeled her office chair over to where her takeout was sitting. She picked up a french fry, dipped it into some ketchup, and said, "And I'm sure she taught her daughter to fear Pat Ludlow too, the same way you'd teach your kid to watch out for copperheads. That's her mission in life: to get that girl launched and keep her safe until she is."

17

JUNE 5, 2021

Noah and I were standing by a swimming pool at the Cardozos' country club in Charleston, under a moonless black sky. Murmurs of conversation came to us from the groups of nicely dressed people chatting here and there, and beyond a plate-glass window at the far end of the pool, I could see caterers manning the buffet. We'd watched Rachael's bat mitzvah service on livestream from the synagogue that morning, and now that the sun had set, the sabbath was over and it was time for the party.

"Check you out," I told him, gesturing to his outfit with my virgin martini. "You look good in a jacket and tie."

With an embarrassed smile, he said, "Whatever."

"You don't want to go inside and dance with the kids? They have a DJ and a light show."

"I'm not thirteen."

"Fair point. Well, you're in the right place. This seems to be where the pretty girls your age are hanging out."

"Yup." He glanced at a few of them.

"In case you need a girlfriend," I said. "Or is that already taken care of?"

He rolled his eyes.

From behind us, I heard Cardozo call out, "Hey, Leland!"

I spotted him emerging from one of the cabanas on the other side of the pool and said, "Hey!"

As he was coming over, I thought I saw Mr. Paramour, or rather Tucker, behind him, getting some hors d'oeuvres with a woman I assumed was his wife. I wondered if every successful lawyer or aspiring politician in the Lowcountry was part of Cardozo's circle.

Cardozo reached us and said, "I was wondering where you two had disappeared to. You get enough to eat?"

"Oh, we were waiting until the buffet cleared out a little bit."

"Don't wait too long."

Noah said, "I can go get us something, Dad. What do you want?"

"A burger, if they've still got some. Otherwise, whatever looks good."

He headed off, clearly relieved to be free of parental company.

Watching him go, Cardozo said, "It is *wild* how fast they grow up."

"Oh, I know. How's it feel to be having your last bat mitzvah?"

He whistled. "A bar and two bats, and now we're all done. It's strange. I keep feeling like I'm going to wake up tomorrow and they'll all be in grad school."

"Uh-huh."

He sipped his drink and said, "How's Noah doing? Back on track?"

"Yeah, he's doing really well. He got inspired—you know Terri?"

"Your PI? Cool woman."

"Very. So, I guess, watching her work, he got inspired to become a PI himself."

"Oh yeah?"

"Yeah. He's doing criminal justice at the community college, graduating in December."

"I remember him spying on me when he was little. Watching out the attic window with binoculars when I pulled up at your place."

I laughed. "Elise got those for him. He still talks about that. And he may look all grown up, but he's young enough that he sees the romance in that career. Like he could be some sort of South Carolina 007."

"Well, good," he said, chuckling. "I've known some very successful PIs."

"What about you? What're you up to? I mean, apart from watching your kids sprint toward adulthood and getting ready for that human trafficking trial."

"That's about all. That trial, my goodness. It's probably my most gruesome one since your sniper guy."

"Oh, Mc—him?" The people closest to us were having their own conversation, not eavesdropping as far as I could tell, but I still stopped myself from saying Dunk McDonough's name.

He nodded. "Yeah. I'm going to need a vacation both before and after. To cleanse my soul, assuming I've still got one."

"Too bad y'all shut down our local yacht charter," I said. "If you could've just overlooked a few dozen felonies, you could've gone for a cruise."

He laughed, shaking his head.

I finished my drink. "Oh, I wanted to run something by you. For a case I've got now, I was thinking about talking to sniper guy's ex-wife."

"Really? What's she tangled up in now?"

"Oh, nothing that I know of. I have some questions about something she might've witnessed a long time ago. But I wanted to run that by you in case there's some reason I should steer clear of her."

He took a sip of his whiskey and asked, "What's the case you want to ask her about? Any connection to mine?"

"No, it's a prisoner-exoneration thing. Do you recall how down my way, about twenty years ago, the local solicitor's wife got killed—"

"Oh, I don't need to recall. I read about it recently!" He laughed. "That has *got* to be annoying, those headlines."

"I try not to read them."

"Good call. Although you might want to have your secretary or somebody keep track of them, in case there's something you need to know about."

"Oh, I like that idea."

Noah walked up with a plate in each hand.

"Thanks." I took my burger and fries.

He gave me a thumbs-up, engaged in some Q&A with Cardozo about his career plans while I ate, and headed back toward the other end of the pool.

Cardozo said, "You know, your exoneration thing, the lawyer that if I'm not mistaken was on that case before you is here somewhere. I think I saw her over in the desserts cabana." He looked across the pool, where four white tents sheltered guests and catering staff, and searched the crowd.

"You're kidding. You know her? I called her a couple of times when I first took the case, but she never got back to me."

He smiled. "I know everybody, Leland. I thought you knew that about me."

I laughed. In law school, he'd been the president of at least three societies that I could recall, and I had quickly pegged him as the most extroverted student in the entire school. His wife, who'd made partner at one of the big local firms, was the same way.

"Still," I said, "federal prosecutors don't normally run in the same circles as prisoner-exoneration types."

"Oh, her husband worked in my office until he went into private practice five or six years ago. Wait, there she is. Come on."

We walked around the pool, which took easily five minutes because he stopped every three or four yards to chat, shake hands, or fist-bump somebody. En route, I asked him, "You know Lawrence Tucker, too?"

"Yeah. At the moment, I'm attempting to mentor him."

"How so?"

"Well, with what happened down your way..." He winced. "He served himself up on a platter to your Mr. Ludlow."

"How'd you hear about that?"

"He sought my advice."

"Oh. Good. What'd you tell him?"

He clapped somebody on the shoulder, introduced us, and told a joke, and then we moved on once more. Between groups of people, he said, "I told him if he still wants a political career, he's got to do the walk-of-shame press conference with his supportive wife by his side. Confess his sins and so forth. Otherwise that sword'll be hanging over his head forever."

"You are the ultimate pragmatist."

"I like to think so."

We reached the other side of the pool and went into one of the cabanas. Leading me toward a heavier woman in stylish red glasses and a black cocktail dress, he said, "Maureen! How's that profiterole? I got somebody I want you to meet!"

"Hi! Oh, it's excellent!"

She stuck her fork into the cream puff in her bowl, freeing up her right hand, and we shook.

"Leland Munroe," I said.

"Maureen Williams. Oh, I got your messages! I am so sorry," she said, laughing. "My whole life was on fire at that point."

"Maureen hit the big leagues," Cardozo said. "She got tapped to be director of one of the biggest prisoners' rights nonprofits in the country."

"Well, congratulations! Oh, is that why you left Found Innocent?"

She nodded.

"I'm going to let you two chat," Cardozo said, "but Maureen, I want you to know I am entrusting to you my best friend from law school. Leland's a very successful criminal defense attorney down in the Lowcountry. Y'all enjoy yourselves, now."

He clapped me on the shoulder and walked away.

Maureen and I talked for a minute about the party. Then she said, "That case, you know, the Maria thing, it was tough."

"Uh-huh." I nodded, although I wasn't sure what she was referring to. "What was the worst part about it for you?"

"Well, there's a lot of things. To start with, I can't blame her for this, given what she's been through, but it's hard to work with somebody who just will not trust you."

"Was it the language barrier, or—?"

"No, we spoke in Spanish. That's what I studied before law school, and I lived down in Mexico for a couple of years."

"Oh, interesting. I wish I could speak like that with her. You know, directly."

"Actually, I almost think it handicapped me, because it gave her free rein to— You know, she's just a very angry person. Understandably."

"Uh-huh."

The cabana was getting crowded, so we stepped out to the poolside. I noticed Noah up at the shallow end of the pool. The light coming through the plate-glass windows was bright, and it looked like he had a tumbler of whiskey in his hand.

I looked back at Maureen. "You mentioned the language," I said, "which reminds me, one thing that's come up recently is a possible issue with the interpreter at her trial. Did you get into that at all?"

"Oh, I thought you were going to say her police statement."

"Well, that, too, but it was already litigated and appealed, so... not much I could do with that."

"That's for sure."

I saw Noah down half his drink in one go.

I looked back at her and said, "Yeah, I'm trying to track down the interpreter. Which, given this was twenty years ago and we've dug up about nine thousand people with the same name as him, isn't easy."

She was shaking her head at me. "I feel for you. I cannot tell you how glad I am that I'm not litigating those things anymore."

"Oh, are you not?"

"No, now I'm, you know, strategy, big picture, the spokesperson."

"That must be nice," I said, keeping an eye on Noah.

"It is. But I tell you what, I still owe you something. You got all my paper files on that case, but not all the electronic ones."

She now had my full attention. "Is that so?"

"Yeah. The thing is, I used my personal laptop there, since we had no budget at all. So when I left, some of that came with me inadvertently. I didn't even realize until I was cleaning my files up the other day. But I can put the folders into Dropbox and get that over to you."

"That'd be great." I pulled out a business card.

She set her dessert down to open her clutch and drop my card inside.

I looked up to where Noah had been. He wasn't there. I scanned the crowd and caught him disappearing behind the building that the buffet was in.

"Maureen, I am so sorry, but I just saw my son over there, and I'm afraid he's going to make a pest of himself. Would you excuse me?"

She laughed. "Kids, my God. It never ends, does it?"

"For sure. Well, it's been great chatting with you."

"It has. I'll give you a call."

"Great."

I headed at speed in the direction Noah had gone.

———

Twenty minutes later, driving home at nearly midnight with my tipsy son buckled into the passenger seat, I worked hard to talk myself out of worrying. It was just a couple of drinks, not drugs. Not, God forbid, opiates. A few years earlier he'd been addicted to the real thing —Percocet or any other source of oxycodone—and I was grateful beyond words that he'd kicked that habit before the street got flooded by fake prescription tablets cut with deadly fentanyl.

And he was twenty years old, within spitting distance of legal drinking age. I was going to have to get used to the occasional sight of my boy with a drink in his hand.

But alcoholism had killed my wife. If it were possible, I would've happily removed alcohol and all knowledge of how to make it from the face of the earth.

Noah, tipping his head back and apparently talking to the ceiling of the car, said, "Oh my God, why did we have to leave? I don't know why you have to be such a hard-ass!"

My nostrils flared. I kept my eyes on the road and tried to remember some of the deep breathing exercises I'd learned during his accident recovery, when we were briefly enrolled in family therapy.

I could not remember any special way of inhaling that the therapist may have taught. I gave up. I'd have to take a different tack.

"Noah, listen. You know why alcohol is a sore spot for me, right?"

He sagged in his seat and nodded. I sensed that sudden shame had sobered him up a bit.

"Okay. And… I'm curious, how does this fit with that straight-edge thing you were talking about?"

"They don't do drugs. Some of them don't drink but it's not, like, a rule."

He sounded defensive. It was not the time to challenge him on that.

"Understood. And I know that you're a young man who just wants to have fun sometimes. Right?"

"Yeah."

"So how about, if I try to put a lid on my reaction to… let's say… your reasonable drinking, you promise me you'll keep it reasonable?"

"Sure. I wasn't going to take it too far, anyway."

"Okay, good."

Maybe he could keep his drinking from getting out of hand. Maybe it wouldn't even be hard for him. Only time would tell.

An idea came to me: if I could keep him occupied, he'd have less time to spend on bad habits.

"You know what," I said, "there's something Cardozo thinks I ought to be doing that I just don't have time to do. You want a little job?"

"A job? What's it involve?"

"Keeping track of any press coverage of any of my cases. Searching for articles and social media posts. Downloading copies, making files of them, letting me know if any of them say something that I ought to know about."

"Huh." He sounded like he thought that might be all right.

"And there's also an online forum I'd like you to search. It's connected with this true-crime podcast that does nothing but North and South Carolina crimes."

"Sounds kind of morbid."

"Oh, you haven't heard the half of it. This podcast is actually based out of the house where Brandon Ludlow's mother was killed."

"My *God*. On purpose? Like, that's why they're there?"

"I doubt that's the *only* reason, but… forget it. That's just a weird detail. Main thing is, I want to know if they're talking about any of my cases, and if so, what they're saying. I basically want to know how things look to the public." After a second, I added, "Might as well keep an eye out to see if anybody there has any interesting ideas or seems to know anything. It's unlikely, but if it happens, I'd want to know."

"Cool."

"Great. Say, ten bucks an hour? You keep track of your time."

"Sure."

18

JUNE 11, 2021

It was a hot morning, and I was on the road back to Elkin Springs with Terri in the passenger seat. The previous day, I'd received documents that were devastating to my argument that Britney LaSalle had shot her husband in self-defense, and we needed to talk to her. More to the point, we needed to look at her cell phone.

No defense attorney wanted to get screenshots from the dead man's phone showing that, in the week before he was killed, his estranged wife sent him half a dozen texts suggesting that they get back together. And I especially didn't want to see a text from the day she shot him, inviting him to come by after the kids were in bed.

If those texts got before the judge at our self-defense hearing, Britney was going to jail, and her kids were going into foster care.

I'd forwarded Terri the email I'd gotten from Fletcher with PDFs of all the texts attached. She was balancing her laptop on her knees as we drove, looking at them.

She read me the number at the top and said, "That's her number?"

"Yeah."

"Okay. And do these all sound like her? How she talks?"

A couple of the texts were pretty salacious. To salvage some humor from the situation, I said, "Well, she doesn't talk to *me* that way."

She laughed.

My phone rang. From the number on the screen, Fletcher had gotten back to his office and was returning my call. I put on my best impression of a lawyer who wasn't worried about his client's case and said, "Morning, Mr. Fletcher. How're you doing?"

After the obligatory collegial chitchat, I cut to the chase: "I was a little mystified, I have to say, by those screenshots this morning—"

"Mystified? How so? They seem pretty straightforward to me."

I ignored his slightly patronizing tone. I needed something from him, and quick, so I had to stay polite. "Oh, in terms of the words in the screenshots, sure, I hear you. But how were you planning to authenticate those?"

"I'm afraid I'm not following you. Her number's right on them."

"I meant authenticating that they're from his phone, when he received them, and so forth."

I wanted to know what forensics, if any, he'd had done on Randy's phone.

As he stammered a response, I glanced over at Terri's laptop, whose screen she had turned toward me. In a giant font, she'd typed questions she wanted me to ask: *Forensics? Chain of custody? Provider? Faraday bag?*

I said, "What I mean is— Well, first off, am I correct in thinking an officer picked up Randy's phone at the scene?"

"Yes, indeed."

"Uh-huh. And how's it been stored since then? Did y'all put it in a Faraday bag?"

If they hadn't, or if there wasn't a clear record of which officers had handled the phone and what they'd done with it, then I would have room to argue that the data on it could've been changed or corrupted since Randy died. I knew the judge wouldn't buy that unless I had a cell phone forensics expert pointing to what had been changed. That wasn't going to happen—Britney couldn't afford to hire an expert—but I needed to kick the tires on Fletcher's case.

"Uh, it's been stored appropriately."

"Great. And did y'all get it forensically examined? Because if so, I'd want a copy of the report."

If they had, we'd get the information we needed free of charge.

"Uh-huh." I could hear him typing. "I don't recall what all we did, but I'd be a little surprised if we did that in a case like this. Sorry I can't give you the yes or no, but I've been in court all morning, and I've got another hearing after lunch."

"Yeah, I hear you. And I'm sorry to have to add myself to your to-do list today. Just one more question: I can see from the screenshots it's an Android phone, but do you recall what provider he got his service through?" I wanted to know which company to subpoena.

"Not offhand, no. You understand, I've got some cell phone issue or other in probably a third of the cases on my desk right now."

"Oh, I'm sure. But you know what, it so happens I'm driving to Columbia today, so I could take a little detour by Elkin Springs to get whatever information from your secretary or paralegal or whoever."

"Well, I don't know about that."

Terri arched a brow at me with a little smile. She was well aware that we had no plans to go to Columbia. I just didn't want Fletcher to know that the reason we were about to show up in Elkin Springs was that his screenshots had blown up my case and I needed to have a come-to-Jesus with my client.

"Yeah, I am going to do my best," I said, "to not impose on you at all. I can just swing by and get the info from your secretary—cell provider, name of the officer who recovered it from the scene, and so forth. And a copy of the report, if you did get one done."

"Yeah, that's— I still have to oversee all that. And I'm heading out at lunch and won't be back until after my hearing."

"Okay, just a thought."

We signed off, and I sighed in frustration.

Terri said, "If Britney says anything other than yeah, she sent him those texts on that day, then even if Fletcher doesn't want us there, I think we should still drop by and see what we can get."

"Yeah." I picked up my Coke and took a sip. It was half water; the ice had melted. "I told you, didn't I, that back in March I looked through her phone myself? I told her it's a totally different case depending on whether they communicated and what they said. She handed it right over. I only looked at the one day, but I didn't see one single text or email from or to him."

"Hmm. And what kind of person does she seem like to you? Level-headed? Honest?" Terri hadn't met Britney yet.

I shrugged. "I haven't gotten any other impression. I just can't see her deleting a bunch of crucial texts before she let me look through her phone. What would be the point?"

She shrugged and said, "People get scared."

"I sure hope she's not lying. I mean, her kids—if she goes to jail, it doesn't sound like their grandma would be able to raise them."

"Yeah, I get tired of these everyday tragedies."

"You and me both."

She looked out her window, thinking. We were passing brown fields with long green stripes heading for the horizon. Cotton, maybe, just starting to come up.

We drove a minute or two in silence, and then she said, "Want to change the subject? Because I did a little more digging on Maria's case."

I smiled. "You solved it? That's great news!"

She laughed. "I wish I had something monumental for you."

"Monumental. Yeah. You got a video of somebody else killing Mrs. Ludlow? Because that might *just about* satisfy Roy."

We laughed.

"No video, sorry, but I found Mrs. McDonough. She and her son moved to a trailer on her grandparents' land in Jasper County. Oh, and the third tenant across the street was some insurance salesman who was never home. He's in Florida now, and he told me he was out of town when she was killed. So we can cross him off the list."

"Did you talk to Mrs. McDonough?"

"Not yet. No listed number. I'll keep looking."

"Great, thanks."

"Oh, I forgot to ask," she said. "Are you through the trial transcripts yet? Anything in there that I ought to be looking at?"

"Not yet. I'm nearly three thousand pages in. Still haven't got to what the defense put on."

"And how's the prosecution's case?"

"Not great, not terrible. Still seems like we need to look at what they didn't investigate, more than what they did."

"Good. That's what I've been doing."

"I'm glad you have because I'm not sure what I can do myself. That front-page smear job kind of threw me off my game. I can't even *tell* you how annoying it is to be... outed, basically, at such an early stage. I didn't file anything, didn't announce anything—I wanted to keep it as discreet as I could that we were looking into this case at all."

"Mm-hmm. And that's why they outed you. Ludlow and Fourth, they're not going to let you control the narrative. Why would they wait until you've got big news to share? It's a lot harder for them to make you look bad at that point."

"Yeah," I said. "And I'm concerned that it might make witnesses scared to talk to me. Partly because if they saw that article, I look like some kind of slimeball. Why trust me? And partly, what normal person going about their life wants to risk getting onto Fourth's radar?"

"Exactly."

"Dammit."

She looked at me and laughed. "I can see you plotting your revenge," she said. "Ludlow obviously doesn't know you all that well. He should've figured this would just make you more determined."

"I may have to consult the attorney ethics rules before I nail down exactly how to wreak vengeance upon him."

———

Britney's house was a one-story box with white vinyl siding that was filthy with age. The porch railings were missing several balusters, and as we went up the steps, I saw some kids' bikes lying on the porch in front of a broken-down couch.

She let us in, and I introduced Terri. Apart from a yapping dog, the house was quiet; I figured the kids were at school. Britney served us iced tea, and we all sat around the counter.

She pushed a stack of papers over to me. "I got these all ready for you." I'd called her that morning before we hit the road to let her know why we needed to come by.

"Well, thank you." It was a pile of wrinkled, coffee-stained phone bills. I started paging through. "Are these in order? Because all I probably need is whichever bill covers the middle of March."

"No, I'm sorry. I'm not real good at that." She took them back and started leafing through them.

Terri opened her laptop and brought up the PDF.

Britney pulled out a few pages and handed them over.

"So, what Terri's about to show you here," I said, "are the texts that Mr. Fletcher tells me he found on Randy's phone."

Terri turned the laptop so Britney could see it. As she read, her head tilted in confusion. "I mean, this one… I think I sent him this sometime last year? We had a fight, and then we, I guess, reconciled right before Thanksgiving."

"Let me just see the date on that." The top text was dated March 18, 2021, at 4:04 p.m. I looked at Terri.

She said, "Do you mind if I just search for that one on your phone?"

Britney hesitated and then said, "No, I guess not." She unlocked her phone and handed it over.

"Okay," I said, "what about these other ones?"

Britney kept reading. Her eyes got wide. She looked at me in what looked like genuine horror and said, "I didn't send those! They aren't real!"

"Uh-huh. So let me just…" I scanned the page of her bill that showed all her calls and texts in March. "Oh," I said. "Do you happen to know which cell phone carrier Randy used?"

"Yeah, same one as me. Sprint."

Terri said, "Oh, good. They respond to subpoenas pretty fast."

In response to Britney's look of incomprehension, I said, "We might need to get some information from them, and the faster, the better."

"Oh, okay."

I went back to her phone bill, looking down the page for the date of Randy's death.

Terri said, "I found that text! November 24 of last year, like you said." She showed me the phone. The first text in Fletcher's PDF, which invited Randy to "come try to make it work," was there on the screen with a date four months earlier than the one on Fletcher's screenshot.

"My goodness," I said.

"Is that good?" Britney said. "Am I okay?"

"Well, we've got to figure this out. Terri, you know how something like that could happen? Or how to show which date is real?"

She said, "It's *possible* it could've gotten re-sent for some reason. I mean, innocently, like a technical glitch. But that doesn't explain the other texts."

184

"I did *not* send those. I don't— I never talk about—" She looked down. Her cheeks had turned pink with embarrassment. I figured she must be referring to the sexy messages.

I looked back at her phone bill and found the right date. "What's this number here?"

She peered at it. "Oh, that's Randy. He called me a couple times that morning."

They were incoming calls, like she said. The only things that went out that day were two calls in the afternoon and a late-night text, all to the same number. She pointed to it and said, "That's my mom."

The time on the text was a few minutes before midnight. "Oh, that's the one you sent her when he was—when you heard an intruder in your apartment?"

"Yeah."

"Well, thank God. I am so glad you saved these bills."

"I don't really throw a lot away."

I didn't comment. The clutter in her house told me that. I asked Terri, "So how does Fletcher have screenshots from Randy's phone on March 18 with her phone number at the top?"

"Well—" I saw an idea appear on her face.

"What?"

"You know how people's names—wait, no, you don't." She explained to Britney, "He uses a flip phone. But okay, Leland, on a smartphone, if you add someone to your contacts, their name shows up on your screen when they text. But you can put anything you want in the name field." She picked up her phone and started typing something. "Give me a call in a second, okay?"

When she set her phone down on the counter, I did.

Her screen lit up, and we all looked at it. A phone number was displayed, indicating who was calling. The number wasn't mine.

"That's my old work number," Terri said. "I went into the contact I have for you, deleted your name, and put that number in the field where your name goes."

"You mean it doesn't display the real number the call—or in Britney's case, the text—was from?"

"It does if you don't have the incoming number in your contacts. But if the number *is* one of your contacts, then it displays whatever you put in the name field for that number. And you can put anything in the name field."

Britney was looking at the screen with her mouth hanging open. "Are you saying Randy did that? Sent himself fake messages from me? Why?"

"Didn't you have a hearing coming up on your restraining order?" I asked.

"Yeah, it was the week after— Oh!"

If Randy had shown up at that hearing with sexy messages from "her" inviting him over, the judge probably wouldn't have granted her a restraining order. Even if she'd denied sending the messages, she likely wouldn't have figured out Randy's trick right there in the court-room, and she might not have figured it out at all.

"We still have to prove this," I said, "to win at your self-defense hearing."

Terri pulled her laptop back across the counter and started typing. "I can get you the subpoena today," she said. "But I can't make them answer it in time."

19

JUNE 11, 2021

It was nearly 11 p.m. by the time I dropped Terri at her house and headed home. To my surprise, there were two cars parked in my driveway: my old beater, which Noah now drove, and right behind it a blue Subaru.

I parked on the street and listened for a minute. I was still edgy because of the home invasion we'd experienced the previous year—if home invasion was the right term for a targeted attack by a gangster who didn't like the way I was handling a case.

I heard crickets and a neighbor's TV. Nothing unusual.

I stepped over to the Subaru and felt its hood. It was cool. That was a good sign. It seemed unlikely that criminals would hang out long enough for their engine to get cold.

As I relaxed, I realized that I was most likely palpating the car of Noah's girlfriend, whoever she was. I had a laugh at myself and headed inside.

I made no effort to be quiet as I shut the door and tossed my briefcase onto the couch. It seemed only fair to give them a little warning, in case they were in a compromising situation.

Heading down the hall, I saw that Noah's bedroom door was open and a light was on. I glanced in and saw him and a girl with long, dark hair sitting side by side with headphones on, playing a video game, oblivious to my presence.

That was a little annoying. He should've known to set the burglar alarm before he went and got so engrossed in a game that he didn't even hear somebody come in.

"Hey, Noah," I said, knocking on his doorjamb.

The two of them jumped like they'd been shocked with a cattle prod. When they turned around, I saw that the girl was pretty… and that she was Isabela Ruiz. Ruiz's second daughter. Who, I was pretty sure, wasn't yet in college.

As they took their headphones off and squeaked out their hellos, I noticed that all she was wearing for pants was a pair of Noah's boxer shorts.

"Uh, hello, Isabela," I said.

She grabbed a pair of jeans off Noah's bed and all but ran into his closet—to get dressed a little more privately, I assumed. I heard the coat hangers clattering as she changed.

"Dad! Uh… hi," Noah said. His eyes looked like they were frozen in wide-open mode.

"Hi. Well, obviously Terri and I decided not to stay the night in Elkin Springs."

Still staring at me with the same stunned expression, he tried to make conversation: "Yeah, so… how'd it go? Your case up there."

"Oh, fine. Learned some interesting stuff about cell phone evidence. Uh… Isabela, you mind stepping back out here when you're done?"

She came out of the closet, still barefoot but decently dressed, and said, "Mr. Munroe, please, I am begging you, please don't tell my dad." She looked like she might burst into tears.

"Isabela," I said, "remind me how old you are?"

"I'm eighteen next week. On Tuesday. Literally in four days."

"Okay." I silently thanked the cosmos that at least their relationship was legal; the age of consent in our state was sixteen. "And where does your daddy think you are right now?"

She looked away, ashamed. "At my friend Kaitlyn's," she said. "Having a sleepover."

"Uh-huh."

I took a second to process the situation.

"Okay," I said. "Your daddy is a friend of mine—"

"Please, he will kill me, he will absolutely kill me!"

"Oh, he won't be happy," I said. "I am sure."

Then I looked at Noah, giving him a hint of a smile, or at least a hint that I might smile again at some point in the future, and said, "You know, Ruiz saved your *life* not that long ago. It'd be a shame if he had to turn around now and murder you over this."

I was trying to dissipate the tension in the room, but it didn't work. Noah blinked hard and gulped.

I shook my head, thinking about what the heck to do.

Isabela said, "Wait, he saved your life? Literally?"

Noah nodded.

"He never told you?" I said. "There was a sniper. Your daddy figured out where he was and stopped him before he could shoot Noah."

Her mouth dropped open. "Oh my *God*."

"Yeah. You might not think much of him, at your age, but your daddy is a hell of a man."

"Dad," Noah said, "no matter what you do, and no matter what happens, you need to know that I love this girl." He was looking at me with his chin up and his shoulders square, like a man speaking his last truth to a firing squad.

I nodded, keeping the look on my face unchanged. There was no expression that could contain what I was feeling: both the heart-lurching emotion of seeing my boy in love for the first time and the sheer hilarity of him being so innocent that he thought his life might end tonight because his dad caught him with his girlfriend.

He said, "So at least please tell that to Mr. Ruiz. Tell him I respect her, and I love her, and I would never mistreat one hair on her head." He closed his eyes like the firing squad was about to shoulder their weapons and shoot.

"Well, Noah, thank you for telling me that."

I snuck a glance at Isabela. She was looking at him like he was her very own Prince Charming.

They were as intense and deeply serious as only kids could be. I knew they wouldn't appreciate my saying it, but if there were an Olympics of cuteness, they ought to win it.

I tried to maintain my gravitas as I said, "Listen, I can see that you two care about each other. I can see you've got something real."

Isabela nodded fast and wiped away a tear.

"So, listen. Isabela, can you get in touch with your friend—Kate? Kaitlyn?"

She looked puzzled.

"I mean, can you call her, or text her, and arrange it so you actually do sleep over there tonight?"

"Oh! Yes!" She lunged onto the bed to grab her phone from her purse.

While she texted, I beckoned to Noah to follow me. We went into the living room because I didn't want Isabela to hear.

"Listen," I said, "are you two being… safe?"

"Of course. I would never—yeah, of course."

"Okay. Good. Now, I cannot… there is no way I can deal with Ruiz while his little girl is lying to him about having sleepovers with my son."

"Yeah. Yeah." He looked down, shaking his head.

"So no more of that. And if you do mistreat her, or get her in trouble, you and I are going to have a major problem. Because I did not raise you that way. Understood?"

"Yes, sir."

"Okay."

We went back to his room to get Isabela and make sure she had all her stuff.

Then we went out—I set the burglar alarm, ragging Noah about it as I did so—and saw her to her car, and then we got in my Malibu and followed her to her friend's house to make sure she got inside safely.

———

When we got back, I went to my office to check the emails I'd neglected all day, and Noah went back to playing video games.

One of my emails was from Maureen. It contained a link to her electronic files from Maria's case. I clicked on it, entered the password, and watched a folder called "Attorney Notes" download itself onto my desktop.

That's all there was, but I was glad to see it. Apart from the intake notes from 2018, when Found Innocent first took Maria's case, there'd been nothing of that type—none of Maureen's thoughts or reflections—in the boxes of case files I'd received.

Most of what I'd just downloaded was Word documents, but one was a huge PDF. I opened it and saw it was over sixty pages of scanned, handwritten notes. Maureen's handwriting looked light and fast, more like squiggly lines than letters. I wasn't up for slogging through that, so I decided to start with the other ones.

The Word docs all had dates in their file names, so I went through them in order. Skimming the first one, I saw that she'd reached out to the public defender who'd represented Maria at the original trial. That wasn't something we could do; Terri had already told me that the man had died in 2020.

I could see from the notes that Maureen had asked about his trial strategy and the vendors and experts he'd used, as well as those he'd chosen not to use. It was clear she'd been gathering information to figure out if she could argue that the public defender had been lousy and Maria should get a new trial based on ineffective assistance of counsel.

Later on, I knew, she'd gone ahead and filed a motion for that, but the court had shot it down. They usually did. It tended to take astonishing levels of incompetence for a court to think a lawyer was so bad that his client deserved a new trial.

On the third page, my eyes zeroed in on one word: "Interpreters?"

Below it were half a dozen bullet points that showed Maureen had done her due diligence on both Ramón Perez and another guy who'd done part of the interpreting for the case. Perez's contact information was there. I copy-pasted it into an email to Terri.

The next file I clicked on had a name in it that I wasn't expecting: Dabney Barnes.

Before I was through reading the first page, I grabbed my phone and texted Terri: *You up?* When she said she was, I called.

"Hey," she said. I heard a smile in her voice when she said, "This better be good. It's past midnight, and I'm throwing a tennis ball for Buster to fetch in my backyard."

"Sorry to interrupt your quality time. It probably won't be as much fun for him to watch you search for Ramón Perez on your laptop."

"Oh, you found something on him?"

"Just some background from Maureen's notes. She got his contact info from the public defender—so it's old, from the time of Maria's trial, but it might help put you on his trail."

"Did Maureen look into him at all?"

"Perez? I don't see anything on him besides his contact info. But the other thing, from her files, is that she talked to our Dabney. Several times."

"Fourth? Really. Why?"

"In her notes, it says she read some news articles from around the time of the trial, and she reached out to the paper to see who wrote them. They were published without a byline, and she wanted to talk to the reporter. Fourth got back to her, saying it was him. And then it sounds like he walked her through his version of events, which was that Maria was guilty. He also said that there was a lot more about Maria that didn't come out—bad stuff that the paper never published, out of respect for her kids."

"What, because they were still young?"

"Yeah, and he said justice had been done, so he saw no point in dragging her name through the mud."

"Fourth sure made himself sound like a real nice guy."

"Yeah."

I heard her getting her dog excited for another throw and launching something across the yard for him. Then she asked, "Did Maureen know that Fourth and Ludlow go way back?"

"Hang on." I ran a couple of Control+Fs. "There's nothing about that in her notes. And she's not from around here, so I don't know why she would have any idea who knows who."

I heard Buster growling near the phone and Terri talking to him again. Waiting for her to return to our conversation, I opened the last file of Maureen's notes.

I read a few lines and said, "Terri? Hey, Terri, you there?"

She came back to the phone, breathless. "Sorry, my Frisbee got caught in a bush."

"No problem. Listen to this. You know that guy, Angelo? Maureen looked into him."

"And?"

"His name's Angelo Cruz. And I guess I know why he disappeared all of a sudden. Maureen did a background check, and the only thing on it happened a few years after Peggy died. Apparently, he got convicted of a burglary up in North Carolina and went to jail."

20

JUNE 16, 2021

Amy McDonough, whose husband, Dunk, was in federal prison up in Bennettsville awaiting trial, had agreed to meet us. She and her son now lived in a trailer on her parents' land in the next county over. The sun was getting low as Terri and I parked in the dirt driveway by the parents' house, a 1950s-style gray split-level. Their spread looked to be a dozen rolling acres or so, or more if they owned the woods at the back of the property.

As she'd instructed, we walked around to the back of the house. From there, we saw her trailer. It was nice, with a raised bed of neatly planted flowers running along the front and what looked like a well-made wooden porch, big enough that you'd almost call it a deck.

She opened the door as we hit the stairs.

"Come on in," she said. "It's too hot to sit outside."

"Well, thank you." We stepped into her shade and air-conditioning. It was a welcoming space, with a living room in front of us and a sunny kitchen to the right.

"My goodness, Mrs. McDonough," Terri said, "what a cute place you've got here. Did you make those gingham curtains yourself?"

"Oh, call me Amy, please. Yes, I did. I do a lot of sewing, on top of my gardening."

She got us all situated in the living room with sweet tea, crackers, and cheese. She explained that her son was at work until eight, so we had time to talk. I munched a couple of crackers while Terri asked more questions about the decor and sympathized with Amy about how hard it must've been to see her life go up in smoke when her husband got arrested.

"You know what, though," Amy said, "it's almost a relief. It's just been such a…"

She pressed her lips together and looked out the window like she was trying not to cry.

"Yeah, it must've been hard," Terri said.

"It was. For a real long time," Amy said. "I don't know if you know this, but Dunk was in the Iraq War. And whatever happened over there, it wasn't him that came back. He got a head injury and all. It took me a long time to accept that no matter what I did, he, or, uh, how he used to be, wasn't ever coming back."

I said, "I'm sorry. I didn't realize he'd been injured."

"Yes, he keeps that to himself." She took a sip of tea, then looked at me and said, "But, Mr. Munroe, I am so sorry for what he put your family through."

"Thanks." Saying more was not in the cards. I did not want to spend even one second recalling the day Dunk had threatened Noah's life.

"Was he in the military when you moved in across from the Ludlows?" Terri asked.

"Not active. He was in the reserves. I met Peggy pretty quick after that—her son wasn't even a year older than Tyler. So we spent a lot of time over there."

"And did you know Maria?"

"A little bit. Not to where we had conversations or anything. She would sometimes watch the boys so Peggy and I could have a good talk."

"Did Peggy ever mention any problems with her?"

"Oh, no. Not that I recall."

"Did you and Dunk ever socialize with Peggy and—"

"Oh, Lord, no. I don't know what our husbands ever would've talked about. Dunk had a chip on his shoulder about men like Mr. Ludlow. He called them 'suits,' no offense."

"None taken."

Terri asked, "But he didn't mind you seeing Peggy?"

Amy winced. "He didn't like me running around. I couldn't drive across town to see my mom. Taking Tyler across the street to see Peggy and her boy, that was about as far as he'd let me go."

"Tell me about Peggy," Terri said. "What was she like?"

Amy smiled. "Well, she was a young mother, we had that in common, but she was real different from me. More vivacious, more... I don't want to say showy, that sounds bad, but..."

"A firecracker?"

"Yeah, a firecracker! Always in bright colors, gorgeous, a real attention-getter. She talked a lot—she had all kinds of ideas. I didn't have much to add, but I liked to listen to her. At first, anyway."

Terri said, "When did that change?"

"Well… I got the impression she wasn't exactly happily married. I don't mean she was sad or he hurt her or anything, but just, it seemed like she was expecting a whole lot *more*, somehow."

"Do you mean she was, maybe, too romantic?"

"Yeah, like a romance novel, honestly. You got to remember, she was young when they got married. And she just… I don't know. She didn't know *men*."

Terri hesitated—I could tell she was deciding whether it was the right time to ask the next question—and then she went for it. "Speaking of men, did you happen to know her gardener? Angelo?"

The openness left Amy's face. "Um, I did, yes."

"And how much did you know about their relationship?"

Amy's eyes flickered wider for an instant. Then she said, "Y'all are good at what you do, aren't you? Nobody's ever asked me about him before."

She didn't go on, so I said, "Well, thank you. We've been taking a close look. So, what do you recall about him?"

"Oh, Peggy was crazy about him. And he *was* gorgeous." She smiled, looking embarrassed and suddenly much younger than her forty-five or fifty years. "My goodness, I mean, the wavy black hair, the muscles… When Mr. Ludlow was at work, Angelo used to garden with his shirt off, and… oh *my*."

She and Terri both giggled. Terri said, "I feel like I've seen him on the cover of some romance novels."

Amy laughed. "Yes, that's exactly what he looked like. And that's all it was to me, just a nice little spark for my day, you know?"

"Oh, I do. But for Peggy it was more, wasn't it."

As Amy agreed, I paused to admire the pure artistic glory of Terri's way of questioning people. It was like she saw what they weren't quite able to say, and then she made bridges for them to get across.

"That's what I meant," Amy said, "when I said she didn't know men. Like, she saw Angelo there, working in the yard, and she wrote a whole story around him and thought it was true."

"What was the story?"

"Oh, you know. True love, he's my soulmate, run away with him."

"Run away? What about her son?"

"That's what I said! I told her, he doesn't want to set up house with you and raise your boy. And even if he did, your son has a father! I also said, at least once, your husband's a *lawyer*, you know? And from a wealthy family. So if this goes into divorce court, there is no way—but she didn't want to hear any of that."

"How serious were her plans?"

"Well, I had my doubts about what *Angelo* wanted, but she was… I wouldn't say serious. I'd say intense. Because she was on the impulsive side. So she might be real excited about something and then change her mind completely. So it's hard to say."

Terri asked, "Do you know where things stood for her, or what she had decided, toward the very end there? That summer?"

Amy sighed, looking off into the distance, her face getting sadder as she went through her memory. "Oh, yes. I remember the very last time I saw her. It was the morning of the day she died. I went over there with Tyler, like usual…" She shook her head and said, "I can't tell you how many times I've wished she would've listened to me. But I guess that just wasn't who she was."

"Mm-hmm," Terri said.

"I remember we went into the kitchen, because it was so hot out, and let the boys play in the living room."

I could picture where she meant, from our trip to the house.

"And she opened a cabinet and pulled out this box, one of those metal cookie tins, and handed it to me. It was pretty heavy. She asked me to keep it for her. And she pulled open the lid to show me this whole mess of jewelry inside."

"Huh," I said, doing my best to sound only mildly curious. I didn't want to interrupt her flow.

She looked at me and said, "Mr. Munroe, I mean the real deal! She never wore costume jewelry. It must've been worth I don't know how many thousands of dollars."

"Do you happen to recall what jewelry was in there? You know, diamond rings, or—"

"No. I'm not really a jewelry person. It just looked like a sea of gold, and rubies, and… She said it was everything she had that was worth anything. And she told me she was fixing to sell it, to pay for her new life with Angelo! She wanted me to keep it at my house while she got things arranged."

"Oh my," Terri said. "So what did you do?"

"I told her absolutely not! Where am I going to put that in my apartment, so my husband and my little boy don't find it? And what am I going to say if my husband *does* find it? Because he was a little… volatile, you know?"

"Mm-hmm. And how'd she take that?"

"She said she understood, but my goodness, she looked like she was about to fall apart. I tried to tell her to, you know, settle *down*, get ahold of herself. Be realistic, be an adult! But that just… wasn't her."

"Wow. And what'd she do with that tin of jewelry?"

"Well, she put it back in the cabinet, for then, anyway. I don't know what happened to it after that."

I asked, as nonchalantly as I could, "And are you pretty sure that was the very day she died?"

"Oh, yes. I'll never forget that because it was so shocking—I mean, to hear about what happened, and to know that a few hours earlier I was talking to her, and… It's just so strange to realize that when we were talking in her kitchen, that was one of the last moments of her life."

Terri nodded. "I know how that feels."

We all sat for a minute without saying anything. It felt like a moment of silence for the dead.

Then Amy leaned forward to get a sip of tea. When she set her glass back down, I asked, "Did she ever mention anything to you about any jewelry of hers being stolen?"

She shook her head like that rang no bells at all. Then her expression shifted; I saw the memory come to her. "Oh, was there something about that at the trial?"

"Mm-hmm," Terri said.

"Oh, okay. I must've read that in the paper. I hardly followed the trial at all. That next summer, when it was going on, I was having a complicated pregnancy, and I ended up losing the baby."

"I am so sorry," Terri said.

"Thank you."

After another respectful silence, I asked, "Am I wrong in thinking you never spoke to the police back then? I mean, the summer when she was killed?"

"No, that's right. Dunk said they'd called, but he told them we didn't know anything. I wanted to talk to them anyhow, just in case anything I knew might help, but he wouldn't watch Tyler for me. He plain refused. And I couldn't talk to the police about a murder in front of my little boy."

"No, that's understandable," I said.

After another minute Terri looked at me, silently asking whether it might be time to go.

I said, "Well, we shouldn't keep you any longer. I know you've got things to do. But is there anything else you can tell us about Angelo?"

"Well... I know he was still around town for maybe a few years after all that. He actually did some landscaping work for my husband's business. And for our house, once we got a place of our own."

Terri said, "Was he close with your husband, do you know?"

"I don't know about close, but they sure saw each other more than I would've liked. After what happened with Peggy, I couldn't stand to see him anymore."

Terri gave her an understanding nod and asked, "Did you ever think Angelo might've had anything to do with what happened?"

"I've thought a whole lot of things," she said. "I just don't know."

———

As we drove back, I was so energized that it was hard not to speed. I flicked my headlights on—it was nearly dark—and shot down a dirt road, saying, "Am I kidding myself, or do we get a new trial on this alone? We've got two huge new pieces of evidence from a witness the police never bothered to interview. One of them more or less destroys Maria's motive, right?"

"Because the jewelry was still there more than a week after she supposedly stole it, yeah. And the fact it was gone after that doesn't prove anything, since Peggy might've given it to Angelo. Or, who knows, to a different friend to keep."

"And the other new evidence actually *gives* a motive to the only other adult who everyone knows was in the house at the time: Ludlow! She was cheating on him!"

"That's not hearsay? What Amy said?"

"Oh, it would be if I was trying to prove Mrs. Ludlow slept with Angelo or really was planning to run away with him. But I don't need to do that. I just need to show that it sure as hell *looked* like she was cheating. Because that's all it takes to make a person go wild with jealousy, and man, jealousy is the oldest motive in the book."

My petition for a new trial was already writing itself in my head. So was a discovery request for anything the police or Ludlow's office might have about the case that they hadn't already turned over.

"That's reasonable doubt," she said, "for sure. But is it enough for a new trial?"

"Yeah, newly discovered evidence is one of the strongest arguments for that." I turned onto an asphalt road. "Evidence that existed at the time of the trial but wasn't discovered until after the conviction—that is *textbook*." I cruised down an entrance ramp and merged onto the highway.

Terri said, "So it could've been Ludlow, or even Angelo. People have committed murder for a whole lot less than forty grand worth of jewelry."

"They sure have." I glanced at my gas gauge. "Aw, heck. Let me know if you see a gas station anywhere."

"Out *here*?" We were in the country, passing nothing but trees and the occasional farm.

"I've probably got ten miles of gas left, but yeah, whenever you can."

"Okay. You are about to see what a smartphone is for."

There weren't many other cars on the road. I did not want to get stuck out here. I slowed down to save fuel. "Anything?"

"It's real slow," she said. "The reception isn't great. But give me a second."

A minute later, she'd found a place at an exit eight miles up.

"Okay," she said. "So, say we get a new trial. We don't just need reasonable doubt, we need an alternate story, right? That the jury will believe?"

"Uh-huh." The law didn't say that—it said the defendant was presumed innocent, so we didn't need to do more than point out the holes in the prosecution's case—but in practice that wasn't how it worked.

"Do we really want to go in there accusing the circuit solicitor of murdering his wife?" Terri asked.

"Yeah, that's a tall order, isn't it? Especially with no physical evidence. So I guess we go with a slightly different angle, like it could've been Ludlow, it could've been Angelo, and we'll never know because the police zoomed in on Maria and never looked anyplace else."

"Mm-hmm. What exactly did Ludlow say at trial? I mean, what'd he claim he saw?"

"Just Maria standing by Peggy with blood on her hands."

She laughed. "*Just.*"

"Fair point. What I meant was, he didn't say he saw her shoot Peggy, or saw her going into the room right beforehand, or saw the gun in her hands. And her prints weren't on the gun."

"They usually aren't."

I nodded. The texture of most pistol grips made it difficult to impossible to get usable prints off them.

"So I'm just thinking," she said, "we might want more on Angelo. And I hate to say it, but I have to wonder if Dunk might know something about him that could help."

"Yeah, I was trying not to think about that."

"I know. Sorry."

———

When we made it to the exit, I cruised up the ramp and breathed a sigh of relief. The gas station, about three-quarters of a mile down, was a shabby little one-pump shop, but its light was on.

"Is that all your smartphone could find me?" I joked. "This little off-brand place?"

Terri didn't answer. She was looking to the side, maybe at her wing mirror.

"You okay?" I asked.

"That truck. It's been behind us ever since we took the on-ramp back near Mrs. McDonough's place."

In the rearview mirror, I could see a big pickup with what looked like two men in the cab.

21

JUNE 17, 2021

We stopped at the last crossroads before the gas station. A traffic light dangling over the deserted road was shining red, and dark fields lay in every direction.

The truck waited behind us.

"I'm going to act like I don't notice," I said, "and just pull in for gas."

"Good. Can you see the badge on the front? The make of the truck?"

I peered in the rearview mirror. The truck was tall, so I could see most of its grille.

"Looks like an oval. So I guess that's Ford."

"Thanks." She pulled out her phone.

"What are you doing?"

"Texting Noah. That way, if something happens, he's got some clues."

"Good." After a second I added, "Don't scare him. There's no point."

"I won't." She read the message to me: "Was driving 170 east with your dad. Want you to help check out a truck we saw. Big silver Ford pickup at exit 16, two guys. Just texting so I don't forget. If I get plate number, I'll text that too."

She looked at me like she was asking permission. I nodded. She hit send.

The light turned green, and I eased forward.

I said, "You should stay in the car."

She nodded but said, "We'll see."

The gas station's cashier window was lit up, but there was no one in it. The attached store was dark. I pulled up alongside the pump.

The truck drove past us. Its red taillights got smaller as it headed down the dark road.

"Goddamn," I said, laughing a little at myself. "Well, I'll be right back."

I went around the car, unscrewed the cap, put my credit card in the slot, and got the nozzle off the pump. When the gas started flowing, I noticed how quiet everything was. Just crickets in the fields and the hiss of the gas.

After a second I thought I heard an engine, but when I looked around, there were no headlights anywhere. The highway was below grade and nearly a mile away; all I could see of it was a glow at the edge of the hills.

But I did hear an engine, getting closer.

Then I saw it. The truck was coming back, fast, with its headlights turned off.

The gas pump was at one point two gallons, one point three, one point four. I needed at least another gallon to get home. I knocked on the rear passenger window and yelled Terri's name.

As the truck veered into the parking lot in front of us, its roof lights came on, blinding white. I put a hand up to shield my eyes as the vehicle screeched to a stop.

A man, or a shadow, leaned out the driver's window. Over the engine's rumble he called out, in an unnervingly calm voice, "You lost, mister? Lost with your lady friend?"

"Nope, we're good, thanks."

"Look at that suit," he said. "I bet you're real far from home."

"Not too far."

"Oh, my buddy and I, we know who belongs here."

He hit the gas, and his truck lurched forward, leaving less than five feet between it and the Malibu. Our only way out now was in reverse, and I was on the wrong side of the car.

As I pulled the nozzle out and jammed my gas cap back in place, the man unleashed a torrent of racist abuse. I saw Terri scooting into the driver's seat.

The pickup driver's buddy opened his door, dropped into the parking lot, and stalked toward her.

She threw open her door, launched herself out, and landed in shooting stance, her handgun pointed at his face. "Freeze! You are under arrest! Put your fucking hands behind your head! And you, hands out the window!"

The truck driver obeyed.

The other guy took a step forward—he was five feet from Terri—then hesitated.

"One more step and you will be shot. I'm a police officer, and you *will* be shot."

He put his hands up and said, "Whoa. Whoa."

"On your knees. Now."

He got down.

"On your stomach."

He complied.

To me, she said, "Get in the car."

I got in the passenger side.

She got back in the driver's side, slammed the door, and handed me the gun. I held it on the driver while she peeled out in reverse, and then we were back on the road and heading for the highway.

———

We got back to Basking Rock about forty-five minutes later, and Terri pulled into the lot outside the truck stop so we could switch seats. We hadn't talked much on the drive, but stretching our legs and seeing familiar surroundings let us both relax a bit.

As I got into the driver's seat, I said, "You know, I've never heard your cop voice before."

"I hope there's no occasion for you to have to hear it again."

"Me too."

I got back on the road.

Her phone dinged a few times, and so did mine. We were back in the land of good reception.

"You think those guys were connected to Dunk?" I asked.

She nodded like that was a distinct possibility. "We were still close to Amy's place when I noticed them behind us. And I certainly wouldn't be surprised if he had people watching his wife."

"Yeah. He kept her on a tight leash before, and being in prison's probably only made him worse."

"If it was him, I wonder how he's paying them." His assets, we both knew, had been frozen by the feds.

"Good question. I'll call Cardozo tomorrow. He at least ought to hear what went down."

I headed to the causeway. Soon we'd get to where I had to either turn toward her house or keep going. I said, "You want to walk off the adrenaline on the beach? Or call it a night?"

"Oh, sleep is not going to happen. Not for a while." She took her phone out of her purse and scrolled through it.

I watched the palm trees cruise past on either side. It was good to be home.

"Huh." She touched her phone screen. "Shannon sent us both an email while we were gone."

"Podcast Shannon?"

"Morbid, true-crime Shannon. Yeah." She read it. "Okay, that's weird. This was about six o'clock. She says they're renovating their bathroom, and the contractors found something we should come see. And they'll be back tomorrow morning, so if we want to see it before the demo is done… What the heck?"

"Lord, I pray they found a cookie tin of jewelry behind the drywall."

She laughed. "And a signed confession from the true killer. I guess we could go over early, before the contractors get there." She sighed in exasperation. "Man, now I'm going to be lying awake staring at the ceiling all night for *two* reasons instead of just the one."

"Did she say we could come by tonight?"

"That's what she suggested, but she sent this almost four hours ago."

I shrugged. "Couldn't hurt to text her."

————

Forty minutes later, Terri turned onto Devonshire Grove. Shannon had texted back with an enthusiastic invitation to drop by, so we'd gone to Terri's to give Buster his dinner and let him romp around in the yard for a few minutes.

Then we'd taken Terri's car instead of mine, just in case the pickup truck guys might still be looking for us in the Malibu.

As we cruised down the long street, I said, "You think we should file a police report? About the gas station?"

"Maybe. But did you want to talk to Cardozo first?"

"Oh. Right." I shook my head to get the dust out. "I think my brain blew a fuse back there. I'm not thinking straight."

"Mm-hmm. I hear you."

We parked and headed for the house. The beveled glass in the front door was lit up, scattering light all over the front porch like yellow leaves. I rang the bell, and before my finger even released the button, Shannon unlocked the door and let us in.

"Hello! It is so good to *see* you!" She threw her arms open, and Terri submitted to an overly friendly hug.

"Thank you so much for letting us drop by so late," I said.

"Oh, not at all!" She shut the door behind us and said, more quietly, like she was sharing a secret, "I just did *not* want this to be touched before y'all could take a look. Even Doug doesn't know. He's in Charlotte until tomorrow night."

She led us to the mezzanine area and up the stairs.

"We're doing a gut job," she said, "because, I mean, I love a nice long bath as much as the next woman, but we've got another tub in the master, and I really want a walk-in shower."

Terri said, "That'll be nice."

"Oh, it's going to be such a game changer for after my workouts. The room that used to be the nursery is our exercise room now."

We followed her down the hall and into the former nursery, which now contained a stationary bike, a rack of weights, and some kind of exercise station that took up about a quarter of the room.

She pushed aside some plastic sheeting, opened a door, and took us into the bathroom. The opposite wall was mostly gutted to the studs, with uneven shark teeth of drywall left around the bottom and top of the wall. In the middle of it was another door. I remembered that this was the Jack-and-Jill bath that connected to the room where Peggy Ludlow had died.

"And will you just look at *that*," Shannon said.

She was pointing to the left of the door we were facing. There, bolted up between two wooden studs, was a pale gray plastic box with what looked like electrical or computer ports on the back and a wire coming out of it. I stepped forward for a closer look. On the side were a black switch and the words "Sony DVR."

Terri said, "A *camera*? Are you kidding me?"

"I know! That's what my contractor said! He saw it when he pulled out the medicine cabinet—that was hanging right here." Her hands framed a space on the wall to the right of the camera. "So he was real careful when he pulled off the drywall over it, because he figured it was something electrical."

Terri was shining her phone flashlight on it, peering close. "What's on the other side of this wall? Because the lens is fitted into, like, a hole in the drywall."

"Just wallpaper. Whatever was there before got covered up, I guess. That's how it was when we bought the place."

"I guess at this height there could've been a sconce on the other side. Or maybe a mirror, since it was Peggy's dressing room."

Shannon clapped her hands together and said, "Oh! A two-way mirror, to spy on her! I like the way you think!"

I did not like the way Shannon thought. She was way too excited about crime. But her enthusiasm was helping us with our investigation, so I knew I shouldn't complain.

I asked Terri, "What vintage do you think that camera is?"

"Oh, it's the right era. Like early two thousands. I remember these from when I was on the beat. This is a nicer one, like you'd see in a high-end retail place. The surveillance cameras in convenience stores were bigger and uglier."

"Oh my goodness," Shannon said, putting a hand on her heart like she was shocked. "I just had a thought. Do y'all think maybe Mr. Ludlow was spying on his wife?"

Terri and I executed nearly identical shrugs. We were not about to invite Shannon into our theories of the case.

"But why on earth would he *do* that?" Shannon asked.

Terri shook her head as if to say, *Boy, it's a mystery.*

"I really do not know," I said. "Oh, Shannon, did you say your contractors are coming back tomorrow morning to finish the demolition?"

"Oh, yes. They would've stayed and finished it today, but when my guy found that, the first thing I thought of was y'all. I thought for sure you'd want to see it. But of course I didn't want to mention y'all's case to him, so I told him I wanted to ask my husband what to do with it before they ripped it out." She smiled, proud of her discretion.

"Well, thank you. That was a good call." To Terri I said, "What did those things record onto? Videotapes?"

"Yeah, but not like you're probably thinking. The little ones." She held her thumb and finger about three inches apart. "That wire there would've run to a box with the tape in it—"

She broke eye contact with me and cracked up.

"What," I said, deadpan. "Is my face funny all of a sudden?"

She laughed harder. When she got ahold of herself, she said, "I'm sorry. I just— You looked so excited. But, Leland, we are not about to find a videotape of the crime, okay? It's been twenty years, and it's inside a bathroom wall, not a bank vault. Even if the killer had held his driver's license up to the camera to help us find him, the tape would've probably fallen apart by now."

I couldn't help but chuckle.

Shannon laughed and said, "Oh my goodness, y'all are so funny!"

Terri, looking at the wall, said, "You know what, though, it's a pretty long wire. Huh." She followed it across the wall, down to the floor, and to the spot where it went through a hole in the stud.

I said, "Is it going *outside*?"

"It might be. Shannon, where are we here? What's right below us?"

"Uh, we're… Well, that window's above the living room window. So if you were facing the front of the house, it's to the left of the front door."

"And what's there? Just the bushes?"

"The hydrangeas, yeah."

"Do you mind if we take a quick look down there?"

"Oh, not at all."

We all went back downstairs, outside, and down the porch steps. The ivy on the front of the house made it hard to find the wire, but— thanks to Terri's flashlight—we eventually did.

It hung down behind the bushes, to a point about three feet off the ground. The metal tip of the cable was so beat up it had completely lost its shine. Whatever it had been attached to was long gone.

Behind us, Shannon said, "Now why would anybody have run it out here?"

Terri and I looked at each other. I was not a believer in telepathy, but I was sure we were both thinking of the landscaper. Angelo.

I looked back at the cable and said, "Well, Shannon, that's the question, isn't it."

22

JUNE 23, 2021

I t had been a hell of a week, and it was only Wednesday morning. I'd spent Monday finalizing and filing a signed statement from Amy McDonough along with the petition for post-conviction relief seeking a new trial for Maria. I'd spent half of Tuesday haggling with Britney LaSalle's bail bondsman to release the liens on her cars. Thankfully, the self-defense hearing had gone as I'd hoped: the phone records we'd subpoenaed showed that Randy had texted the flirty messages to himself, so there was no evidence that Britney invited him over that night. Judge Merriweather had agreed with my point that, if anything, the fake texts suggested cunning and malevolence on Randy's part. Britney was now a free woman, and one of the concerns looming over me was gone.

I was in my home office, getting ready for a 10 a.m. pretrial hearing in Clay's case, when Noah knocked and asked, "You want to see these before you go?" He held up a black binder.

"Is that media coverage?" I was not in the mood, but for a lawyer, ignorance was never bliss. "Yeah, maybe just whatever you found about Clay, if there was anything."

"Oh, there was. That's at the second tab." He opened the binder to show me how it was organized. "And tab four is everything I found on that true-crime forum. It's actually really good, and they talk about that Maria case a lot."

"Is that so."

"Yeah. Cool stuff. Oh, Terri also said I should give you an invoice."

He handed me a piece of paper. I wrote a check for seventy-five dollars, handed it to him, and he left for class.

I stared at the binder he'd left like it might be booby-trapped. I did not want to get thrown off my game by some Dabney the Fourth hit piece right before a hearing. But it was irresponsible to risk walking into court not knowing if some explosive piece of news had just come out. And I couldn't trace any leaks by the other side if I didn't know what the press was saying.

I went to the coffee maker to top up my cup, then came back and flipped the binder open.

I was glad I did.

The first printout from our local news site, dated this morning, had a photo of Emma Twain below the headline "Boat Crash Witness Touts Lie Detector Results." It said she'd taken a polygraph "to put rumors to rest," and she felt "vindicated by the results."

Both the South Carolina and United States Supreme Courts had ruled that lie detector tests were not admissible in a court of law because they weren't considered scientifically reliable. But Dabney either didn't know that or didn't see fit to let his readers know.

I pulled up my hearing outline on my laptop and sketched out an argument. If Fletcher was behind the release of these polygraph results, that would be a clear violation of the gag order.

I flipped to the next page and froze.

Yesterday, another article had come out. Noah had handwritten several exclamation marks above the headline: "Destroyed by Wife's Alcoholism, Ex-Solicitor Seeks Revenge."

I took a deep breath.

I decided not to read that one right before the hearing.

———

On the bench, Judge Chambliss adjusted his spectacles and said, "I have before me the motions in limine of both parties. The State wants to kick out defendant's psychological expert, and the defense wants to kick out your fingerprint expert and the breathalyzer results."

"Uh, Your Honor, just part of the fingerprint expert's report," I said.

"Right, thank you. And I understand counsel met and conferred on these?"

"Yes, Your Honor," Fletcher and I said, almost simultaneously.

"Okay. Now, I've read your briefs and determined that on this psychology expert, I don't need to hear oral argument. I agree with the State's position that there's no justification here for any alleged expert on the psychology of memory. This isn't the type of case where we've got an eyewitness picking a stranger out of a lineup months after the crime. It's a young woman stating which of her longtime friends was doing what, two days after the accident—"

"Your Honor," I said, "if I could direct your attention—"

"Mr. Munroe, I'm excluding that expert. That's my determination. I don't see how it's relevant in a case like this. But now, why don't you go ahead and speak first on the other issues."

"Yes, Your Honor. Before we get to that, though, it's come to my attention that there may have been a violation of the protective order. This morning, the local news ran an article stating that Mr. Fletcher's star witness had taken a polygraph test and what her results allegedly were."

I pulled a printout of the article from my binder. The bailiff took it over to Chambliss.

After skimming it, Chambliss said, "Uh, Mr. Fletcher, do you have an explanation?"

"Your Honor, I honestly— This is the first I've heard of this. May I— is there a copy I could read?"

"I'm happy to share mine," I said, and handed it to him.

After giving him a few seconds to glance at it, Chambliss asked, "Now, Mr. Fletcher, what aspect of this were you not aware of?"

"Any of it, Your Honor. I had no part in any of this."

"Are you telling me this witness procured her own polygraph?"

"Your Honor, I don't know. Matter of fact, I don't even know whether this article is accurate."

"If I may, Your Honor," I said, "I find it hard to believe that a twenty-year-old kid who lives in a trailer park took it upon herself to locate and pay for her own polygraph examiner. For one thing, I seem to recall that those tests cost on the order of six or seven hundred dollars."

Chambliss nodded. "Mr. Fletcher, would you disagree?"

"Your Honor, standing here today, I don't have the facts at hand to speak to that. And I'm not sure we should be addressing this when we haven't even confirmed whether the story is accurate."

"Do you have reason to doubt that it is?"

"Just, as Mr. Munroe pointed out, it seems unlikely she did it herself, and I certainly didn't direct her to."

"Okay. Well, we've got to get clarity on that. Do you think you can reach her today?"

"Uh, I'll certainly try, Your Honor. And whether she confirms or denies what's in the story, I'll remind her of the terms of your protective order and her obligation to comply with it."

"Very well. When you do, schedule a conference with my clerk, and we'll determine how to deal with it. Okay, Mr. Munroe, back to you. I've read your brief, so can you just summarize real quick what relief you're seeking?"

"Certainly, Your Honor. I've sought to exclude certain evidence, and as I mentioned, Mr. Fletcher and I weren't able to reach agreement as to two things. Number one is Mr. Carlson's breathalyzer results, and number two is our objection to the part of the report that Mr. Fletcher's fingerprint expert submitted about the overlapping prints."

"In other words, his opinion that those prints show your client was the last person touching the wheel of the boat?"

"Yes, Your Honor."

"Okay. Now, as I see it, that's a *Daubert* issue. Is this guy's method scientifically reliable or not?"

"That is the question, Your Honor, and I think the scientific consensus is that it's not."

He nodded. "Okay, well, that's something I think we save for a hearing immediately before trial, or maybe the morning before this expert's supposed to testify. Because, thank you for attaching the literature, but I didn't see you cite any cases that specifically rejected this expert's method. So I'm going to want to hear from him directly what support there is for the methods he used, what the peer-reviewed literature says, and so forth."

Fletcher said, "That makes sense, Your Honor."

It did, but it was annoying, because it gave him more time to prepare.

Chambliss moved on. "So, to your other point, Mr. Munroe, am I correct in thinking your argument on the breathalyzer comes down to lack of probable cause?"

"Exactly, Your Honor. That test was administered at 1:51 a.m., just six minutes after the police arrived and before any accusation was made by anybody that Mr. Carlson had been driving. I've reviewed the body-cam footage from officers on the scene, and as I expect Mr. Fletcher will agree, none of it shows anybody accusing my client. There is no point in that footage where anybody states that he was driving or, for that matter, even points at my client. And since there was no basis for thinking that he was the driver, the police had no probable cause to perform the breathalyzer."

"Mr. Fletcher, is that how you'd characterize the body-cam footage?"

"No, Your Honor. Mr. Munroe is trying to prove a negative. He's saying that if there's no recorded footage where we hear that accusation made, we ought to conclude that no such accusation was made. But this was a chaotic emergency situation, with basically every hand on deck trying to rescue kids from the water, attend to the medical needs of the survivors, calm people down who were in the middle of a very traumatic event—so there's a lot of background noise, a lot of moments where the audio or the video was obscured because the officer was physically engaged in rescuing somebody, and so forth. So I don't think we can conclude that if we don't hear it, it's not there."

Chambliss looked at me. I said, "Mr. Fletcher and I do seem to be in agreement that we don't hear it. There's no evidence my client was accused at the scene, whether in the footage or in the police reports. Matter of fact, there's some evidence otherwise: there's footage where we see the female survivor, the girl whose boyfriend was killed, crying on the beach, and the other boy who survived, Jimmy Ludlow, apologizes—"

"Your Honor," Fletcher said, "that's misleading. We've all told somebody 'I'm sorry for your loss,' and that doesn't mean we caused the loss."

"You can address that at trial, if it comes up. Anyway, Mr. Munroe, were you done?"

"Very nearly, Your Honor. To conclude, there's nothing to support probable cause at the time the breathalyzer was done, which law enforcement records show was at the scene, at 1:51 a.m."

Chambliss said, "What time do we know for a fact that an accusation was made implicating Mr. Carlson?"

I said, "Three a.m., Your Honor. Which, I have to note, was about forty-five minutes after a *highly* unusual move on the part of the circuit solicitor, who very understandably came to the hospital to see that his son was okay, but then proceeded to leave his son's bedside and conduct private interviews with my client and the other survivor in their hospital rooms. And before talking to them, he actually asked their nurses to leave."

Chambliss nodded. "I saw that in your brief. Okay, Mr. Fletcher, what's your argument on probable cause?"

"Your Honor, as I said, Mr. Munroe is trying to prove a negative, and on the facts we have, I don't think he can. But to my mind, the more important point is that boating under the influence was not the only thing that police at the scene were investigating. All three of the survivors were under the legal drinking age, so whether Mr. Carlson was driving the boat or not, any outward sign of intoxication would've provided officers with probable cause to suspect him of underage drinking."

"Mr. Munroe?"

"Your Honor, an officer wouldn't need to perform a breathalyzer before he could cite a kid for underage drinking. That's a summary offense that requires no more than a single sip. It certainly doesn't require scientific proof that a certain blood alcohol threshold is met."

Fletcher said, "Now—"

"Excuse me; I'll finish in just a moment. My point is, there was no probable cause to believe my client had committed any crime that required accurate measurement of his blood alcohol level or proof that he was legally intoxicated. And besides that, with regard to the under-age-drinking idea, I also didn't see on the body-cam footage anybody asking any of the survivors their ages or checking their ID. The evidentiary record indicates that for at least two of them, their ID was at the bottom of St. Helena Sound. So it seems to me that Mr. Fletcher is trying to retroactively justify actions that weren't justified at the time."

"Mr. Munroe," Chambliss said, "your client doesn't deny that he was intoxicated, does he?"

"Your Honor, I don't think anything he says now can create probable cause after the fact. It's well established, under *State v. Holt*, that if the police arrive after an accident, after the survivors have gotten out of the vehicle so nobody's sitting in the driver's seat, there's no prob-able cause to breathalyze any of them unless one of them points the finger and identifies somebody as the driver. They can't even breathalyze the owner of the vehicle—which, I might add, in this case was not my client, but Pat Ludlow."

"If I might speak to this, Your Honor," Fletcher said, "I understood your question differently. It's not about creating probable cause after the fact. It's just about the fact that if he was intoxicated—and whether it's admissible or not, standing here in the courtroom today, we know that he was—then he might've been acting like it. He might've been stumbling around or slurring his speech, or there might've been a smell of alcohol on him. And any of those outward indications would've given an officer probable cause to suspect him of drinking. Add to that the fact that he looks like he very well might be underage, and I think there's probable cause to suspect underage drinking. Which, while it's true an officer doesn't *need* to do a breathalyzer to prove underage drinking, he certainly *can* do one."

"Yeah," Chambliss said. "Yeah, I'm inclined to agree with that."

"Your Honor, may I respond to what Mr. Fletcher said?"

Chambliss nodded.

"Mr. Fletcher said that my client *might* have been stumbling, or slurring his speech, or he *might* have smelled of alcohol. But he doesn't point to any evidence that he *was*. It's all speculation. He's had my brief in hand for ten days now, so if there were evidence that any of that were true, he's had time to gather it and bring it here today. But he hasn't pointed to anything—no police report, no body-cam footage, nothing. He could've had an officer testify, but he didn't. And there is no basis for a finding of probable cause based on after-the-fact speculation."

"Your Honor," Mr. Fletcher said, "the officer who performed the breathalyzer happens to be on vacation right now. He specifically planned that for before trial so that he could make himself available anytime he's needed during trial. But as a result of that, he's not able to be here today."

"Okay. Well, as Mr. Munroe points out, I can't admit your breathalyzer evidence based on speculation, so you are going to have to put him up to testify as to what led him to conclude there was probable cause. And if he can't point to specific facts, then that evidence won't come in."

Fletcher nodded as if he'd been chastised. "Understood, Your Honor."

I gritted my teeth. The chastised posture was an act. We both knew Chambliss had given him a road map: Get the cop to say Clay had alcohol on his breath, and the breathalyzer evidence comes in.

Clay was still looking at twenty-five years.

————

I turned my phone back on and went out onto the courthouse steps. A crowd of twelve or fifteen people stood on the sidewalk below. I noticed a camera, and then another one, and a news truck parked off to the side. I turned and looked behind me, wondering who they were waiting for.

"Mr. Munroe!"

I looked back at them. Another person called my name, and then another.

"Mr. Munroe, do you have any comment?"

I gave a professional smile and a curt nod before heading down the steps. There'd never been crowds at Clay's hearings before, just the one journalist who sat in the back of the courtroom. This morning's hearing, I realized, was my first scheduled public appearance since

Dabney's hit piece had come out; maybe they were here to ask about that.

If so, I would be leaving with nothing more than a "No comment." I was as happy as any other trial lawyer to stand on the courthouse steps creating good PR for my client, but answering questions about my own life was something else entirely.

I felt my phone ringing in my pocket, but I didn't answer it. As I reached the bottom of the steps, a young woman thrust a microphone at my face and said, "Mr. Munroe, any comment about the video? Is it your position that the violence was justified?"

I had no idea what she was talking about. But I wasn't about to let her know that.

I said, "No comment," and stepped past her. I had to say it again to a few more people, and then, as I walked half a block in silence, the crowd followed me to my car.

I felt a pang of embarrassment as I unlocked the door. Clay's father's comment on what a lawyer ought to be driving came back to me, and for once I saw what he meant. Escaping a pack of journalists in a black BMW somehow would've looked better than hightailing it out of there in a silver Malibu.

At a red light a few blocks away, I looked at my phone. The call had been from Noah. I called him back.

I barely had time to say hello before he said, "Dad! What the hell! Why didn't you tell me about this gas station thing?"

"What?"

"It's on YouTube. And old Dabney put it on his site, too, of course. What the hell? Why'd you guys do that?"

His question didn't make sense. I said, "Listen, Noah, I don't know what's up, but I'll be home in ten."

After we hung up, I called Terri. It went to voice mail.

———

Noah and I sat at the kitchen table with his laptop. The home page of Dabney's local news site displayed a photo of me pumping gas below the headline "Controversial Lawyer, PI in Bizarre Gun Attack."

He clicked play.

One of our local newscasters, a cute young woman with blonde hair and a serious expression, said, "Our newsroom received this shocking dashcam footage this morning. We've since confirmed it does appear to show controversial local attorney Leland Munroe and his private investigator, Terri Washington, pulling a gun on some Good Samaritans who stopped to help them at a gas station in Jasper County last week. Neither Mr. Munroe nor Ms. Washington has commented, but local law enforcement tells us the investigation is ongoing."

The gas station came on-screen. I saw myself standing beside the Malibu, looking toward the camera while Terri sat in the passenger seat. The perspective was from the pickup truck. For a dashcam, the resolution was excellent. Anyone who knew me would recognize my face.

The audio, on the other hand, was bad. It was impossible to make out what the driver was saying or to hear his menacing tone. The video had subtitles, but they didn't include any of the threats or racist epithets that I remembered. They had him saying, *Evening, are you folks lost? Need any help? The highway's right over there.*

On-screen, I put the gas nozzle back on the pump. Terri scooted into the driver's seat.

The truck's passenger appeared, walking toward the Malibu. The subtitles said, *My buddy's got a map if you need one.*

Terri jumped out of the car and held the passenger at gunpoint. This audio, for some reason, was loud and clear: "Freeze! You are under arrest!"

She swore at him. He hesitated. She yelled, "I'm a police officer, and you *will* be shot!"

We watched the Good Samaritan obey her instructions, get down on his knees, and lie flat on the asphalt.

As Terri and I peeled out of there, the light glinted off the gun in my hand.

Noah looked at me and said, "What the *hell*?"

"That— Hang on a second." I pulled out my phone and dialed Terri. Voice mail again.

I took a deep breath and said, "I don't know what they did to the soundtrack on that, but that isn't what happened."

"What isn't what happened?" He looked baffled, and then his face cleared. "Are you saying that's a deepfake?"

"The soundtrack," I said. "That's not what that guy was saying, at all."

"But that *is* what Terri was saying?"

"Listen. You got a text from her last Wednesday night, right? About a truck we saw?"

"Oh. Yeah."

"That was the truck in this video. They followed us onto the highway, after we left the house of a witness we were talking to, and eight or nine miles later they followed us back off when we exited to get gas.

Terri sent you that text so that if anything happened to us, you'd have a location and a description of the truck."

His eyes widened. "Whoa."

My phone rang. To my dismay, it wasn't Terri's cell; it was some downtown exchange that I didn't recognize.

I picked up.

"Leland," Terri said. "I'm at the jail. I'm under arrest."

23

JUNE 23, 2021

I didn't have a spare ten grand lying around. So I'd called one of my credit card companies to get a cash advance, destroying much of the progress I'd made in paying off debt, to bail Terri out about five hours after her arrest.

She could've used a bail bonds service to get herself out, but that would've taken at least twenty-four hours; I'd even seen cases where it took a couple of weeks. I did not want her spending a single night behind bars. I remembered the broken jaw Noah's friend Jackson had gotten when he was in jail, back when he was my client. The drug cartel I'd been up against then had planted some of their own people inside just to keep him in line.

And I knew Terri's arrest was a setup.

I had no doubt about who was behind it. We—Noah, Terri, and I— were all sitting in my living room watching him on TV. The pizza I'd had delivered was on the coffee table, but none of us had any desire to eat. That would have to wait until Ludlow's press conference was over.

He was on the courthouse steps, standing in the sunshine with a breeze in his hair, saying with great indignation that "this brazen act of violence" was "contrary to everything that we believe in here in Basking Rock, and in America."

"I was particularly shocked," he said, "to hear Ms. Washington claim, falsely, to be a police officer. Impersonating a law enforcement officer is a crime." He looked from camera to camera to let that sink in. "And impersonating an officer while threatening a civilian with a gun is beyond my comprehension. But we've all seen that video evidence with our own eyes, and rest assured, my office has filed charges against her for that crime."

Noah said, "He's really doing it. I can't believe this." He looked at Terri and said, "This is insane. I'm so sorry. At least you've got, like, a built-in lawyer."

I said, "I actually can't represent her. I'm a witness. Can't be her lawyer in the same case."

"Oh, man!"

"I'll make sure she gets a good one, though."

Terri didn't say anything. She was glaring at the TV like she wished she could murder Ludlow. Slowly.

On-screen, he answered a reporter's question: "Yes, my office is also investigating Mr. Munroe. We're reviewing the evidence to determine whether charges should be filed, be it for the brandishing of the gun or for other acts. I will keep everybody updated as the investigation proceeds."

I'd been up against Ludlow enough in the past few years to read between the lines. He was letting me know that if I toed the line, he could make those charges go away. Quid pro quo.

Noah said, "I just want to take this guy *down*. Isn't there some way to?"

I laughed, although it wasn't funny, and said, "I'd sure love to find one."

"Yeah! He's a total waste of space. Even his own son hates him."

I looked at him in surprise. "You been talking to Jimmy Ludlow?"

"No. I meant Brandon. But if Jimmy hates him, too, I'm not surprised."

While I was mentally reminding myself to keep my trap shut instead of sharing confidential case info with Noah, my phone rang. It was Ruiz, so I went into my office to answer.

"Hey there." I closed the door.

"Hey. I'm watching the news. What in the name of God is going on?"

I looked at the corkboard on my wall: the photos of Ludlow's dead wife, his troubled son, Maria and her family. The strings connecting them now looked to me like so many trip wires.

I said, "I stepped on one of Ludlow's land mines, I guess."

He sighed. "Sure seems that way. Look, I know it's weird for me to call right now, since I work for him. If you don't want to talk, that's fine. But knowing you, I thought this *cannot* be what he's saying it is."

"Well, I appreciate that. And you're right, it's not."

"Thank God. Well, if you're up for it, I want to hear your side."

I hesitated. I didn't want to tell him where Terri and I had been on the night we were attacked, or who we'd been talking to.

So I skipped that. "Well, long story short, that video got doctored. Those subtitles are not at all what those men were saying. They'd followed us for ten miles and cornered us in the middle of nowhere when we were out of gas, yelling things I don't even want to repeat. There was no doubt in my mind that we were about to be attacked."

"Goddamn. I'm sorry. But that at least makes some sense."

"You mean how we reacted? Yeah."

"You know what, I should've realized what was wrong with that video. That's dashcam footage, right? So why would the voices inside the car be all muffled, when Terri's voice outside was clear?"

"Exactly. And if you could hear them, you'd know why we reacted that way. Just being followed, even before they blocked us in at the gas station, scared Terri bad enough that she texted Noah a vehicle description and location so he'd have a lead if we went missing."

"Scared *Terri*? I don't think I've ever heard those two words together before. I thought that woman was bulletproof."

"Right? Yeah, no. But fortunately, when she's scared, she goes into cop mode instead of panicking."

"The training kicked in. You spend as long on the force as she did, it's never going away."

"Nope."

"Okay. Well, thanks for letting me know. Now, with my boss on a rampage about this, I'm going to be a little limited in terms of what I can do to help, but if you need something, I'll do what I can."

Ruiz was not the kind of guy to ever knowingly break a rule, and with his office prosecuting my PI and possibly me, there were going to be some rules hemming him in.

"Thanks," I said. "But I'm not going to put you in the middle of this."

Then a thought came to mind. "You know what, though, I might actually need a little hand. Not about Terri or any of this, nothing your office is prosecuting. This might be outside your bailiwick, but I sent your office and the police department a couple of discovery requests over a month ago and haven't heard back. It was on my prisoner-exoneration thing, just looking for whatever might be left in the archives or the evidence room from twenty years ago."

"Oh, I can ensure compliance with lawful discovery requests, for sure. Especially if Ludlow's too, uh, *busy* to get around to it." He laughed. "I'll see what I can do."

"Great. And, uh, thanks. For having my back, I mean."

"I have to now, right?" I heard a smile in his voice. "You're Noah's dad. My little girl would never forgive me if I didn't."

"Oh! Right. Man, that's something, isn't it."

"Yeah. Kids." He sighed. "I can't believe it. In my head, she's still a baby. I don't know how I was ever supposed to be ready for this."

"Right? It goes so fast. But so you know, I've talked to Noah. Among other things, I told him that if he ever mistreats her, he'll have to answer to me."

He laughed and said, "Well, good. Good. Because if you don't take care of it, I will."

"Oh, I meant it. I raised him to do the right thing, you know? At least I hope I did."

"Yeah, he's a good kid. Way I look at it, I'm not ready for her to grow up—and I might never be—but there's plenty of boys in town that I wouldn't even let step into my *yard*, much less... Better him than them, is what I mean. How's he taking all this? The gas station thing? And Ludlow?"

"As well as he can, I guess. It's a real education, and not in a good way. I mean, to see just how easily we could've been done for, out there in the middle of nowhere... And on top of that, Ludlow? It's a side of the world that he's a little young to see, although I guess it had to come sometime."

"You guys file a police report yet? Your version of events on the gas station thing?"

"Doing that tomorrow. I'm interested to know who was behind it. With that dashcam footage going straight to Dabney and Ludlow, I'm inclined to think we were set up."

He was quiet for a second. Then he said, "Sorry, my brain kind of had to reorganize itself there. It's a lot to take in." After another pause, he said, "I wish that didn't make sense. And I wish I could think of anybody other than Ludlow that might've had some reason to set you up like that."

"So what's Ludlow's reason, in your view?"

"Well... You ever notice how when he walks in, it's got to be all eyes on him? There's no room for anybody else. And there sure as hell isn't room for anybody who makes him look stupid. If it was up to him, that'd be a capital crime."

"I made him look bad, so he's returning the favor?"

"And then some."

I thought for a second about how to respond. Ruiz was a friend, and he'd never liked Ludlow, but he did still work for him.

I decided to speak to the friend, not to the assistant solicitor.

"You know what, you're right that that's part of it, but I don't think it's that simple."

"No?"

"No. Making me look bad, getting his friend to publish hit pieces on me, is one thing. But it's a big leap from being a vindictive jackass who only cares about his own ego to bringing criminal charges against my PI that could get her license yanked and put her in jail. And threatening me with the same thing."

"I'll give you that," he said.

"That's where you start to wonder if you got a psychopath on your hands. I mean literally."

I was also thinking of what Terri had told me about Ludlow's abuse of Emma's mom, but I wasn't about to tell that to Ruiz or anybody else.

"Well, I don't like to armchair diagnose anybody," Ruiz said. "I'm no psychologist. But I've worked under him for more than a decade, and it's a fact that every time I hear that old quote about how absolute power corrupts absolutely, I think of him."

"And he's a third-generation circuit solicitor. That position's been occupied by a Ludlow for, what, going on eighty years now? In these parts, power doesn't get much more absolute than that."

"For sure."

"If he's willing to do that to me and Terri, what else would he do? And what else has he already done? Who else has he railroaded?"

Ruiz didn't say anything. I pictured him, sitting at home or in the home office in his garage, thinking on that. He was probably still wearing his suit; I'd never seen him wearing anything else. Suits were traditional, and he was a man who never questioned the idea that rules and traditions were there for a good reason.

I knew that about him. So I said, "Ludlow swore an oath to seek justice and protect the innocent. We all did. That's supposed to be our guiding rule. And I just don't see him doing that at all."

Ruiz heaved a sigh and said, "I hear you."

After a second, he added, "I tell you what, I think we got a hell of a problem on our hands."

"Yeah. I think we do too."

24

JUNE 30, 2021

I parked in Roy's little lot and strolled up the walkway in the flimsy shade of the palm trees. There was a breeze, but in my shirt and tie—I was dressed for Zoom meetings—I was already hot.

As I came in, Laura looked up from her desk and said, "Oh, hello. I just made a fresh pot of coffee. And I got your desk set up for your talk with Mr. Bertini."

"Thank you. I don't know why I need my coffee hot no matter what the temperature is outside."

"Oh, I'm with you. It's not *coffee* unless it's hot."

I set the bag from the donut place on her desk. I was still only coming into the office about once a week—the pandemic had changed how we worked, maybe permanently—and I always brought her favorite kind.

"Thank you. Do you know what, Leland, I'm taking that home with me." She folded the bag up neatly, taped it shut, and put it into her purse. "I'll have it tonight, while I'm listening to my podcast."

"Oh? What is it you listen to?"

"*Carolina True Crime*, of course! What else? She's going to be talking about you—I'm not going to miss that!"

"Well, that's nice. I guess I ought to listen to it too."

"Oh, yes! I've been listening to it for a couple of months now. It's fascinating."

I smiled and headed to the coffee maker.

Terri and I had filed our police report a few days earlier, and afterward, she'd suggested calling Shannon and telling her our side of the story. As she saw it, Dabney was out to ruin us, and Shannon was the closest thing we had to a media connection, and we needed to fight fire with fire.

Shannon had responded with passionate indignation. She was in our corner instantly. It seemed as if she felt genuine outrage at the injustice, but I couldn't help but think she'd also do whatever it took to get us on her podcast at some point, whenever—if ever—we were free to speak.

I went into my office and saw that Laura had put a fresh legal pad and three different-colored pens on my desk. The pens were exactly parallel to each other, and I was pretty sure that if I got out a ruler, I'd find that the legal pad was within a sixteenth of an inch of the dead center of the desk.

She'd also set out a stack of photographs that I recognized as being all the officers we knew had been present at the scene of the boat crash, and all the ones who'd interviewed the various witnesses. Each photo was labeled with their name and title. I flipped through and then tucked them into my briefcase. They were going home with me, to be pinned up on my corkboard.

I hadn't realized until I started working with Laura how much I valued a compulsively organized legal secretary. Even if she did go a little overboard sometimes.

I leaned out my doorway and said, "Laura, this looks great. Thanks much. I was wondering, do you have time to do a little project for me this week?"

"Most likely. What is it?"

"I got a bunch of electronic files from Maria's former counsel—her interview notes and whatnot. One of them is a long PDF, a scan of her handwritten notes. And her handwriting's not the best, so—"

"Oh, you want me to type it up?"

"If you could, yeah. Everything else she sent was in Word, but that one I haven't had time to slog through yet. For all I know, it's just the handwritten version of the Word docs—I'll send you them all so you can check. If it is, then I don't need it typed up."

"Okay. You know what, even if you don't need that one, I'll read through everything and create an index of all the people's names that she mentions, and the locations, and all the issues that come up in her notes. That way, when you're looking for anything in her files, you can just check that index."

I stared at her. It was like looking at the Grand Canyon or Halley's Comet or some other natural wonder. I said, "You are a godsend."

She laughed.

———

A few minutes later, I fired up Zoom for my meeting. Mr. Bertini, my fingerprint guy, wasn't there yet. I turned off my camera so I didn't have to stare at my face while sipping coffee.

My phone rang. It was Ruiz. Before I could answer, Bertini appeared on my screen. He was in his fifties, with steel-gray hair and heavy jowls. Behind him was a low bookshelf and a framed poster of Sherlock Holmes.

"Afternoon, Mr. Bertini. How's Atlanta?"

"Hotter than the Devil's armpit, as per usual. How you been?"

"Oh, can't complain."

I'd already told him about the doctored video, to avoid him finding out from someone else or from Google. He'd taken it in stride. Bertini had spent twenty-odd years as a police detective and then retired from that to go into the expert-witness business. He taught classes in crime scene investigation at one of the Georgia police academies. I had the impression it would take at least a neutron bomb to shock him.

He said, "Trial prep going okay?"

"Yeah, it's coming along. Twelve days to blastoff."

That was way too soon. I'd never liked having the amount of time available to investigate a case be dictated by a judge—I always felt like I could use another six months—but it was part of the territory.

"So," I said, "the reason I wanted to touch base is that we're going to have basically a *Daubert* hearing on that part of the prosecution's fingerprint opinion where he looked at overlapping fingerprints and decided my client's print was on top, so my guy's hand was the last one on the wheel of the boat."

"When you say 'basically'... Do y'all do things a little different there?"

"Yeah, technically here we apply what's called the *Council* standard. I just say *Daubert* because it's pretty much the same thing and everybody knows what that means."

Daubert was a federal case, so lawyers and experts nationwide used that term all the time.

"Well, you'll have to tell me how this *Council* thing works. Under *Daubert*, at least, claiming you can tell which fingerprint in an overlapping print was on top is just a flaming pile of BS, as far as I'm concerned."

I chuckled. One of the reasons I'd chosen Bertini as our expert is that I thought his plainspoken, beat-cop attitude would go over well with the jury. "I mean, I didn't use the term 'flaming pile of BS' in my brief, but that was the gist. And we don't bear the burden of proof in the hearing, but I do need to be able to rebut the solicitor's points as they come up—which is to say, the prosecutor's points—so I'm hoping you can give me what I'll need to do that."

"Sure."

"Okay, so at the hearing, the solicitor bears the burden of showing that what his fingerprint guy wants to say is scientifically reliable. He's got to hit four points. First, what do peer-reviewed publications have to say about his technique? Second is prior application of the technique in other cases. That's mostly on me, since I can search the case law databases, but if you know of any cases where it's been used or rejected, let me know."

"I go to conferences on crime scene investigation twice a year, I do six or eight trials a year, and I keep up with the literature, obviously. I don't recall anybody ever talking about doing this for real, in a publication or at a conference or otherwise."

"Good to know. But what do you mean, for real? Are you saying their guy basically made this up?"

He winced like that went too far. "Naw, what I mean is, it's a thing we'd like to do. It's a thing people have tried various ways of figuring out. But I haven't heard anybody claiming that they've actually solved the problem in a systematic, reliable way. About a decade ago, there were a few articles about algorithms some folks had come up with to try to separate overlapping prints."

"Meaning what, run the overlapping print through a computer program?"

"Right. And supposedly, the program would separate it into the two different underlying fingerprints. The idea being, then you could run them both through IAFIS looking for a hit. Or compare them to your suspects, or whatever."

"Uh-huh." IAFIS was the FBI's nationwide fingerprint database.

"But even that never took off. It just wasn't reliable enough."

"Good to know."

"More recently I've heard people talking about different fluorescence profiles, separating prints that way. Putting them under UV light, recording the hyperspectral data, et cetera. But that's still experimental at best. And these approaches are only the first step. Figuring out which overlapping print is which. So we haven't even mastered step one, much less step two, where you would figure out which print was laid down first."

"Yeah, in my experience, we were never able to use overlapping prints at all. Now, the third factor is what quality control procedures their expert used to ensure reliability—"

"What quality control can you do on an unreliable method? You put lipstick on a pig, it's still a pig."

"Exactly. Okay, and the fourth factor is how consistent the method is with recognized scientific laws and procedures."

He shook his head, making a face. "It's just not. I mean, if we don't even have a recognized scientific way of separating out which overlapping print is which, how can you say which one was laid down first?"

"Uh-huh. Makes sense. Okay, so what I'm going to do is email you a list of those four points, and if you could write down, for instance, that you searched whatever database you search for literature and found nothing, or you only found such-and-such article and here are its flaws—that's the kind of thing I need."

"Sounds good. You shoot that over, and if I've got any questions, I'll reach out."

We signed off.

———

My next meeting was with Terri and a criminal defense guy up in Charleston that Cardozo had recommended. She needed a lawyer, and with Ludlow's sword hanging over my head, I was probably going to need one too.

We all showed up on time and said our hellos. Cardozo's guy, Max Rubin, was sitting in a leather armchair in front of bookshelves containing what looked like every legal treatise ever published.

I'd sent him links to the video of our attack, Ludlow's indignant speech on the courthouse steps, and Fourth's inflammatory articles. He knew the background, and now he needed to prepare for Terri's preliminary hearing.

"So, before we get started," he said, "I've got to point out the obvious: you're two different people who were involved in the same incident, and were charged or might be charged for that incident. Which means we have to consider whether your interests are aligned. Because there might be some scenario where your best outcome, Terri, would require letting Leland take the fall, or vice versa."

"Oh," Terri said. "I hadn't thought of that."

"For example, one of you might be offered a plea to testify against the other, or your police statements might not match up in some critical detail. And if that's the case—if a conflict developed down the line—I'd have to stop representing one of you. So that's something we need to discuss."

"Yeah, of course." She looked worried.

"But you're the one who needs a lawyer right now," I told her. "So Max is your guy. Max, my take on this is, we got attacked together, we're getting dragged through the mud together… and besides that, Terri is my friend. We stand or fall together."

He smiled. "I like that. I'm sure you'll understand—just as one professional to another—if I tell you I don't get a lot of particularly honorable people sitting across my desk—so I like that. But I do have to let you know, when it gets real—when a person is faced with potentially life-altering or career-ending charges, as you both may be since you're both in licensed professions—things can look very different."

"I hear you. But things are never going to look different enough to me to throw Terri to the wolves. If Ludlow puts me in a position where I have to choose between my law license and my *friend*?" I shrugged. "Being a lawyer isn't the only way to make a living. I could open a bakery, drive for Uber… who cares? I'd wash dishes before I'd sell her out to Ludlow."

Terri's smile told me my words meant something to her. But she wasn't the type to ever say that out loud. She teased me instead: "Leland, you don't even know how to bake!"

I laughed. "I can make pancakes. That's a start."

Max smiled and said, "It's a step above making toast, maybe."

I liked this guy.

"Anyway, listen," I said. "Max, that's an important issue, and I'm glad you raised it. For now, Terri's the one who needs your help, so I'll get off the call to avoid messing up your attorney-client privilege. If I do get charged, I'll call you back and we can figure things out at that point."

————

As two thirty approached, I checked my camera to make sure everything looked professional: no fast-food containers in the background, nothing stuck in my teeth. It was time for a quick chat with Fletcher and Judge Chambliss—the kind that used to be held in the judge's chambers, until the pandemic made us all realize that a ten-minute conversation shouldn't require an hour-long courthouse trip.

Once we were all on-screen and Fletcher figured out how to unmute himself, Chambliss said, "Okay, counsel. Now, what'd you find out about that polygraph?"

"Well, Your Honor, I spoke to Ms. Twain, and she unfortunately confirmed that it did happen. It was not an error on the part of the newspaper."

Chambliss sighed. "And here I was hoping you were going to make my life easier."

"I apologize, Your Honor. I did chase it down in terms of finding out where the test was conducted and reaching out to them. Unfortunately, they informed me that the test was paid for in cash, which obviously is pretty unusual, and the record shows it was requested by a Mike Smith, which, being an extremely generic name—"

"Are you kidding me?" Chambliss said. "Did some guy at a bus stop somewhere order a polygraph for your witness? What is going on here?"

My best guess was that Dabney was behind it, but I wasn't going to speculate out loud. Especially not when that might distract the judge from being angry at Fletcher.

"Your Honor, I asked her that, and she showed me a letter she had received. And I'm having my secretary email a copy to your clerk, as well as to Mr. Munroe here, because this is a bizarre situation. As you'll see, it appears to be on the letterhead of the polygraph provider, although they've assured me they didn't send it. Matter of fact, they never send letters like that. But it claims that my firm arranged for this test and Ms. Twain should present herself on such-and-such date. And unfortunately, she didn't call my office to check with me. She just went ahead and complied."

Judge Chambliss stared at Fletcher for so long I thought my screen had frozen. Then he shook his head and said, "Mr. Fletcher, this is not happening in my courtroom. I am not—"

"Your Honor—"

"Hang on, Mr. Fletcher. This is not the *Jerry Springer Show* or Geraldo Rivera or any of that. I'd like you to go on digging up what happened here, but everybody in Basking Rock probably saw that story, and it never should've happened. Unless you want to start all over and transfer this case to a different venue—"

"Not at all, Your Honor."

"I didn't think so. Now, obviously, I'm going to have to address this in voir dire and then instruct the jurors we seat to disregard it. Mr. Munroe, what are your thoughts?"

"Your Honor, I agree it has to be addressed. And I have to say, while I accept Mr. Fletcher's representation that he didn't order this, it happened on his watch. And it could've been avoided with proper instructions from him to his witnesses."

"Yes, it could have."

"But I also agree that ideally we should avoid the expense and delay of a venue transfer. So I could agree not to move for that if we're able to craft some way to put this in context for the jury—"

"Are you talking about your memory witness?"

"Yes, I am."

"Your Honor, we—"

"Mr. Fletcher, if you have a better idea, let me know. But bear in mind, you brought this on yourself."

After a little more back-and-forth, my expert witness on the psychology of memory had her toes in the door. For the limited purpose of explaining why a polygraph result could be meaningless, she was in.

When we got off that meeting, I felt like I'd won the lottery. I basked in that for a minute and then remembered that Ruiz had called. I called back.

He picked up quick. "Hey, Leland. How's it going?"

"Oh, fine. At the office. Same old, apart from the whole Ludlow apocalypse."

"Yeah, I'm at work too."

Meaning, *now is not the time for us to trash Ludlow.*

"So, I looked into those discovery requests about the Guerrero case," he said. "I'll be sending you a download link. As it turned out, the evidence room guy managed to find a couple of things from the case, one of which was a VHS tape of Mrs. Guerrero's police interview—"

"Oh yeah?"

"Yeah, which, it being as old as it is, I assumed was physically at high risk of falling apart. Normally, I'd suggest a time for you to come by and review it, but I didn't want to try that and end up damaging it. I've got a duty to preserve the evidence."

"Of course. And do you even have a VCR to watch it on anymore?"

"I doubt it. Anyway, I took it to this vendor we use and got it digitized. That's what's at the link."

I waited, but he didn't go on.

I said, "Anything interesting?"

"Well, it's not my place to discuss your case with you. But I can tell you that they used a Spanish interpreter to interview her. And you may need an interpreter of your own to help review it."

Something in his tone told me there was more to his message than what he was saying out loud. "You speak Spanish, don't you?"

"Yes, I do."

"Do you happen to recall offhand if the interpreter they used was a Mr. Ramón Perez?"

"Yes, I believe it was."

"Okay, thank you."

25

JULY 4, 2021

A little before 9 p.m. on Independence Day, Terri and I drove over to one of the narrow beaches overlooking Port Royal Sound. From there, you could watch the fireworks on Hilton Head Island without having to deal with the traffic or the crowds. We'd both been lying low since the PR catastrophe of the doctored video and Ludlow's speech. Ludlow had charged me for the same incident—with a single charge of assault, for brandishing the gun, but I took it as a warning. I knew he could add more charges any time.

So being out in public was not on our wish list.

Noah was coming to join us later, possibly with Isabela Ruiz, if her daddy let her come.

I parked, and we got out.

"Man, it's nice to get some fresh air," I said. "I would've passed out from the DEET if we'd been in the car much longer. We should've waited to put the bug spray on until we got here."

Terri laughed. "They would've eaten me alive in the time it took to put it on. I just tried to focus on the smell of the food."

She put our bag of Mexican takeout on the hood of the car. I got a blanket and the camping chairs out of the trunk and set them up.

"Oh, did you happen to have any luck with Miss Paramour?" I asked. "Sorry to talk shop, I just thought we ought to get that over with before Noah gets here."

"At least she didn't shut the door in my face this time. She let me in, I think because her folks were out of town, and we talked for maybe ten minutes, max. She's a nice girl, but she's sticking with her story. I really don't think she knows what she's getting into."

"How do you mean?"

"Well... after I'd established some rapport, I asked her how she could identify a stranger from forty-odd feet away, at night. And then I asked, you know, given what she and Tucker were in the middle of doing at the time, was she really paying attention to the boat? And she got this look on her face—this, like, choir-girl, holier-than-thou look—and she said that was offensive and not true and not my business."

I stared at her. "Does she not realize that's going to come up at trial?"

"I don't think she does. I really don't. I mean, from her social media and everything, I think she's had a sheltered life. For someone her age to be that I... It's not something I've come across much."

"Wow. And I guess you couldn't tell her that if she gets on the stand, I'll have to grill her on that."

"No! My goodness, I'm not going down for witness tampering. 'Ms. Washington, is it not true that you attempted to dissuade the witness from testifying?' No. Not happening."

I laughed and went to get the drinks. I thought it was a little shady for Fletcher not to have prepared Kayla for that line of questioning. My first impression of him as a straight shooter kept getting chipped away, although it was useful to learn that he was willing to humiliate a witness on the stand in order to win.

As I hoisted the cooler out of the trunk, I wondered why Tucker hadn't warned her. He was a lawyer; he knew how things worked. Maybe he'd been telling the truth when he said he hadn't spoken to her since the crash.

Setting the cooler down between our chairs, I asked, "How are things going with Max Rubin? Don't tell me anything privileged, obviously."

"Oh, he is *methodical*. He does not miss a detail. And he's going straight for the jugular as far as the authenticity of that video."

"Great. That's the right place to focus. Although if the guys in the truck testify that it's real, I guess you'd need a deepfakes forensics guy. Which isn't cheap, but what can you do?"

"Without the money to prove yourself innocent? I guess you can spend your life in jail," she said. "Like Maria."

"Oof, yeah. Thank God for that police interview, though. That's as close to a slam dunk as you can get in a case like this."

"It sure is."

I'd sent the video of it to an interpreter up in Charleston, and she'd told me two things. First, he sounded Dominican. Knowing that, I hoped, might make it easier to find him. But even without finding him, the second thing she told me was explosive: During the police interview, she said, Ramón Perez had been doing exactly what we'd suspected he did at Maria's trial. He subtly mistranslated some of the questions and a few of her answers, in order to make her implicate herself in the crime.

I'd filed a supplemental petition for a new trial on that basis within twenty-four hours of my phone call with Ruiz.

Terri, sitting in her camp chair, reached into the cooler and fished out a bottle of beer.

"Thanks for bringing this," she said. "If there's ever a time when you just can't deal with watching somebody drink alcohol, or, I don't know, the smell of it, please tell me. I'm fine going without."

"No problem." I opened my bottle of Coke. "I've seen you stop after only one or two enough times that if it's *you* drinking, it doesn't bother me."

"Good. It just really hits the spot when I'm having Mexican food. Oh, look!"

Balls of light shot into the sky over Hilton Head trailing red, white, and blue tails. When they reached their full height, they exploded into patriotic flowers of fire.

From across the water, we could faintly hear the oohs and aahs of the crowd.

I unwrapped my tacos and started eating.

Terri said, "As soon as I see Noah's car in the distance, I'll stop talking about the case—or any of the cases—but I still think we ought to try to talk to Dunk."

More fireworks launched. High overhead, green webs spread across the sky.

I sighed. "I wish we could run the prints on Shannon's bathroom camera."

"Yeah. But that would just show who installed it, not who *had* it installed."

We'd dusted the camera, since Terri had a kit in her car, and she reminded me that prints could last for decades on an undisturbed surface. She'd picked up two that looked semi-usable, but without a suspect to compare them to, we couldn't do anything. Only law enforcement could run prints through IAFIS.

"I've got to admit," I said, checking my phone to see if Noah had called, "it doesn't make sense for Ludlow to have installed a camera that fed to a tape deck outside the house. If he wanted to monitor his wife, he could've just fed it to his study or something."

"Mm-hmm. It had to be somebody who wouldn't normally have been inside. And that's why I don't think there's any way around talking to Dunk. Or Angelo, if we can find him."

At the crack of another firework, I looked up. It looked like spinning white raindrops, or tiny fish, were falling toward Hilton Head.

"Angelo would be my preference," I said, "but I can't think of where to look for him that we haven't already tried. The man could be dead by now. I know he's probably only forty-five or fifty, but a guy who works with landscaping equipment and pesticides, and has a record for breaking and entering, and does something as stupid as sleeping with the wife of the most powerful guy in town—that's not a guy I'd expect to reach a ripe old age."

Terri laughed. More fireworks shot up. When they burst, fiery blue nets spread across the sky, seeming to capture the falling white fish.

Something hit me. *Blue.* Boys in blue. Two of the men in the photos Laura had printed out for my corkboard were Basking Rock police officers.

"Terri... why were there municipal police officers at the boat crash? That was miles outside the city limits."

She went still. "It was DNR jurisdiction, wasn't it," she said. "On the water. And on land, the county sheriff..."

"Right, and that's who responded to the scene. Apart from the ambulance, nobody else should have."

We looked at each other. Fireworks exploded overhead. We ignored them.

She said, "But they were there. And on top of that, the paramours both said it was a police officer that collared them."

"And Tucker's a lawyer. He knows the difference between a police officer and a deputy sheriff."

Most people did—their cars and uniforms were different—and a lawyer, one who wanted to be circuit solicitor, certainly did.

She nodded slowly. One side of her face lit up red as another firework burst overhead. "Tracking people, trying to catch them in compromising positions, that's PI work," she said. "Back when I was a cop, there were a few who would moonlight as PIs. They weren't supposed to, but for a discreet job that paid well, some of them would."

The puzzle pieces in my head clicked into place. "So you think Ludlow hired one? To shadow Tucker and find dirt on him?"

"Oh my goodness. To destroy him in the primary."

"Or convince him not to run. Man, he sure got the dirt."

"He sure did," she said. "And then when the boat crashed, the cop called in a buddy who was on duty, to help with the rescue. Which was the right thing to do, but—"

"The right thing as a human being and as an officer, yeah. So his buddy came in a cruiser, with his partner. That's the two cops whose names are in the reports."

"Mm-hmm. So the guy who nabbed the paramours must be friends with at least one of them. I mean, to have their number, to know they were on duty... And he had to be close enough to Ludlow that he's who Ludlow would hire as his PI."

"Yeah! This is— Oh, hang on." My phone was ringing in my pocket. I pulled it out, expecting Noah to be calling to let me know why he was running late.

It wasn't him. The number was vaguely familiar, but I couldn't place it.

"Hello?"

"Mr. Munroe, this is Jackson. I'm sorry, I'm so sorry. You've got to come to the hospital. It's Noah."

"What? What happened?"

"Sir, I got him here right away. I called the ambulance. And he's— I'm outside right now—they don't allow phone calls in the ER."

I dropped my food on the ground and jumped into the car.

———

When we got to the hospital, Jackson was standing at the emergency room entrance waiting for us.

"Mr. Munroe! I want you to know, I was with him just a minute ago, and he was still alive. Come on this way." He plowed through the door with us at his heels.

"Masks are right there," he said, putting his own back on and pointing to a sanitation station just ahead. "They're required."

We put ours on. I had no words. The only question that mattered was whether Noah was going to be okay. Jackson couldn't answer that, so there was nothing to say.

He got to a security guard and explained who we were. The man asked for my hand, wrapped a papery green wristband around my cuff, and then did the same to Terri.

Jackson took off down a bright white hallway and looked back at the guard, who buzzed open the doors at the end. We hurried to make it through.

He said, "I got to tell you so it's not a shock. They put him on a ventilator. But that's what saved his life."

———

My son was unconscious in a hospital bed, hooked up to a machine that was pushing air into him with loud, robotic sounds. Wires came out every which way from his hospital gown, and a TV screen on the wall displayed his blood pressure, breaths per minute, and the jagged lines of his beating heart. Jackson got us a couple of chairs and went to find the nurse.

We didn't sit down. I held Noah's hand and noticed he was restrained, with white cloth-and-Velcro cuffs attached to the railings of the bed. Terri stood on the opposite side and held his other hand. She saw what I was looking at and said, in a low, calm voice, "These are probably to keep him from pulling out the vent tube when he wakes up."

I took a sudden deep breath, like she'd hit my reset button. For half a second my thoughts were organized and calm: *They expect him to wake up. That's why they put these on him.*

A nurse stopped by to say Noah's nurse was with another patient, but she'd be over soon. A police officer came to the door, holding a cup of vending-machine coffee and looking like he wanted to talk to me, but maybe something in my face changed his mind. He turned away and took a sip. A respiratory therapist came in to check the numbers on Noah's ventilator. Terri moved her chair around to my side of the bed so he could do his job.

Another nurse came in, wearing scrubs covered with cartoon characters, and said she was caring for Noah. When she introduced herself, her name went through my head without leaving any trace.

She said, "I'm sorry, I know this is hard. So, your son was brought in here by ambulance in full respiratory arrest at about ten o'clock, but we were able to intubate him and restore the airway."

Terri asked, "Do you have a sense when the sedation will wear off?"

"Oh, he's not sedated. We do normally sedate patients while they're on the vent, because it's a pretty distressing experience for them otherwise, but due to the potential drug interactions, we don't do that with patients who've suffered an opiate overdose."

I said, "Overdose?"

"I'm sorry, I thought—" She looked at Jackson.

"Sir, it was an accident. He didn't know."

"How... What happened?"

"We were at Brandon's apartment. Brandon Ludlow. We were just playing OtherWorld all afternoon, and then he was going to drive over to the fireworks with you. But Brandon was smoking—cigarettes, I mean—and it was kind of driving Noah up the wall, because he's trying to quit."

"Uh-huh?"

"So he found—he went to the bathroom, and I guess he found a box of nicotine patches in there, so he came back to ask Brandon if he could have one. But Brandon was out on the porch talking on the phone, so Noah just went back in and put some on. He said the ones he uses are... I forget what dose, but a higher dose than it said on the box he found, so he put three of them on. And, uh..."

He looked over at the cop, who was leaning against the doorjamb watching us talk.

"Evening, Mr. Munroe," the cop said. "I'm Officer Andrews. I responded to the scene along with the ambulance and another patrol car. We're awaiting forensics, but at this point our understanding is that what your son found in that box was fentanyl patches."

"Patches? Of an illegal drug?"

"They're legal for pain relief," the cop said. "With a legitimate prescription."

I'd seen so many cases involving fentanyl overdoses in my time as a prosecutor, so much heroin and cocaine cut with the stuff, that I'd forgotten it even came in a legal form.

Jackson said, "Noah started getting real sleepy. Brandon was just, like, whatever, but I know Noah—I could tell something was wrong. He fell asleep on the couch, but his breathing sounded weird, like he was wheezing. I got in almost an argument with Brandon because I was trying to figure out what was going on and he just wanted to keep playing the game. I was, like, thinking out loud, trying to remember everything Noah had done that day, and when I mentioned the nicotine patches, Brandon freaked out and said that was where he kept his stash of fentanyl."

The cop said, "You the one who called 9-1-1?"

Jackson nodded. "I wish I'd called them faster. I got some paper towels first and tried to pull the patches off his arm without, like, getting any of it on my hands."

Terri said, "You did good."

To the nurse, I said, "Wait, so... you said he's not—that's not sedation? You don't have him on anything?" My brain felt like it was wrapped in gauze; I knew she'd told me this not five minutes ago, but nothing was processing. Noah was completely limp. He hadn't moved so much as an eyelid since we'd arrived. "Is that—is he in a coma?"

"At this point, we can't say. There's some evaluations that would need to be done, but that's more a question for his doctor."

"But how's his brain?"

"Um, that's... Our immediate concern was the airway. The first responders administered naloxone on the scene, and it was effective, but it wears off pretty quick. So the priority was keeping him breathing. Since there wasn't any indication of traumatic injury—I mean no car crash or anything like that—the doctor didn't feel a CT scan was indicated."

"But should we do one anyway, to check on his brain activity?"

"Oh, I see. No, for that the doctor would need to order an EEG. That would have to wait until tomorrow, since we don't have any neurologists on the night shift."

"You don't?"

"No, sir. We're a smaller hospital, so—maybe up in Charleston or Columbia they could do that tonight, if it was indicated, but here, that kind of non-emergent testing would be done tomorrow."

———

The next few hours were a blur. The ventilator hissed like a tractor trailer, with a metallic click at the end of each breath. Monitors beeped. Terri asked Jackson if he'd called his mom, and if he was safe to drive home, if he'd drunk anything or taken any drugs. When she was satisfied he could drive, she thanked him again and told him to go get some sleep.

The nurse came in and out. A patient was rushed past on a stretcher. A doctor signaled from the desk that he'd be with me in a second, but when I looked again, he was gone.

I sat in the chair, reaching under the bed railing so I could keep holding my kid's hand. I woke up falling over, stopped the fall, tried to stay awake. Terri came around the bed and made me scoot my chair to where I could lean against the side of Noah's mattress without letting go of his hand. She found a pillow in a cabinet and wedged it between me and the bed.

The next time I woke up, my head was on the pillow. A white sheet was draped across me that she must've put there.

The next time, it seemed like dawn. Terri was asleep on her chair in the corner, leaning against the wall.

I drifted off again but woke when someone started shaking me. It was the bed shaking, I realized, and then I saw Noah's arm flailing and slamming against the railing—as much as it could in the restraints. I stood up and grabbed his hand. I thought he might be having a seizure.

Terri had his other hand. She was smiling at me from across the bed. "He's fighting the vent!" she said. "He's coming around!"

I looked at his face. His eyes were squeezed tight shut, and then he opened them. He looked at me in a panic and made as much noise as he could, a muffled yell.

I put a hand on his forehead and said, "It's okay. You're okay. You're in the hospital, but you're okay."

Terri went to the door and called out, "Bethany? Nurse Bethany? He's coming around!"

26

JULY 9, 2021

Noah had come home three days later, exhausted but, thankfully, with no brain damage or other permanent injury. He set up camp on the sofa, sleeping and watching TV, and I worked from home. At lunch on the second day, eating cold pizza, he told me sheepishly that he'd been trying to help with Maria's case. "I figured Brandon was there when his mom died," he said. "I thought he might know stuff, and if I got him to trust me, he might tell me."

"Oh, God." I stared at him. "Noah, please don't ever do that. I'm sorry if I made you feel like you ought to. I would never expect that of you."

"It's not your fault. I wanted to do it."

There was something meaningful, probably, in the fact that his friend Jackson, who I'd defended against trumped-up murder charges a couple of years ago, had been the one to pull the patches off Noah's arm and call 9-1-1. I'd been glad anyway that Jackson wasn't serving a sentence for a crime he hadn't committed, but I couldn't deny I was even more glad he'd been there to save Noah's life.

We caught up on the local news. Ludlow's star was on the rise with another indignant speech about Terri and me, and his ability to protect his sons from the consequences of their actions was undiminished: despite the fentanyl, Brandon Ludlow hadn't been arrested. Meanwhile, Tucker had sent his own star into the scripted freefall that Cardozo had advised, with a humiliating press conference where his wife stood by as he confessed his adultery.

I wondered if anyone but him, me, and Ludlow realized what that meant. As far as I knew, Tucker was now a free agent, with nothing left that Ludlow could threaten him with. I wondered whether he'd challenge Ludlow for the solicitor position after all; he had six or seven months to polish his reputation back up before the primaries began.

On Friday morning, Terri and I were in my home office, drinking take-out coffee she'd brought and eating cheese and crackers from the food basket Roy had sent. A fruit basket from the Ruiz family, minus the banana I'd just eaten, was perched on top of a stack of legal pads.

I looked up from my computer screen, where I was working on my opening statement for Clay's trial, and looked at Terri. She was at her laptop, finding out everything she could about the two police officers at the scene of the boat crash, probably up to and including their conception dates and grandmothers' maiden names.

It felt right to see her there. And it had started to feel strange, I noticed, when she wasn't around.

My phone rang. It was Victor Guerrero.

"Morning, Victor," I said. Terri looked over, her brows raised.

After his sympathies about what I'd been through with Noah—apparently the entire town knew about it—and a few seconds' chitchat, he said, "Hey, so, I was going to drive up by Columbia, but I thought I should check with you first. I got a call out of the blue from Angelo Cruz."

"Angelo? Really?"

Terri, wide-eyed, pointed at my phone and mouthed the word "speaker." I pointed past her, toward the office door; she shut it.

I set my beat-up old Nokia on my desk and hit the speaker button.

"When was this?" I asked.

"Last night. After dinner. It was a blocked number, but my cell is my work phone: I always answer. And of all the damn people, it was Angelo Cruz. Said he'd called the office, got my number that way."

"I'm assuming he didn't say where he was?"

"Oh, no. I didn't even think to ask, because he went right into—he said he'd seen in the news that my mom filed for a new trial. And he said he always felt bad about that, and he knew somebody who could help."

"Who's that?"

"That's the thing. I should've called you last night, but I wanted to sleep on it. He said there was this neighbor, who I don't remember at all, called Dunk McDonough. He said the guy was in prison now but would see me if I went. And this morning I googled the guy and realized, you know, it's the guy who ran the truck stop until the feds shut him down, and he's in prison for some bad stuff. *Real* bad stuff."

"Yeah, he sure is. So… are you asking me for advice? Or seeking my blessing for you to head up there, or—"

"Advice, I guess. Like, do you think he really might know something?"

"Well, he was a neighbor, that much is true. He lived across the street from the Ludlows." I looked at Terri. She nodded, so I said, "His wife was friends with Mrs. Ludlow. And apparently, Angelo did landscaping work for him."

"Oh my God. So he might really know something? Then, you know what, I got to go. If he could help my mom get home… What do I have to lose, right? It's not like he's asking me to come meet him in a dark alley someplace. Yeah, I'll call the prison, and if I can see him today, I'm going up."

Terri had written me a message in all caps on a legal pad: YOU GO? I STAY WITH NOAH?

"You know what, Victor, I have a thought. Would you mind if I came with you?"

———

We drove northeast in Victor's Subaru, which was full of dog hair and had a lawn mower rattling in the back. Since his mom's prison was about an hour closer to us and we expected to be near her a little before lunchtime, we decided to pay her a quick visit en route and grab sandwiches after that. I brought my laptop and read through some of my files to get ready for our talk with Dunk.

We were passing tobacco fields under a clear blue sky, listening to some music Victor liked, when I noticed the notes Laura had typed up from Maureen's PDF. I'd been too busy preparing for Clay's trial to get around to reading them.

The sixty-plus handwritten pages had become thirty-two typewritten ones. A lot of it was redundant, but some went into useful detail on issues that mattered. Maureen didn't say one word about Dunk, and her notes of prison visits showed that it had taken her four visits before Maria even mentioned Angelo.

I had a moment of feeling superior about that—it always felt good to find out you'd gotten to the heart of the matter faster or more effectively than someone else—but then that feeling shriveled up and died.

According to Maureen's notes, Maria had told her that when she worked for the Ludlows, she'd been dating Angelo. They'd broken up, she said, "for other reasons, but also partly because of Peggy."

Since I was in the passenger seat of her son's car, I couldn't shout and swear like I wanted to. And I couldn't call Terri to discuss this bombshell.

My client, for whom I was seeking a new trial on the grounds that there was no evidence of her alleged jewelry-heist motive for murder, turned out to have a different motive that I hadn't known about. And a much stronger one: I was well aware that in the history of criminal law, far more people had been murdered over jealousy than over jewelry.

Victor, switching lanes to pass a tractor, asked, "So, how're things coming in my mom's case? We just waiting on the court to make a decision about that petition you filed?"

I said, "Yep, just waiting."

———

At the women's prison, Victor and Maria had a happy reunion. Since I was her lawyer, and I fudged a little by saying Victor was there as my Spanish interpreter, I was able to get us the private room. I did not want to discuss what I had to discuss in public.

I stood there watching them hug and chatter away in Spanish as Maria wiped tears of happiness from her cheeks.

We only had about fifteen minutes to visit her if we wanted to see Dunk that day, so at the ten-minute mark, I said, "You know what, Victor, I actually have something I want to discuss with your mom—"

"Oh, you need me to go out? So it can stay secret? Yeah, I seen that on TV."

They had a final hug, and he stepped into the hall.

I sat at the table, and Maria sat down across from me. Her face was still glowing from the pleasure of seeing her son.

"Okay, Maria, since we're short on time, I have to get straight to the point. So tell me this: Back when you worked for the Ludlows, did you have a romantic relationship with Angelo Cruz?"

A storm cloud passed over her face.

"Can I take that as a yes?"

She nodded.

"Okay. Why didn't you tell me that before?"

She huffed. "Because I knew what you would think! You wouldn't believe me. You wouldn't fight hard enough. Like that other lady, Maureen."

"Well, look, be that as it may… Actually, how did that not come up at your first trial?"

"We were…" She shrugged. "Secret, you know? I have five kids. I wasn't going to tell them, hey, I am doing this with this man. So I wasn't going to let anyone see."

"Did Peggy Ludlow know?"

"Oh, no." She shook her head with certainty. "I don't think she even saw me that way, as a woman. She was so beautiful, and to her, I was just this… maybe a little bit fat, Mexican mother. To her, I was nothing. And we were careful, Angelo and me. We both worked for them. We didn't want them knowing anything."

"And did he cheat on you with Peggy?"

Another shrug. "Of course. A woman like that offers herself, what do you think?"

"Were you jealous of her?"

She looked me square in the eyes. "Mr. Munroe, everything about her, I was jealous of. She's rich, I am poor. She doesn't work, I have to work hard. She is beautiful, I am not. Everything, okay? But what can I do about how God made my life? If she's dead, am I rich and beautiful now? No, I just don't have a job. And I had children to feed. I think it was an accident, if you want my opinion. But all I can say for sure is that it wasn't me."

I took that in. It was time to go. If we needed to talk more about it, that would have to wait.

The last thing I said before leaving was, "You knew that Angelo was visiting your kids for a few years after you went to prison, right?"

"Yeah. He felt bad. He helped out. He was a better man than I thought."

———

The high-security men's prison was much larger and more imposing than the one Maria was in. The security check deprived me of my phone and my laptop; I was a lawyer, but not Dunk's lawyer, so there were no special privileges. The slamming of metal doors echoed off the cinder blocks and tiles of hallway after hallway, and finally we were there.

We got a stall in the general visiting room, with two phone receivers hanging on either side of a bulletproof window. The place was noisy as hell.

Dunk, sporting an orange jumpsuit and a crew cut, shouldered his way into his side of the stall. Before prison, he'd reminded me of an angry bull. Now he'd hit buffalo proportions. I figured he must be spending a lot of time in the weight room.

The chair disappeared behind him as he sat down. He stared at me with his arms crossed over his chest. It occurred to me that I hadn't asked Victor whether he'd told the prison that both of us were coming.

We all picked up our phones.

Dunk said, in a tone like a cold blade, "Hey, Mr. *Law*-yer. Ain't you sitting high on the hog now."

I wasn't necessarily expecting an apology for what he'd done to me and my son, but that was still bracing. "If the two of you would rather talk alone," I said, "I can step away."

"You step your ass right where it is. It might actually be a good thing that you came."

I could all but see gears turning in his eyes, calculating my utility.

Victor said, "Uh, Mr. McDonough, I'm sorry I wasn't able to check with you beforehand if it was okay to bring him. I just thought, since he's my mother's lawyer, he'd need to know whatever it is that you wanted to share with me."

"Share ain't the word," Dunk said. "Nothing's free."

"Oh. Okay, yeah, of course. Well, I've worked all my life to try to bring my mom home, so I'm prepared to do what I've got to do."

As long as it's legal, I thought, although I wasn't about to make that unwelcome contribution to the conversation.

"First I'll tell you what I got," Dunk said. "That way, you'll understand the price."

Victor said, "Okay."

"So, back when your mom got arrested, my wife and I lived across the street. Not my part of town, but Ludlow lived there, and I'd been told to keep an eye on him."

"Oh yeah?" Victor asked, sounding puzzled. "By whom?"

I wanted to kick him under the table, but I didn't have to. Dunk said, "You think this is a fucking interview?"

"Oh. No. Sorry."

"The point was to get dirt. Of any kind. So when the Ludlows were doing some remodeling, I had an associate on the team who did a little extra work on the house. A few cameras installed here and there, wired to boxes outside where my other associate could come get the tapes and change them out for new ones."

Victor said, "Okay, wow."

"Mr. Lawyer," Dunk said, staring at me, "you got a look on your face like you might know what I'm talking about."

My neutral expression had apparently failed. I nodded.

"Well, good."

"Is that true?" Victor said. "You didn't tell me that."

"I'm sorry, but I'm not allowed to tell you everything. Your mom's the client."

I didn't mention that I hadn't told her either. That conversation, I figured, would have to be had.

Dunk said, "Mr. Lawyer knows every rule in the goddamn book."

I ignored that. I said, "Are you telling us you've got tapes?"

"I've got *the* tape. And it's only been played once. Back then, before the trial, to Ludlow."

"Ludlow knows you taped him?"

"If I don't tell him what I got, what's the point?"

Beside me, Victor seemed confused, but he didn't dare ask this crew-cut minotaur for clarification.

I wasn't confused. I knew what Dunk had been convicted of, as well as a lot more that hadn't come out at his trial. Victor didn't. He was trying to do algebra, but all I had to do was put two and two together.

That equation told me that Dunk had been tasked with gathering any dirt available so that Ludlow could be blackmailed. He'd followed those instructions, and he had succeeded. In the decades since Peggy's death, Ludlow had been, essentially, turning tricks for his black-mailers—the cartel Dunk was involved with, I assumed. Whoever owned that video owned Ludlow.

That explained a lot about how the solicitor had handled certain cases.

"What does the video show?" I asked.

"Depends how much of it you watch."

We stared at each other for a second. Apparently, Dunk wanted me to beg a little.

"Which part did you show Ludlow?"

"The short version. Without sound. Which looks real bad for him."

"What does the long version show?"

"Oh, his wife having one of her breakdowns. She had a lot of those. This time she got out her revolver and was going to end it all. Ludlow came in, they argued, he tried to take the gun from her, it went off. You know the drill."

"Can you see on the video," I said, "that Maria didn't come in until after that?"

"You see everything. After the shooting, Ludlow hears something and disappears into the bathroom, Maria comes in, and a minute later Ludlow comes back in through the main door. It's all there."

Victor and I sat there, letting it sink in.

I said, "She had a bad interpreter. I mean the guy translating the Spanish. You know anything about that?"

"Dominican guy? Yeah. I told Ludlow I could arrange that, and he grabbed on to it like a goddamn life raft."

If Dunk really did still have that video, it was a silver bullet. Proof of Maria's innocence—and of Ludlow's corruption. Even without any evidence of the blackmail, without Dunk testifying that he'd provided the interpreter, without any need to show that Ludlow had spent twenty years putting his thumb on the scales in favor of Dunk's cartel, the video would show that he'd framed a woman he knew was innocent. That was a crime.

If we got our hands on this thing, I could set Maria free and take Ludlow down for good.

Victor cleared his throat and asked, "How much?"

27

JULY 12, 2021

My phone rang at a few minutes past seven on the morning of Clay's first day of trial. It was Fletcher. I was sitting in my office. I took a sip of coffee and picked up.

"Morning, Leland. Bryce Fletcher here. This a good time?"

"As good as any. How're you doing?"

"Fine. I've got a final offer for you, if your client wants to get some control over this instead of rolling the dice at trial."

"Okay. What're you thinking?"

"If he'll plead on the felony reckless homicide by boat, we'll drop the other charges, including the BUI, and we'll recommend a sentence of one year plus a $5,000 fine. And loss of his boating license for five years."

"Hmm. Just recommend?"

"Just recommend. If he hadn't been drunk, I could see my way to a firm deal. But I can't get past the fact that he drank and then chose to drive, and neither can the boy's parents."

I knew Clay had done that much. The only dispute was which drunk boy was at the wheel when they crashed.

And if the jury convicted him of felony boating under the influence, one year was the absolute minimum sentence. The max was twenty-five years. And the fine could be twenty grand.

If Clay had been guilty, if he'd caused the crash, that offer would be generous as hell.

I said, "Well, I can tell you, the fine is not what matters to him."

"You don't have to tell me that. I know what his daddy does for a living. But I cannot go below the felony. I cannot look that dead boy's parents in the eye and tell them I went below that."

"Can you tell them you want to send Clay to prison even though it was Jimmy Ludlow at the wheel?"

"I'm not playing this game, Leland. Let me know before opening statements what your client wants to do. After that, this deal is off the table."

"I will. Oh, one question: if he took the plea, would you let him serve his sentence under house arrest, with an ankle monitor?"

"You mean, would I let him sit in his bedroom for a year, eating pancakes and playing video games? No."

We hung up.

I called Clay. It went to voice mail. I spelled out Fletcher's terms.

"I'd rather have told you in person," I said, "but I wanted you to be able to think about this, and discuss it with your folks if you want, as soon as possible. Give me a call, or we can talk about it at the courthouse."

———

Terri arrived at seven thirty, suited up for court and carrying a paper bag that smelled delicious.

"Oh, thank you," I said. "Let me get you some coffee. Noah will be up in a minute."

He was coming to court with us, as a spectator. Courts were allowing that again, he was curious about the case, and having him there would keep me from worrying about him.

I handed her a cup of coffee, and we headed to my office. "Did you send those photos to Tucker?" she asked.

"Not until last night, but yeah. Thanks."

While I'd been up visiting Dunk, she'd been putting together a very short list of Basking Rock police officers that she thought might fit the bill for being the guy who collared the paramours.

I shut the office door behind us and said, "You know, Victor called me six times over the weekend. I told him I have to focus on this trial and Dunk's not going anywhere, but he wants this so much... I bet if he thought he could get away with it, he'd take a helicopter up to that prison and fly his mama out. Buying exonerating evidence from a felon must seem like a no-brainer."

"Wait. You explained the problem to him, right?"

"I explained *all* the problems. I don't think he even cares if it's illegal —he didn't say that, it's just my impression."

"So what'd you tell him?" She produced some napkins and pulled still-warm ham-and-cheese croissants out of the bag.

"I focused on the point that you can't trust a mobster who's serving life for murder."

"Which is kind of a big point!"

"Right? I mean, I pretty much believe that Dunk saw what he described. We saw the camera setup ourselves, so it seems likely he had that tape. But that was twenty years ago, and he was doing the surveillance for somebody else, not on his own account. So what are the chances he's still got the tape, and that it's still usable? I said all that, but Victor didn't want to hear it. He just wants his mama home."

I took a bite of my croissant. When I glanced up, Terri had her head cocked like she saw right through me. She took a sip of her coffee and set the mug down. "You want it just as bad, don't you," she said. "I bet if you owned this house, you'd sell it to get your hands on that tape."

I laughed. "Look, I'm trying to stay focused on the fact that we can't trust Dunk. Because if I thought he'd really give it to me, I'd... If there was a way to get it without going to prison myself, I'd cash out my retirement, sell everything down to the clothes on my back, and show up at court in my boxer shorts."

———

By the time we got to the courthouse, Clay and his dad had called me twice to discuss the plea offer. Trial wasn't starting yet; I told them it would take at least the whole morning to get through jury selection. They decided to go for a drive and talk about the offer as a family.

Chambliss liked to handle voir dire himself, so the only thing counsel could do was tell him which jurors we wanted to exclude. I preferred judges who let attorneys do the voir dire, and I was sure Fletcher did, too, but we didn't get the choice. Instead of facing the pool of our fellow citizens, looking from one person to the next and putting the exact inflection I wanted on a question so I could gauge their response, I sat there while Chambliss recited our written questions robotically. Terri and I did our best to get a read on the good citizens who'd been summoned for the chance to decide Clay's fate, but on that point, my only comfort was that Fletcher was having just as hard a time.

Actually, Fletcher probably had it harder. Terri had psychological X-ray vision—and, unlike Fletcher, who'd parachuted in from a halfway across the state, she had a mental catalog of the personalities and histories of a startling number of folks in our town.

When lunch rolled around, jury selection wasn't quite done. I told Clay to meet me in the war room for an attorney-client-privileged talk while his dad, Terri, and Noah went out to grab us all lunch.

On the way to the men's room, I felt my Nokia vibrate. I pulled it out and saw a text from Tucker: *#2 is the guy.*

I laughed. The second cop on the list I'd forwarded him from Terri was Detective John Blount. I'd had dealings with him before, and his involvement made things interesting.

I'd long since given up trying to type texts on my flip phone, so I called her. "Terri! Got a message from Mr. P. He says your number two is it."

"Does he? Oh, hot damn, hot damn!"

"You sound like I just managed to score us Prince tickets. To see him resurrected for one last show."

She laughed. "If only. But listen, if you don't need me for trial prep tonight, let me work on that a little bit."

"Sure."

———

When I got to the war room, Clay was in there by himself. The suit and tie I'd told him to wear made him look even younger than he was.

In a small voice he said, "If I... If we... When a person loses, what happens next? How long do you have before they take you to jail?"

"They take you then and there. From the courtroom."

That hit him hard. After a second, he asked, "Right in front of my mom?"

"Yeah. Clay, what'd you talk about with your folks? Do you want to take the plea?"

"I don't want any of this. But if I have to be in jail, a year isn't nearly as bad as five or ten or twenty-five."

"Okay. Would you like me to go talk to Fletcher?" I didn't like the idea of this boy going to prison, even for a year—but it was his life on the line. He had the right to make the decision.

"No! I... Mr. Munroe, do you think you can win?"

"If I didn't think I could, I would've strongly advised you to take a plea a long time ago. Because, yeah, ten years is a lot worse than one or two. But Fletcher's still not offering a negotiated deal, so pleading guilty wouldn't guarantee you'd only get the one year. You probably would, or something close to it, but it's not certain."

He took a long while to answer, but then he said, "He really thinks I killed Hayden, doesn't he?"

"Yeah, I think he does."

"But I didn't," he said to the wall in front of him, or to himself. Then he looked at me and said, "So let's prove him wrong. Or at least let's go down fighting. I've got no other choice."

———

Fletcher faced the jury and began: "What happened on the night of March 7, 2020, was every parent's nightmare," he said. "It was a Saturday. Four friends, all sophomores at USC up in Columbia, were home here in Basking Rock for spring break. Three of them told their parents they were going to a friend's house for a cookout, and that's what they did. But after that, they thought they'd have a little more fun. One of them used her fake ID to buy alcohol. One of them borrowed his daddy's boat. They went out on the water, and they all got drunk. And one of those four kids never came home."

He heaved a sigh and walked toward the jury box, shaking his head.

"Now, which of y'all doesn't know that it's dangerous to drink and drive? We all know that."

The jurors nodded.

"And I know from what y'all said this morning, in voir dire, that y'all are like me: we're all from right here in the Lowcountry. And down here, we know our boats. Now, do any of y'all think it's okay to get drunk and then drive a boat?" As the jurors shook their heads, he agreed: "No, we don't. We know that's dangerous. We know that it can get folks killed. That's why it's against the law."

He started pacing along the jury box. "Now, this is not a murder case. The defendant, who you see there"—a gesture to where Clay sat stiffly next to me—"didn't mean to kill anybody. He didn't lie in wait. I'll be the first to tell you, he did not have the state of mind that we call malice aforethought." He stopped pacing, for emphasis. "But the State of South Carolina does not have to prove that he did. Because we're not charging him with murder. We're only charging him with what he did: He decided to get drunk, even though he was underage. He decided to drive a boat, even though he was drunk. And because of those decisions, in the wee hours of the morning on March 8 of last year, he plowed into a concrete piling on the Sea Island Bridge, and Hayden Parker died."

His assistant hit a button, and Hayden's face appeared on a sixty-five-inch monitor facing the jury. The photo looked to be from his senior prom. He was wearing a tux, smiling radiantly, and had his arm around a beautiful girl.

Fletcher went on in that vein for half an hour, and then it was my turn.

A trial is two competing stories. And since the prosecution goes first, telling my own compelling story wouldn't be enough. I also had to convince the jury that the first storyteller got it wrong.

"Ladies and gentlemen of the jury," I began, "as Mr. Fletcher said, we're here because of a tragedy. We're here because a young man lost his life, and his family lost their son."

I stood in front of the jury box. A forty-something Black woman, a grandmotherly white lady, a younger guy who looked vaguely familiar—it was a small town. I knew most of them were parents. That would make their hearts hurt for Hayden's family, but I thought they'd also recognize their sons in Clay.

"These kids from Basking Rock, four young people with everything to live for, got together on a Saturday night for a cookout and some beers, and a boat ride under the stars. A Saturday night like most all of us have had at least a few times in our lives."

Terri clicked, and a photo of all four teens appeared on the monitor. I pointed them out. "That's Hayden Parker, the boy who lost his life. That's Emma Twain, and Jimmy Ludlow, the son of the circuit solicitor. And that's Clay Carlson, with the fishing rod."

I paused so we all could look at them.

"Four young kids. All of them good students up at USC, looking forward to bright futures. And on that night, they decided to get some beer. All four of them were underage, but one of them, Emma there, had a fake ID. So off they went to the grocery store, and then they drank that beer. They shouldn't have, since they were all a little over a year shy of the legal drinking age. They shouldn't have, but as any parent knows, kids sometimes do things they shouldn't do."

I sighed and looked at the floor.

"Even good kids," I said, looking at the jurors again. "Even real good kids. Because not *one* of us gets through this world without making any mistakes. Not one of us is without sin."

A few of the jurors nodded. We had veered, for a moment, almost into revival-meeting territory—I was preaching, and I felt them respond— so I said, "And the wages of sin… is death."

"*Mm.*" One juror agreed so strongly that, in that instant, she'd had to make it heard.

My voir dire questions had included one prompted by Terri, on church attendance. Six of these twelve jurors went every Sunday. I needed only one of them on my side to prevent a guilty verdict.

I decided to speak my truth, in their language.

Pointing up at the picture, I said, "All four of those children made their mamas proud. All four of them just wanted to get together with their friends and enjoy themselves one Saturday night. But they were walking through the valley of the shadow of death. They didn't know it, and they didn't mean for it to happen, but that night one of them was going to the Lord. Hayden Parker left us that night. He slipped into the black waters of St. Helena Sound, and he left us. And not one of his three surviving friends will ever be the same. Not Emma, not Jimmy, and not Clay Carlson here."

I pointed to Clay. The jurors turned and saw him looking like a child in his daddy's suit, with the stark, sad, humbled expression on his face that I'd expected my words would produce. The kid had a heart, and I knew they'd see it if I could bring it out.

"Now, Mr. Fletcher has told you he doesn't have to prove malice aforethought, and that's true. This is not a murder case. What took Hayden Parker from us was an accident. A mistake. And most mistakes are not crimes."

"Objection." Fletcher stood.

Objecting during an opening statement was highly unusual. Chambliss said, "State the grounds?"

"Misstates the law."

Fletcher, I figured, had sensed that I was connecting with the jury, and he'd objected just to interrupt that flow.

I said, "Which law did I misstate?"

After a second of silence, Chambliss said, "Overruled."

"Ladies and gentlemen," I said, "I apologize. As I was saying, we all make mistakes, and most mistakes are not crimes. And Clay Carlson, sitting here today as a survivor of that terrible accident, is presumed innocent of any crime. Because that is the American way. That's how our justice system works. He is presumed innocent."

I turned to appraise Mr. Fletcher, sitting in his chair at the prosecution table.

"And Mr. Fletcher over there," I said, turning back to the jury, "has to meet a very high standard before you can set that presumption of innocence aside. He has to prove to you, beyond *any* reasonable doubt, that alone among those four kids, Clay here bears the blame for Hayden's death. He's got to prove that Clay did something uniquely heinous. That out of those four kids, all drinking beer when they were underage, all going out on a boat at night—that Clay, alone among them, is *criminally* responsible for Hayden's death and deserves to be cast down."

I let that reverberate.

"And he's got to prove to you every element of that, beyond *any* reasonable doubt."

I looked from one juror to the next. The revival feeling was still there. My notes for this opening statement went into detail about the charges Clay was facing and what Fletcher had to prove for a guilty verdict on each one, but I didn't think this jury needed that. We could get there when I closed. For now, I needed to hit the final chord and leave them in the mood they were in.

"Ladies and gentlemen of the jury, I've seen the evidence that you're about to see, and the proof is just not there. By the time this trial is over, I believe you'll agree that Clay Carlson is no worse a sinner than the other three kids who went out that night. He's no worse than my son, or yours, or any of the rest of us sinners. And in our system of justice, that means he is not guilty."

28

JULY 13, 2021

At 6 a.m. on the second day of trial, I would not normally be having a heated argument about an unrelated case, but while I was shaving, Victor called.

In the mirror, I watched myself drag the razor across my face while saying, "Dammit, Victor, it's not money laundering all by itself, but that's where it's going. And once you go into business with a mobster, once you sink your own money into something of his—"

I rinsed the razor and brought it back to my cheek.

"—you can't just change your mind and back out. They don't take that too well."

I nicked myself and swore.

"But Leland, I've been waiting my whole life for this! Absolute proof my mom is innocent!"

"You think she'd be happy to get home and then watch *you* get carted off to jail? You've got to be patient. The court's looking at our petition probably as we speak."

In reality, our petition was most likely at the bottom of a very tall stack, but I had to talk him off the ledge. He was up there because some associate of Dunk's had used a self-destructing message app to send us both a three-second clip of the video. We'd seen the Holy Grail, and then we'd seen it disappear.

———

In court, Fletcher surprised us by calling Emma to the stand. The previous day had ended with the usual fairly dull testimony that cases like this started with: the investigating officer, in this case the DNR guy. I'd scored some hits about the lost evidence and the fact that he'd never investigated any type of homicide before. This morning, I'd expected to challenge the sheriff's deputy who'd done Clay's breathalyzer test. Casting doubt on the accuracy of the testing equipment was standard fare for a DUI case, and when the crash occurred, his equipment had been a month overdue for its annual calibration. If the State couldn't prove Clay was legally drunk, the most serious charge against him would go away.

I requested a sidebar.

We both approached the bench, along with the court reporter, and Chambliss's clerk turned on the white noise machine so the jury wouldn't hear us.

"Your Honor," I said, "we agreed to today's order of witnesses yesterday afternoon. I prepared for those witnesses, not Miss Twain. I'd like to know what's going on here."

"Unfortunately," Fletcher said, "Deputy McDonald's had a family emergency. I didn't want to waste the court's and the jury's time by asking for a continuance until he can get here."

Chambliss looked at the witness list. "What about Mr. Tucker? He was after McDonald."

"Your Honor, candidly, I may need a subpoena for him. I've had some trouble confirming his continued participation."

That was good news, though not entirely unexpected. It made sense that Tucker wouldn't agree to testify anymore, now that the sword Ludlow had been holding over his head was gone.

"Well, how long do you think it'd take to try to get him in here?"

"I don't know, Your Honor. But I'm happy to proceed with Ms. Twain."

Chambliss told me he'd grant a recess after Emma's direct if I felt I needed more time to prepare her cross. That wasn't ideal, of course, as it left the version of the story Fletcher had elicited in the jury's minds longer. But we'd probably be coming up on lunchtime by the time he was done with direct anyhow, and the difference between one hour and two wasn't likely to make much of a difference. As I walked back to my seat, I spotted Noah in the back corner of the courtroom, now with company: Isabela Ruiz. I also noticed Shannon Pennington, no doubt gathering material for her podcast.

As Fletcher called Emma to the stand, I sent a quick text to Tucker: *Pls text me or Terri ASAP.*

Emma was wearing a blue-gray dress, businesslike but feminine, dark enough to contrast with her long blonde hair. She wore hardly any makeup, so she looked even younger than she was—like what I'd called her in my opening: a good kid. A good, heartbreakingly beautiful kid.

Fletcher led her through an introduction that probably made every juror wish they could have such a wonderful daughter. Although she was a little shy about her accomplishments, he made it clear she was a good student, dedicated to a health-care career so that she could help people. She came across as a genuinely nice person, and when she talked about losing Hayden, she apologized because she kept crying.

Fletcher brought her a box of Kleenex. She cleaned herself up, and he walked her through the story of their relationship, the plans they'd had, and how those plans had been cut short.

Then he said, "Now, I am so sorry to do this, Miss Twain, but we have got to talk about that night."

"I know. I've got to do it. For *him*."

"Okay. Now, before y'all went out on the boat, where were you?"

"At Jimmy Ludlow's house."

"And did you observe anybody drinking there?"

"Yes. There was a bottle of wine, and I saw all three of the guys have some."

"When you say all three—"

"Clay, Hayden, and Jimmy."

"And where had that wine come from?"

"I don't know."

"Did you have any?"

"I didn't. I don't really like red wine."

"And can you tell me about the boat ride? Where'd you leave from?"

"Jimmy Ludlow's dock."

"Do you recall about what time?"

"It was a while after midnight. I remember it being midnight when we were all still at the house."

"And at that point, when you first left, who was piloting the boat?"

"Jimmy was. It was his dad's boat, so he got the key and we went."

"And did that change at some point?"

"Yeah, when we got out of sight of his house, we started taking turns. One person would drive while the rest of us just, you know, hung out and talked and drank beer."

"And did you drive?"

"Just for, like, a minute. With Hayden showing me. The guys all had their boating licenses, but I didn't. I still don't. I haven't been out on a boat since. I just can't."

"That's understandable. So, while y'all were out on the boat, was it friendly the whole time? No arguments?"

"No. I mean, at first it was. We were having fun. But when we got out on the sound, I got a little scared because you could hardly see any lights on shore, and Hayden was getting sick."

"Sick in what way?"

"Well, he'd drunk some beer, so there was that. But also, I think he was a little seasick. It's disorienting to be driving around in circles at night trying to figure out where you are, especially on such a small boat, where you really feel the waves. So he wasn't feeling well at all, and I was saying to the others that we needed to get back to shore."

"The others being who?"

"Jimmy and Clay."

"And what was their response?"

"They started arguing."

"Do you recall about what?"

"Oh, things like... which way to go, where to try to land. I don't recall the specifics, because Hayden was just not well, and I was mostly trying to help him out."

"And do you recall how the boat came to be near the Sea Island Bridge?"

"Yes, sir. We saw the lights on the bridge, so we knew where we were, and I remember Jimmy saying that from there, he knew how to get us back to his house. So he started taking us toward it."

"And where was Clay Carlson at that time?"

"He was driving. Jimmy had come over to help me get Hayden over to the side to where he could... I'm sorry, sir, but to where he could throw up."

"And did he stay with you?"

"He didn't. He went back to drive, but Clay kept arguing with him. It was Jimmy's boat, or his dad's, but Clay was insisting he ought to drive it."

"And did there come a point where you realized the boat was in danger?"

"Yes, sir. We were pretty close to shore—I remember seeing through one of the arches under the bridge to what looked like a little restaurant. And seeing that, I realized how fast we were going. I yelled that we ought to land there..."

"Who'd you yell that to?"

"Whoever was driving. I was looking at the shore. And I thought—I was so relieved—"

Her voice broke.

"I thought we were safe. Because we were so close to shore. But we kept going, and—" She covered her face with her hand. "They didn't listen to me. I looked at them to yell again, and Clay was at the wheel. I yelled at him to land, and that's the last thing I remember before—before—it just exploded, and I was in the water."

She started crying.

Fletcher gave her a moment to collect herself. Then he said, "Miss Twain, could you repeat for the jury who was at the wheel of the boat just before it crashed?"

"Clay Carlson."

"And do you see him in this courtroom?"

"He's right there." She pointed.

"And how do you know it was him?"

"Sir, I've known him since the ninth grade. I know who I was looking at."

———

We broke for lunch, and Clay, Terri, and I went to the war room. As soon as we shut the door, Clay fell apart. He asked me if the plea offer was still on the table and begged me to go talk to Fletcher when I said it wasn't.

Terri touched his shoulder. "Clay," she said gently, "this is normal. This is how trials are. It's a roller coaster. You have to hold on."

He nodded. His dad came in, and they decided to go for a walk to try to calm down.

As soon as they left, Terri said, "I talked to Blount last night."

"Yeah? Any revelations?"

"Nothing that directly helps Clay. But I asked him about working for Ludlow to get dirt on Tucker, in a tone of voice like I knew more than I was letting on, and from his reaction it's clear that's exactly what he was doing."

"Did you get a read on why he did it? Is he just a Ludlow loyalist?"

"Oh, he's not anybody's loyalist. If the ship he's on starts sinking, he's not going down with it if he has any other options."

"Huh." I pulled my phone out and dialed Tucker's number. "So you think he'd turn, if anybody ever gets around to investigating Ludlow?"

"In a hot second."

I let Tucker's phone ring a dozen times. No answer. "You know where Tucker lives, right?"

She laughed. "Of course. Heck, I know where he went on his honeymoon. That's my job."

I smiled. "So, at sidebar," I said, "something interesting came up. Looks like he's bailed on Fletcher. I guess now that he confessed his sins in that press conference, he's got no more incentive to commit perjury."

"Oh, that's fantastic."

"Well, it would be, if Emma hadn't just about destroyed us."

"Yeah. I didn't want to tell Clay, but sometimes the roller coaster doesn't go back up."

"Exactly. I'm putting the memory expert on to try to cast doubt on Emma's recollection, but that's days away. It's a long time for the jury to marinate in what she said."

"So why do you want Tucker?"

"He's listed as a prosecution witness. And he was supposed to testify today, so if we can get him here, Fletcher ought to call him. I want him to get up there and surprise Fletcher by telling the goddamn *truth*."

Terri looked dubious. "I don't think he actually saw who was driving, from that distance."

"I mean the truth about Ludlow. If my alternate theory for the jury is that Jimmy was the one driving, it sure helps if his daddy was blackmailing a witness to get him to say it was Clay."

"Would he testify to that?"

"He might. What I'd tell him, if he'd answer the phone, is that just by getting up and saying that, he could take Ludlow down. What Ludlow did ought to cost him his bar license, and when you add to it that he was also trying to blackmail his political opponent into getting out of the race, I don't think it's a stretch to say he might face federal corruption charges."

"I'm pretty sure you just described the top two things on Tucker's Christmas list."

I laughed. "If you find him, tell him he can make Christmas come in July. For himself, and in case he cares, for Clay."

Terri pulled her laptop out of her briefcase, handed it to me, and said, "If you need to show the jury any slides this afternoon, the Power-Point's the first file in the Clay folder. And all the photos we had that aren't in the slides are there, too, in a subfolder."

"Thanks."

"I'll go find him," she said, "if I can."

29

JULY 13, 2021

After lunch, I stayed in the war room with Clay and his dad, taking the hour-long recess that Chambliss had offered to prepare for Emma's cross. I was also trying to buy Terri some time. Clay was back in meltdown mode, so scared that I thought he might get sick.

"She's lying!" he wailed. "Why is she doing this? Even if I *had* sent that nude around, I wouldn't deserve to go to jail!"

His dad stared at him. He had apparently not heard about the falling-out Clay and Emma had had over her nude photo.

I said, "Clay, I don't think she's lying—"

"What? Do *you* not believe me now? She is *lying*! You have to get up there and rip her apart!"

"Clay, I'm sitting here because I believe you. I think Emma is simply remembering it wrong. It happens. And because she thinks she's telling the truth, I have to cross her in a much gentler way than I would if she was a liar. Okay? So I need you to know that, and I need you to sit there in the courtroom and stay calm while I do it."

"Come on," his dad said to him. "Leland's got a point. Just hang on, and we'll get there." He gave Clay an encouraging whack on the shoulder.

When the hour was up, there was still no news from Terri. We headed back to the courtroom. Before the jury came back, I explained that my assistant had left due to an emergency, so I was going to be putting the evidence up on the screen myself. Chambliss sympathized.

I set Terri's laptop on my podium. The jury came back, and Emma took the stand again.

"Afternoon, Miss Twain. I want to thank you for coming down here today to tell the jury what you remember."

"Of course. I have to, for Hayden. I owe him that."

"Yes. We all owe him that. Our presence, and our good faith. Now, about that night. You said the four of you left from Jimmy Ludlow's dock, right?"

"Yes, we did."

"And y'all brought three six-packs of beer with you on the boat?"

She looked ashamed. "Yes, we did. I'm so sorry."

"I understand. A lot of mistakes were made that night, and they had the worst possible outcome. If you need a moment—"

"No, I'll be okay."

"All right. Now, I believe you said that before leaving, Hayden, Clay, and Jimmy had drunk some wine? But you hadn't?"

"I hadn't, no."

"Okay. And we agree that after y'all went out on the water, but before the accident, Hayden was sick, and even vomiting, and you were helping him?"

"Yes."

"I believe you said he was vomiting partly because of the wine and beer he'd drunk?"

"I think so, yes."

"You think that's why?"

"Yes."

"Had he drunk a lot of the wine?"

"He—honestly, he had most of it. Clay and Jimmy were more into the beer."

"Okay. And can we agree that out there on the boat, you had no idea that an accident was about to happen?"

"Of course not. It came out of nowhere."

"Uh-huh. And, if you don't mind looking at the screen, does this appear to be the boat, on the day after the accident?"

Everyone looked at the white motorboat with its splintered hull, sitting on a DNR trailer.

After a moment of emotion, she said, "Yes, sir, it does."

"And I believe the record shows, and we can even see part of the name on the side of it there, that it was a nineteen-foot Nautica Sport-craft. Does that sound right?"

"I... I wouldn't know," she said, looking over to Fletcher.

Fletcher said, "Your Honor, the State will stipulate that it was."

Chambliss nodded.

"Thank you," I said. "And, Miss Twain, this next picture is that same model of boat off the manufacturer's website. The boat you were on, like this one, was a five-seater, correct?"

"I guess so, yes."

"One seat for the pilot, facing forward, obviously, and then two pairs of seats, each pair facing off to its respective side?"

She looked at the screen. "Yes, and we were—Hayden and I—we were on that pair of seats there, the one that's, like, farther from the camera."

"So you're saying you two were facing left? Looking off the left side of the boat?"

"Yes."

"And you were talking to him?"

"Yes. About how bad he felt and what he needed me to do."

"And did you happen to have your arm around him at all?"

She thought for a second. "Yeah, I did. To comfort him and kind of help him stay upright, you know?"

"Yes, that makes sense. And you were listening to whatever he was telling you?"

"Yes. And also talking to Jimmy and Clay, though. Because I was telling them he was sick, and we needed to get to shore."

"Uh-huh. And would it be fair to say you didn't get up and leave Hayden and go up to talk to either of them by the driver's seat?"

"I didn't— Oh, you mean— Yeah. I didn't leave Hayden. I talked to them from where I was."

"And that was, like you said, sitting in that left-facing seat?"

"Yes."

"And I believe you said on direct, at some point Jimmy came back to help you with Hayden?"

"Yes."

"Because Hayden was throwing up, and you were trying to help him get to where he could throw up over the side?"

"Yes."

"Uh-huh. He threw up in the boat?"

"Some, yes."

"And I'm sorry for this detail, but did he throw up on you at all?"

She winced. "It was—yes, it was a little bit of a mess."

"Okay. And as you sit here today, under oath, are you absolutely certain that it was Jimmy who came and helped you with Hayden?"

"I mean... yes?"

"You sound—I might be misinterpreting, but you sound a little uncertain there?"

"No, I'm just confused why you're asking me. I already said what happened."

"Meaning, you said what you remember is Jimmy coming to help?"

"Yes. That's what happened."

"Okay. Well, let me just show you something."

I went into Terri's folder of photos and found the two I needed.

"Miss Twain, does this appear to be Jimmy Ludlow on shore shortly after the accident?"

"Yes."

"Okay. And does he appear to be soaking wet, but not visibly injured?"

"Yes, he got shook up, but he was lucky. We all were, except for Hayden."

She got emotional. I gave her a second to compose herself.

"And apart from what looks like mud on his pant leg, do his clothes appear to be clean?"

"I mean… I guess?"

"Do you see any stains?"

The laptop pinged, and a text message appeared on-screen, with Terri's name at the top. It said, "We're here." I guessed she was trying to message me using the only device she knew I'd have in front of me.

"Pardon me, Your Honor." I closed the message. "Anyway, Miss Twain, besides that mud, do you see any stains on Jimmy Ludlow's clothes?"

She squinted. I blew up the photo. "No, I guess I don't."

"Okay. And now, does this photo appear to be Clay in the same place, right after the accident?"

"Yes. Oh."

She was seeing the same thing I had. "Miss Twain, what is it that you see on his shirt?"

"Some kind of stain, maybe?"

"Some kind of stain. And what color— Well, first off, what color is his T-shirt?"

"It's white."

"And what color does the stain appear to be?"

"I guess… reddish-brown?"

"Okay. And what was it that you said Hayden was drinking that night, besides the beer?"

She was quiet.

"Miss Twain? Didn't you say he'd drunk most of the red wine?"

After a second, she said, "Yes."

"And would a stain that color be consistent with red wine?"

"Objection!" Fletcher was standing at his table.

Chambliss said, "What grounds, counsel?"

"Assumes facts not in evidence, Your Honor, and in addition, he's asking opinion testimony from a fact witness. It's improper to seek her opinion as to what a stain in a photograph might have been."

"Your Honor," I said, "the reason that T-shirt is not in evidence so we can test the stain is because the State's investigators failed to properly secure the evidence at the scene. I went over that in my cross of the DNR agent, and it's improper to let the State benefit from its own failure. And I'm not asking Miss Twain to opine as to what the stain was, I'm asking her a common-sense question about its color."

Chambliss considered that. "I'm going to allow that last question. But let's move on to something else, counsel."

"Thank you. Okay, Miss Twain, is the color of that stain consistent with red wine?"

"I guess so. Yes."

"And would it be fair to say that if Clay had come back to help you when Hayden was vomiting, he might've gotten some of that red-wine vomit on his shirt?"

"Objection! Same grounds."

"Move on, Mr. Munroe."

"Okay. Miss Twain, you said you were facing the shore, and as the boat approached the Sea Island Bridge, you saw what you thought was a restaurant on the shore, correct?"

"Yes, I did."

"So you were looking at the shore?"

"Yes."

"And can we agree that means you were looking off the side of the boat?"

"Yes."

"Not toward the front of the boat?"

"Not... no."

"So you were not looking toward whoever was driving?"

She hesitated.

Chambliss said, "Miss Twain, please answer the question."

"No, I... At that moment, no," she said.

"And then, as I believe you put it, everything exploded? The boat struck the bridge, and the impact took you by surprise?"

She nodded and reached for a Kleenex. "Yes."

"And it took you by surprise because you were looking toward the shore, not toward the front of the boat?"

"Yes, I…"

"So can we agree looking at the shore means you weren't looking at the driver?"

"I… I guess so."

"Yes, we can agree you weren't?"

"Yes."

"Thank you. I have no further questions."

As Emma left the stand, I saw Fletcher looking toward the back of the courtroom. Mr. Tucker was making his way forward. I didn't see Terri.

Tucker came to Fletcher's table, and they conferred quietly.

Fletcher stood and said, "Your Honor, the State calls Mr. Lawrence Tucker."

———

After having Tucker state his name and profession, Fletcher asked him, "Mr. Tucker, where were you at approximately one forty in the morning on March 8, 2020?"

"I was down by the Sea Island Bridge."

"And, briefly, what were you doing there?"

"I, unfortunately, was betraying my wife. I'm not proud of that, but I was with another woman."

Several of the jurors looked shocked. I guess they hadn't heard about Tucker's press conference.

"Okay. And what did you observe there?"

"Not much. A light hit us from the direction of the water, which I believe was the masthead light of the boat we're talking about, and then I was—we were—interrupted by a police officer who informed us that we were under arrest for indecent exposure."

"And—and—before that, did you observe anything else about the boat?"

"No. Immediately *after* that, I heard a crash. I turned around and saw that the boat had collided with one of the bridge pilings."

"Uh… Prior to the impact, can you tell us who you observed at the wheel of the boat?"

"I cannot. I was looking at the police officer, and in any case, it was nighttime, and I must've been forty feet away."

Fletcher stiffened. "Your Honor, permission to treat Mr. Tucker as a hostile witness."

"Mr. Tucker," Chambliss said, "you were called as a witness for the State. Are you claiming you didn't see who was driving the boat?"

"I am. I did not."

"Permission granted."

"Mr. Tucker, isn't it true that you gave a statement to a sheriff's department investigator shortly after the crash, stating that the driver of the boat was a blond male?"

"I did—"

"And isn't it true that you later specifically identified Mr. Carlson here, the defendant, as the driver?"

"Yes, but—"

"And haven't you represented to both law enforcement and my office, repeatedly, that Mr. Carlson was at the wheel?"

"Solicitor Ludlow blackmailed me into—"

"Now hold on—"

"Let the witness answer," Chambliss said.

"Thank you, Your Honor," Tucker said. "As I was trying to say, Solicitor Ludlow, whose son Jimmy was on that boat, blackmailed me into making false statements to the effect that Clay Carlson was at the wheel. I never saw Mr. Carlson at the wheel. To be clear, I never saw Jimmy Ludlow there either. I did not see who was driving the boat."

I heard people shifting, papers rustling—mayhem was on its way.

Fletcher turned and looked at me. Something had just occurred to him.

He turned back to the witness stand. "Mr. Tucker," he said, "have you been in communication recently with counsel for the defense, or with his assistant, Miss Washington?"

"Yes, I have."

"Did you see Miss Washington today, outside this courthouse?"

"I did."

"Where?"

"At my house."

"Did she ask you to come give this testimony?"

"She did."

Mayhem had arrived.

"And did she suggest some benefit might accrue to you if you did so?"

"She indicated it might help bring down the circuit solicitor, who I believe to be utterly corrupt. So to the extent that's a benefit, yes."

For a second, Fletcher's mouth hung open in shock. Then he said, "Your Honor, I move for a mistrial. This is witness tampering."

Chambliss said, "Mr. Munroe?"

"The defense strongly opposes a mistrial, Your Honor."

Chambliss asked, "Mr. Munroe, you represented to this court that your assistant had left due to an emergency. I would remind you of your duty of candor toward the tribunal."

"The emergency was the need to bring in a recalcitrant witness, Your Honor."

Fletcher said, "I don't see anything recalcitrant about this. I don't see any emergency. I see a witness doing a one-eighty on facts he previously swore to, and perjuring himself, and making outrageous claims about the circuit solicitor, who's the father of a witness, in open court with the jury present. I do not believe this case can be fairly tried before this jury, and I demand a mistrial."

Chambliss said, "Mistrial granted. This jury will be dismissed."

30

AUGUST 23, 2021

I t was early evening, and I was walking with Terri up the tree-lined street where Victor lived.

As I'd explained to Clay, and as we'd established in court proceedings two weeks after Tucker's testimony, there was an interesting rule about granting the State a mistrial over the defense's objection. The rule was that if it turned out the State was wrong—so, in our case, since there'd been no witness tampering and no perjury—then the double jeopardy rule applied. The State had taken its shot at convicting Clay, and it wasn't allowed to try again. He was free.

Tucker's shocking testimony had been the subject of an entire podcast, and a number of people had come out of the woodwork with their own accusations about Ludlow's misbehavior over the years. The state ethics board had launched an investigation—and so had Cardozo, for violations of federal anti-corruption laws. In the space of about ten days, Tucker went from being the poster boy for pathetic adulterers to being the dragon slayer who'd triggered the downfall of a Lowcountry legal dynasty.

Ruiz was now the acting circuit solicitor, although to keep that spot, he'd have to defeat Tucker in an election the following year.

Whether either of them would try to get a confession out of Jimmy Ludlow or would find some other way to bring charges against him for the boat crash was an open question. But that problem was not mine to solve. Moreover, with Ruiz running things, the trumped-up charges against Terri had been dropped, so all in all, I was feeling pretty good about life.

I opened Victor's ornate cast-iron gate, and we went up his walk. Two of his daughters were sitting on the porch, and they went to bring him out before we even got to the steps.

"Hey there," he said, shutting the screen door behind him. "What brings y'all here?"

"Got something for you." I handed him an envelope.

"You open this already?" He stuck his finger in where I'd ripped it open. "What is it?"

"It's about your mom," I said. "It's from Ruiz."

"Oh, damn." His face fell. "Did he decide when her trial's going to be?"

The court had granted Maria a new trial on the grounds that mistranslation of material testimony by the State-provided interpreter meant her trial lacked the fundamental fairness that the Constitution requires. After his initial euphoria at that news, Victor had realized that meant his family had to go through the ordeal all over again, and pay tens of thousands, if not more, in legal fees. Worse, they had to face the possibility—however slight—that she might be convicted a second time.

"Read it," I said.

"Man," Victor said, "I've been looking forward to this for so long, but now I think the stress is going to kill me." He pulled the letter out and looked at it. "Wait, what?" he said. "Looks like some kind of legal form. Did Ruiz fill this out?"

"Yeah." I stepped closer and read Ruiz's scraggly handwriting out loud: "Due to the age of the case, certain witnesses and evidence cannot be located. As a result, the State of South Carolina is unable to proceed."

"What's that mean?"

"This is what we call a nolle pros. It means they're not going to try her again. It's over."

He looked at me. "Over?"

"There isn't going to be another trial. Your mom is coming home."

————

After spending forty minutes or so celebrating with the Guerreros, Terri and I walked back down their walkway by ourselves. It was sunset, with a gorgeous blaze of oranges and pinks ahead of us and deep blue overhead.

Terri said, "You've made that family *so* damn happy."

"*I* have?" I stopped and looked at her. She turned to me. Behind her, a huge rose bush framed her face with about fifty red blooms. "It's not like I could've done it alone."

She smiled and looked away, a little embarrassed. "Mm-hmm," she said. "We work pretty well together."

"We do."

In the sunset light, everything was glowing. The flowers, the beads in her hair, her little gold earrings.

I said, "Can I take you out to dinner? I mean a proper dinner. A nice place. Maybe on the water."

She looked back at me, still smiling. "Yeah," she said. "Let's go."

I opened the gate, let her through, and followed.

On the sidewalk, I took her hand.

I wasn't naive. I kept making enemies, powerful ones, and chances were this was the calm before the storm. But I was going to enjoy it while I could.

END OF INTERPRETING GUILT

SMALL TOWN LAWYER BOOK 3

Defending Innocence

Influencing Justice

Interpreting Guilt

Burning Evidence

PS: Do you enjoy compelling thrillers? Then keep reading for an exclusive extract from ***Burning Evidence***.

ABOUT PETER KIRKLAND

Loved this book? Share it with a friend!

To be notified of Peter's next book release please sign up to his mailing list, at www.relaypub.com/peter-kirkland-email-sign-up.

ABOUT PETER

Peter Kirkland grew up in Beaufort, South Carolina. While he had always loved writing, his academic and debating skills made law seem like the obvious career choice. So, leaving his pen and paper behind, Peter worked as a defense attorney for many years. During this time, he saw both obviously guilty clients and a few that he felt were genuinely innocent of the crimes that they were accused of. But no matter what, Peter was always determined to give the best possible defense for his clients and he's proud to say that he won more cases than he lost.

But the more he practiced in criminal law, the more he found himself scribbling away at the end of a hard day to clear his mind and reflect on his current cases. One day, years later, he found himself absent-mindedly reading through his old journals and found he had the beginnings of a story hidden inside his notes. That the tales from the courtroom were deep and rich in characters, twists and turns, and he remembered how much he enjoyed writing before studying law. Peter began reading legal thrillers voraciously and turned the reflections from his journal into a fictional manuscript and decided to try his luck at being published.

New to the industry, Peter would love to hear from readers:

PETER KIRKLAND

BURNING EVIDENCE

SMALL TOWN LAWYER · BOOK FOUR

BLURB

In a small town, it's all too easy for secrets to stay buried…

When a young woman dies in a late-night restaurant fire, the owner, Bobby Carter, is charged with arson and murder. The evidence is stacked against him, but something doesn't add up. And his only chance for justice rests on the shoulders of small-town lawyer Leland Munroe…

Leland's client insists he's innocent. But the local media is quick to demonize Carter, and powerful forces behind the scenes are determined to keep the truth from coming out. Leland must navigate a web of corruption and deceit to expose the real culprit.

Meanwhile, defending a young athlete accused of selling drugs has Leland facing off against a former colleague with an axe to grind. The two cases seem unrelated, but in Basking Rock, things are rarely as straightforward as they appear. Can this quick-witted lawyer outsmart the real killer? Or will he become their next victim…

Grab your copy of *Burning Evidence* (Small Town Lawyer Book Four) from
www.relaypub.com/blog/authors/peter-kirkland
Available October 26, 2023.

———

EXCERPT

Chapter One:
March 6, 2022

The building where the girl had died was coming down. I'd driven past it since the fire, but this time the traffic light was red. I stopped. A bulldozer sat on the far side of the rubble, waiting for its operator to return on Monday. Two intact doorways jutted out of piles of fallen bricks, their closed doors protecting no one.

My son, driving behind me so he could continue up to Charleston after the appointment we were heading to, honked his horn. There was nobody behind him urging us on—it was a minor street in a small town—but the light had changed, and he was impatient. He was too young to know you ought to make time for the dead.

We pulled up in front of a large, fine house. The front door and the underside of the porch roof were haint blue, the pale aqua shade that some folks believed kept evil spirits away and others painted on their houses just in case.

We went up the front steps. I couldn't remember what color anything had been the last time I'd been here. That must've been thirty-five or forty years ago, and I might not have seen the porch back then at all, since the family that had lived here didn't let my mother and me use the front door. They had us come in through the servants' entrance.

Before I could ring the doorbell, Chance Carpenter, the realtor I was working with despite his ridiculous name, waved to me and Noah through the beveled glass and let us in.

After the customary chitchat, I smiled and looked around appreciatively at the woodwork Chance was pointing out. I clearly could not afford this place, even though I was doing much better than I had been when I first moved back to my hometown. I wondered whether Chance had gotten some numbers transposed when I told him what my budget was.

I didn't tell him how wrong this home was for me. There was no sense in being rude; it wasn't his fault I hadn't recognized the place when he'd given me the address. I'd never thought of it in terms of an address. When I was a kid it had just been the fanciest of the many houses that my mother cleaned to keep us fed.

Apparently, Chance saw me as the type of man who came home to a beveled-glass front door. The master of a house like this, in a neighborhood full of doctors and lawyers.

I couldn't blame him for that. He wasn't from around here. I'd only met him a week ago.

"The high ceilings give it so much light," he said.

"Sure do." I noticed a smoke detector up there, about twelve feet above the hardwood floor, and said, "I'd hate to have to change the battery on that thing in the middle of the night."

Noah laughed.

"Oh, you won't have to," Chance said. "This whole system here is hardwired. It only goes to the battery backup if the power goes out. I doubt you'd have to change it more than once every ten years."

"That actually is the safest setup," Noah said. "Whatever house you get, you should probably get a hardwired system installed."

I looked at him. "Since when are you an expert in fire alarms?"

His face turned somber. "Oh, it's that arson case. I learned some stuff researching it."

"My goodness," Chance said, matching Noah's serious tone. "Are you working on that—the fire where that poor young lady so unfortunately passed away?"

"No, not that one," he said. "Man, that poor girl. No, this is something I'm helping a professor with."

Noah had graduated in December and was working as a researcher for one of his former teachers while peppering every detective agency in Charleston with resumes, trying to land his first real job.

The fire Chance was asking about had been all over the news, but there hadn't been any finding of foul play. Not yet, anyway.

It had nothing to do with me, apart from happening in the town I lived in. But I'd stopped trying to lose the habit of having my ears prick up at any hint of tragedy or crime. Seventeen years as a prosecutor and another three doing criminal defense had left marks that would never go away.

I knew useful information sometimes came from unexpected places, so I said to Chance, "That's a hell of a thing, isn't it, that fire. You hear someplace it was arson?"

"Oh, it's just—" He waved one hand, like the idea had floated to him through the air. "I don't know anything personally. It's just, people talk. And she was the same age as my little sister. I saw that on the news. So I think it hit me harder because of that."

We all shook our heads. It was a terrible thing. A pizza shop had gone up in flames in the middle of the night, and the girl who lived in the apartment above it—a beautiful girl, from the pictures, who, if I recalled correctly, was only twenty-two—had been killed.

Chance said, "Anyway, look. I am so sorry, Mr. Munroe, I do not want to waste your time—"

"Not at all. Call me Leland."

"Leland. I will, thank you. So, obviously we're not here to talk about the news and how it makes me feel..." He flashed a smile. "We're here to find you a house, and I brought you to this one, even though it's bigger than what we'd talked about, because I know how deep your Lowcountry roots go, and—"

"Oh, yeah," I said, nodding. "This is a real Lowcountry house, that's for sure."

It was a pale-yellow Victorian, with deep porches across the front and down one side. Strong beams framed the doorways, and every corner was crammed with woodwork so delicate it looked like lace. It had to be more than a hundred years old—the big old oak out front looked at least that age—and both the house and the tree seemed like they'd been built with only two purposes in mind: to look beautiful, and to withstand hurricanes.

Chance led us into the kitchen, which was straight off some cooking show, perfectly curated to look homey and inviting while also letting you know that the remodel had probably cost north of eighty grand. I'd feel like an ass using this kitchen to reheat the pizza or takeout shrimp I ate most nights.

Noah pointed to the far wall and said, "That there's a stove, Dad. Those red knobs are how you turn it on."

"Oh, shut your mouth," I said, laughing.

Chance caught our mood and said, smiling, "Okay, I'm sensing this house doesn't exactly hit the mark?"

"Not unless it comes with a chef," Noah said.

"It's a beautiful home," I said. "And I do have a soft spot for true Southern style. But I'd hate a kitchen like this to go to waste. And anyway, this is a four-bedroom, right?"

"No, it's three. Although, you know what, there probably were four back in the day—the master suite upstairs is stunning, and I'm guessing they got that by combining two of the original bedrooms."

"Uh-huh."

I had a memory of ceiling fans, one in every bedroom, turning slowly, stirring the hot, heavy summer air—there was no air-conditioning back then. I remembered they'd been hard to clean.

"Well," I added, "even so, three is a lot for me, with Noah moving away. I mean, I don't think my Yorkshire terrier needs his own bedroom."

Chance laughed. "I hear you. I knew it might be a little large for you, but since you didn't love that mid-century place yesterday, I thought looking at this one might help us pinpoint your style."

Noah said, "His style is, if there's a coffee maker and a desk, he's good to go."

I said, "And a microwave. I do need *some* luxuries."

As they laughed, I thought how strange it was going to be not having my son around to crack jokes with. I'd been thinking that a lot, and then shaking off the thought. I shook it off again.

As we headed back to the front door, the beveled glass shot rainbows all over the foyer. I wasn't able to enjoy the sight of it much. There'd come a point about twenty years ago, after I'd been through a few trials and heard some stories, when any front door with that much glass in it started looking to me like it had nothing there at all. Anybody with a glove on could just punch right through.

Right now I was representing a kid up in Charleston who'd picked the wrong roommate, one with drug-gang connections. I liked living an hour and twenty minutes away from people like that, but I wasn't sure it was going to be far enough. It definitely wouldn't be far enough if I lived in a fragile bauble like this place.

I silently crossed cute Victorian houses off my list.

"You know what, Chance," I said, "I know there's not that many of them around here, but if you could keep an eye out for a stone house, or a brick one, I do have a little bit of a preference for that."

"Okay, I'll do that. Good to know." As he took us back out onto the porch and turned to lock the door, he said to Noah, "See? Your father does have a style! Everybody does."

"Yes, indeed," I said.

If I'd felt like explaining it, which I didn't, I would've told him my favorite style was any type of architecture that was resistant to fire, intruders, and bullet holes.

———

**Grab your copy of *Burning Evidence* (Small Town Lawyer Book
Four) from
www.relaypub.com/blog/authors/peter-kirkland
Available October 26, 2023.**

Made in United States
Troutdale, OR
01/08/2024

16788519R00186